CW00521196

DEATH AND TRANSFIGURATION

Philanderer Ken Crossland goes missing and his abandoned car is found on DCI Alec Stainton's turf. A serial killer known as the Carver is terrorizing women across the country. As the hunt for Crossland intensifies, so the suspicion grows that he and the Carver are one and the same person. But the truth is different: Crossland is himself the victim of a deranged personality, someone whose fantasy life is spiralling dangerously into violence.

With the police hunt now concentrating exclusively on the search for the serial killer, it looks as if Crossland may not survive ... A complex, atmospheric and ultimately terrifying new novel featuring Alec Stainton and DS Liz Pink.

DEATH AND
TRANSFIGURATION

Stephen Murray

HarperCollins*Publishers*

Collins Crime
An Imprint of HarperCollins*Publishers*
77–85 Fulham Palace Road, London W6 8JB

First published in Great Britain
in 1994 by Collins Crime

1 3 5 7 9 10 8 6 4 2

A catalogue record for this book is
available from the British Library

ISBN 0 00 232511 X

Set in Meridien and Bodoni

Photoset by Rowland Phototypesetting Ltd
Bury St Edmunds, Suffolk
Printed and bound in Great Britain by
HarperCollins Book Manufacturing, Glasgow

1

The day her mother died, Anita Simpson wept.

Had anyone called to commiserate they might, observing the traces of her tears, have been touched by the presumption that through the old woman's long and demanding decline and the indignities of the sickroom, daughter had loved mother to the end. Anita's eyes appeared larger and softer than usual, her skin pale as if newly washed, and her drained limbs almost languorous with the abrupt cessation of her mother's demands. Her brother Keith drove down from St Albans the day after the death.

'Anita's looking almost pretty,' he remarked to his wife as his sister left the room to answer the telephone. 'Now that Mother's gone perhaps she'll do something about sorting her life out. Getting married.'

His wife Jan gave him a hard look, then smiled without humour. How like Keith to speak as if Anita had *elected* to nurse her mother; as if choosing to do so had been another whimsical quirk of her embarrassing . . . eccentricity. How like him to obliterate the memory of how deftly *they* had wriggled out from under the burden, as soon as it became apparent that it was a burden, of looking after his mother. God knows, it had suited them well enough that Keith had an unmarried sister available to undertake the task. Supposing Keith had been an only child? It didn't bear thinking of! All the things they had been spared! Nursing homes. Endless tedious journeys on the motorway round London making pointless visits. Money following money on fees. Jan herself knew precisely what they had been doing in leaving Anita to do the caring: taking eight good years out of her life instead of out of their own. She certainly didn't regret it for one moment, but it did amuse her that Keith could talk as if those eight years had never been; as if Anita was not eight years older, as if the strain of nursing a cantankerous old woman had left no mark! She could see her sister-in-law through the open hall door: square freckled face; hair the weak colour of ginger; a reasonable figure clumsily displayed; gesturing as she spoke on the phone, at once emphatically and uncommandingly. Hardly a woman likely to leap off the shelf into the arms of a delighted suitor.

'I don't think so,' she replied.

At the end of a wet September sodden leaves already clogged the gutters, and puddles of muddy water lay in the lane, reflected in the glossy black coachwork of the hearse and the undertakers' stretch-limousine. A cousin was there with his wife, and the dead woman's brother-in-law had been brought over, himself decrepit and with the odour of decline on his breath, by one of his sons. With Jan there was a respectable minimum of cars to follow the limousine in which Anita and Keith and the old man travelled. Along the lane and up the hill; winding down into the village; waiting in the queue to turn on to the Lewes Road and the other drivers waving them through in atavistic, superstitious homage to the dead. Up the long hill to East Grinstead, keeping a steady, reverent twenty-five miles an hour, the traffic building up behind. Round the ring-road. Through Felbridge, and then the swirling leaves to Copthorne and the orderly crematorium.

The journey back was swifter. Keith travelled with his wife. In the limousine, Mrs Simpson's brother-in-law gazed vacantly out of the window at the trees shedding leaves and the bustle of traffic and shoppers, and Anita in the other corner sat composed and silent, calculating how much the few mourners would drink and when she might have the house to herself. She had something she wanted to do out of doors this afternoon; and although the clocks had not yet changed, already darkness seemed to come early.

Once back at the house, the atmosphere veered dangerously towards elation as if a tedious guest at a dinner party had at last taken her leave. It wasn't long before the conversation reached the topic of the latest murder by the killer the media were now calling the Carver. Nobody suggested this was a poor choice of subject on such a day. There was discreet speculation about the nature of the signature the Carver left on his victims—discreet, but not without lubricity, because it was known it was sexual. One or two of the women present crossed their legs uncomfortably.

'She should have been married years ago.' Finding herself momentarily alongside her husband Jan reverted to the conversation of several days before as longstanding couples, even unhappy ones, so easily do; observing Anita dispassionately across the room passing dismal fish-paste rolls on a willow-pattern plate. 'Too late now. She'll find the world a tough place.'

One of the advantages of the country, insufficiently prized by those who do not realize how irrevocably it has been surrendered by town dwellers, is that it is a place where things may still be burnt.

No need to expend effort and fuel taking rubbish to municipal tips—a messy, sordid business of spilling plastic sacks, queues and odorous skips. All that is required is a match and the ancestral art of fire. And fire is a living thing, cleansing and sacred. Rubbish need not be merely moved from one place to another: it can be annihilated.

Anita annihilated everything associated with her mother that afternoon on the waste patch beyond the vegetable plot where bonfires had always been held when she was a child. It was overgrown now with bramble and bindweed, reminding her how long it had been since she had known the freedom to enjoy so simple a thing as a bonfire.

Clad in her wellingtons and an old jersey over her funeral clothes, Anita's appearance would have disappointed Keith and reinforced his wife's pessimistic estimate of Anita's chances of romance. Her eyes, the softening influence of tears long fled, had not the individuality that might have redeemed her face from plainness. Her cheeks flamed in the cold, robbing all colour from the ginger hair that straggled over the collar of her jacket as she bent to her toil. JoJo watched incuriously over the half-door of his stable as she stamped the brambles flat and kicked a clear circle into which she scrunched four sheets of newspaper. On top went torn strips of card, and over these, wigwam-style, she tented the debris of a wooden orange-box. Beside her lay, valuable but necessary, a double handful of the cloven billets they sometimes burned on the fire, taken from the back of the wood pile; and a scuttle half full of house coal. She felt herself grow in stature with the access of remembered skills.

A single match lit the paper, and within a very few minutes Anita was dropping the first of the coal into a fire which, though compact, was already burning with greedy intensity. Hot gases shouldered aside the autumn haze of moisture. Anita felt the heat beat on her cheek and nursed the flames until they seemed to pulsate as angrily as the hoarded resentment within her.

She let the fire burn back to a pile of ash whose incandescence was almost invisible in the pale autumn light before she fetched the commode. She made no attempt to smash it; simply placed it with one leg firmly in the glowing heap, stood back and watched the varnish begin to bubble and steam. The first flicker of flame, yellow with chemicals, darted up. She smelt disinfectant. The ugly piece stood four-square even as it flamed, acrid smoke wreathing it as if a ghostly occupant might be concealed. The bowl cracked with a sharp report and fell in two pieces through the disintegrating plywood base into the heart of the fire.

The commode was stoutly made, and by the time the legs and seat collapsed inwards the afternoon was waning. Happily, Anita made her way to the back porch.

I'll burn you too, she thought, looking up at the house: at the shabby windows, the missing tiles, the lichen-stained brickwork. I would, if I didn't need to live in you! For a moment she was tempted. A flaming brand, thrust into the rubbish piled ready in the porch, was all it would take. The ultimate cleansing.

A well-made fire will burn anything. After the papers and the photographs and the mantelshelf gewgaws, Anita burnt the make-up sticks and the bottles of medicines and the nightdresses, delighted at the vivid colours which flamed from the shrivelling plastics. She left the tops on the bottles and some, of glass, exploded like miniature grenades, making Anita laugh aloud.

The afternoon darkened into evening, but within the circle of light cast by the bonfire, time had ceased to run; or rather, was running backwards, cremating the days, weeks, months, years Anita had been forced to squander. They couldn't be had again. But you could burn them, and then get on with the rest of your life. The flames leapt and died and leapt again, consuming the years of Anita's young womanhood, and she watched them hypnotized.

At last only the mattress was left in the porch, flopped against the wall like a soiled drunk. The bed itself had defeated Anita's strength and her ingenuity and in the end she had looked at it and told herself with half-formed anticipation that after all it was a double bed, the only one in the house, and new mattresses could be bought. But the old mattress she cajoled down the stairs, its aura of urine and faeces disgusting her as it folded lasciviously over her; its impenetrable map of stains in which, perhaps, if she had known where to look, she might have made out the spilled seed of her own conception, filling her vision. And now she dragged it through the darkening weed-grown garden to the beckoning fire, held it up and let it tip, with a woomph and a blast of ash, on to the flames. With the toe of her boot she lifted a corner so that the air could get beneath; but the fire was greedy and eager and already the top surface was scorching and receding round a circle of flame.

It was the last relic, and Anita watched it burn while around her the dusk gave way to definite night. From time to time a car passed on the road, or an aeroplane drifted overhead in a slow jewelled winking of lights. The fire died, and cold crept forward out of the shadows, and Anita kicked the untouched corners of debris into the inner circle of flames, watching them rear up, only to die back. She would have liked to prolong the fire or build it again, but there was nothing left to add. And with the incursion of the cold came a flattening of the spirit of release which had flared up in her all afternoon. The fire seemed in retrospect too clean a fate by far. It had to some extent satisfied her immediate need to defile what had so long defiled her—she wished herself a man, she would have liked to urinate upon these failing embers—but whatever one did to inanimate objects could not redeem the wasted years nor cleanse the mind of the memory of drudgery. The thought recalled Keith: self-satisfied Keith, who had not visited their mother from one year's end to the next. With his executive house and his somnolent conscience and his hard brassy wife. It had been some consolation to see how little love was lost between them. Perhaps it was *his* house she should be burning down.

Indoors she felt no desire to eat. She stripped off her jacket and boots. Beneath, the things she had worn to the funeral were crumpled and stained and the skirt had been caught by a spark which had burnt a neat round hole in it. Good. Tomorrow, in the final cremation, she would burn them too.

In the dingy living-room she turned on all three bars of the electric fire but left the lights off save one small lamp, preferring the shadows to the stark illumination of the comfortless room. The room above, which had been so warm so long to cosset the invalid was empty and cold and, but for the chest of drawers and the stubborn base of that double bed, bare. Anita thought about that bed, encouraging fantasies in which it served a different purpose and bore more active figures. She had been denied too much too long. Now her mother was dead—she uttered it out loud. Dead. Dead! She shouted it up at the ceiling—everything should come her way.

*   *   *

10

Crossland leaned against the roof of the car, pressing the telephone closer to his ear against the roar of the machines racing along the churned, roughly aligned waste that would by next summer be a dual carriageway carrying holi-daymakers to the Cornish resorts.

Even as he made his call abruptly all activity ceased. Half-past five: he checked his watch automatically. The contract had eight months still to run. Nobody was paying double time now that the onset of winter had slowed the pace of work. Ken, casting his eyes round, judged that the contract was well on schedule. To the uninitiated it might look as if a thousand children with an endless supply of water had been set to play in the mud; but there was not, in fact, so much more to do. Periods of favourable weather through the winter would enable modest progress to be made on drain-age, kerbing and lighting, and once spring came the final and most visible parts of the work, the roadbeds and blacktop, would follow in a matter of weeks. The bonus for early com-pletion would be paid, he was in no doubt.

He dropped the phone into the pocket of his jacket and crossed to the site office. Covers were going on typewriters, the coffee machine being unplugged, cupboard doors shut and locked. Crossland, in his suit, queue-jumped a handful of donkey-jacketed section foremen.

'We'll have the fitter here on the dot of eight tomorrow, and he'll have the alternator with him,' he reassured. 'You'll have that 'dozer back on line by nine latest. Can't say fairer than that, can you?'

Financial penalties started to operate as soon as any of the contract-hire machines had been idle for more than half a day. The site manager's surly acknowledgment communi-cated that he knew this as well as Crossland; but Crossland prided himself on his skill as a fixer—that is, as an arranger, because he himself never wielded a spanner—and took plea-sure in the fine gradations of gratitude he was able to evoke from site managers to whom idle machinery meant idle men, late completion and looming penalty clauses.

'I'll look in next week,' Crossland said. 'See everything's

OK.' Another way he nourished relationships with clients, and another reason his own employers paid him large bonuses. He nodded farewell, embracing in his bonhomie the waiting foremen, some of whom might themselves be site managers next year.

The site manager's secretary was shrugging on her coat, and smiled at him. Young and pretty after the local manner, with dark hair cropped short except at the back where it straggled to the nape, a fresh face, alert brown eyes and good teeth round which she was just now running the tip of a pink tongue in a promising sort of way. She was eyeing his suit appreciatively, and the smart white shirt Sarah had ironed at the weekend—he used them up at the rate of two a day, always changed his shirt at lunch-time; one of the lessons he had learned a long time ago which paid dividends.

'I'll stand you dinner,' he declared. 'I'm staying at the Post House. How about it?'

On construction sites long spiels were superfluous. Direct propositions were the way, and Crossland had found that with the younger women particularly the casual mention of hotels and expense accounts was far more efficacious than personal compliments. If that betrayed a rather mercenary outlook on their part he didn't resent it; and he relished the implication that Ken Crossland was visiting the site from his proper station in a superior, more genteel white-collar world.

She nodded towards the manager's desk, round which a knot of men still waited patiently for his attention. 'I'd better just stay until he goes.'

Crossland made a play of consulting his watch; gold, behind an immaculate cuff.

'I've some phone calls to make, and a letter to dictate,' he said provisionally.

'Shan't be long,' she replied with a wink. 'He likes to be away by six.'

Crossland nodded. 'Be in my car, darling. Red Audi estate. Six on the dot or I'll be gone.'

A few minutes short of his stipulated time, Ken Crossland bumped his car over the ruts and past the cones out of the site compound on to the road, the girl by his side. It was automatic in him to accelerate fast away: he didn't pay for the fuel; he drove that way even when he wasn't out to impress.

'It's a nice car,' she said, wriggling her hips back into the leather. She managed to make the action both appreciative and inviting. She was wearing a skirt: it was one of the first things he had noticed, when he first entered the site office that afternoon. He liked a girl who took a bit of trouble—who brought a bit of class to a site. And it was certainly not a long skirt. When she crossed her legs, as she did now, it revealed her thigh almost to the turn of the buttocks.

Crossland changed up into top, and as his hand came off the gear lever it was no surprise to either of them that it found a resting place on her knee.

Life was good. Back home tomorrow, to a couple of days with his daughters and a supply of freshly ironed shirts and home cooking and a spell tinkering with his latest model aircraft project. And tonight, the company of this pretty little darling who already showed promise of being brighter than most and very pleasant company. He had plans, he definitely had plans, for that pretty little—or rather, well-developed—body. Life was very good.

2

It had been an indifferent summer and a wet autumn, but as autumn shaded into winter, brisk, clear days went some way to restore the balance. Clouds pushed high and fast across the sky from the south-west. Underfoot the ground had dried and on the open uplands the forest tracks ploughed up by hooves and boots earlier in the year had fossilized into sharp ridges from which JoJo's hooves kicked little puffs of chalky dust. Anita's spirits soared like an unpredictable Guy Fawkes rocket. In the rapidly shortening days she rode from early morning to late in the afternoon, roaming further than she had ever dared to do in the days when her mother's sickness limited her absences to a snatched hour or so. Together with JoJo, she ranged as far afield as Fairwarp and Maresfield, the two of them padding companionably along the narrow bridleways, or cantering on the open rides; avoiding as much as possible the places where people were to be found; crossing the roads quickly and with horror of the rushing, lethal, impersonal traffic.

From these heady expeditions Anita returned to Bracken Ghyll with reluctance. It was then, when early dusk had closed around the house and the stable chores were complete and there was nothing to do but leave JoJo to pull hay from the net in his box, that Anita's spirits plummeted all the more leadenly from the gunpowder heights they attained during the day. The shabby house, with the gloomy furniture with which her father had equipped it forty years ago, seemed to contract around her. The lights never seemed able to push the gloom out of the corners. She bought some 100-

watt bulbs and replaced every one, and the only effect seemed to be to reveal more dismally the faded pattern of the wallpaper, the scuffed paintwork, the stains and threadbare areas of the carpets.

Anita complained to herself, at first silently then increasingly out loud, about the *bloody* house. It was as if it stubbornly refused to be hers, though probate had quickly come through and Anita was its legal owner, clinging instead to the ghost of its former mistress.

So she sank, after the uplift of her day-long rides, into the slough of her own solitariness; left with the tedious business of watching bad television each night until, with the end of the *News At Ten*, she could make her way to bed. Lying in her lumpy bed waiting for sleep, Anita was resentfully aware that apart from JoJo her life was sterile and without profit.

The weather continued to call her out and for a week she was on horseback every day, ranging far and wide, returning sometimes dangerously in the dark to the dingy house where the food-encrusted dishes lay on the draining board and the dark hours stretched endlessly towards morning. She went eight days without speaking to a human being.

The thing to do, Anita decided, was to get a job.

It was extraordinary that she hadn't thought of it before. That the money would be useful was a weaker argument. The shop, which had provided the steady profit on which she and her mother had lived since her father's death fifteen years before, still brought in ample for her needs, though she had an idea that the figures were a good deal less healthy now than they had been a year or two back. That bastard, her father, had been financially competent. There was no mortgage on Bracken Ghyll, and included in the inheritance from her mother she had found more than one deposit account with a growing balance as unspent interest accrued year by year. Her mother had made a will, so it all came to Anita and very little had to be paid in tax. There was now no Mother to require endless fussy foods and incontinence pads and expensive non-prescription nostrums.

15

But there are other reasons for working, and Anita set about the business of finding a job with determination. She knew what she was looking for: a place where she would be part of an active and sociable office life. She saw herself blooming and sparkling; and she saw her out-of-office life sparkling too, as her new friends included her in trips to the theatre, summer parties, cosy dinners, happy groups in pubs and restaurants. And she chose in her fantasy from the many men she came in contact with special ones to know better, more intimately.

And yet, sometimes her resolution wavered and her heart misgave her. When she went out, to shop or to see the solicitor or to buy petrol, when she saw men in the streets, the shops and the garage and strove to imagine them in relation to herself, they seemed impenetrably other. How did you bridge the gap? Even she knew that she could not just go up to these men and say, 'Come home with me now.' There were men all around you, busy with work or the daily round and you never met any of them. Despite the television serials, despite the short stories in her magazine and in the Sunday supplements, in which people picked up partners as casually as a pair of tights and threw them away as quickly when they found them to be flawed, she herself returned every evening to solitariness.

She looked round the dingy living-room, seeing all the things that were usually so familiar that they didn't impinge on her consciousness: the tears in the wallpaper, the paper lampshade turned from white to grey with accumulated dust, the mantelpiece crammed with those items that had no other home, or which had long outlived their purpose. What sort of message would this room convey when a man *did* come back here? Hardly a very enticing one. There were books, as an indicator that she was not an unintelligent woman—her library of true crime, her set of Virginia Woolf and D. H. Lawrence. But otherwise the message conveyed was not a very captivating one. Supposing she did use her comparative affluence towards her new social ends; supposing this afternoon, as well as buying the papers which advertised jobs, she spent some time in the furniture and DIY stores. (There was her mother's bed upstairs, after all, waiting for a new mattress. That was a nice room. New wallpaper, fresh paint and pretty curtains would make it a room suitable for any of those scenes of freewheeling love which the television assured her would eventually come her way.) Would it ever happen? She was used to imagining the two of them, herself and her lover, sporting together; she knew from living the experience in her mind just how his weight would feel, pressing on her rib-cage. But when she tried to conjure the scene not as a fantasy but as a rational prevision of what the future held, it slipped elusively away like a negative held too long in the developer, which shows for a brief moment a wavering image, which clouds and darkens into obscurity once more and is lost for ever.

Sometimes she hated men. The hate and the frustration were difficult to distinguish, and she became accustomed to them being a permanent feature of life. She felt no particular regard for men in general; had never seen anything in any man she wanted to get close to; had, indeed, the example of her brother Keith to remind her what offensive beings they were; but every other woman had men at her beck and call. The sense that she was somehow abnormal became itself normal, and there were periods of black depression when she knew for certain that she was destined never to enter into the common experience of other women.

Finding a job proved harder than she anticipated, and more of a drudgery. It took perseverance to discover where jobs were advertised. She learned that you had to respond quickly; and she experienced brush-offs and casual hurts which she resented with a deep fury. Meanwhile, in her perusal of the newsagent's shelves, she came across a women's magazine she had not seen before, and out of curiosity bought a copy. The girl at the desk gave her a grin as she paid for it. Back home, in front of the television, she riffled through it with growing astonishment, and then began to read it with fascination as she felt her body tingle. That night she fell asleep in the silent house with the magazine on the bed-cover, and when she woke she reached for it again and marvelled afresh that such a thing should be so readily purchased, over the counter, in the newsagent's in the village. How innocent she had been!

Buoyed up by temporary optimism she decided that as well as finding a job, she should get out in the evenings. The papers she had bought for the job advertisements had a 'what's on' page. Anita scanned them, only to be bitterly disappointed by the absence of anything at all suitable.

There was, however, an announcement of a meeting of something called FIGHTBACK, in Tunbridge Wells next week; an organization set up to counter the threat posed by male violence in general, and the Carver in particular. It was time, the advertisement declared, for women to stand against male selfishness and aggression. Anita, thinking of her brother's propensity for egocentricity, agreed whole-heartedly. She liked the idea of control. Control of horses provided her with the only enduring sense of fulfilment she had ever known. Power over men was heady in prospect. Her future, the advertisement told her, was in her own hands and the first step was to attend the inaugural local meeting of the Feminine Initiative to Beat Attacks on Women.

Anita ringed the advertisement in biro, abstracted the page from the paper, added it to the pile of papers and post await- ing attention, and within three minutes had forgotten about it.

The new mattress for the double bed was delivered that after- noon. The men backed their van over the grass, churning it into the mud in which they casually let the mattress sag as they unloaded it from the van. Anita pointed this out, whereupon they retorted that it was plastic-covered anyway. They showed some reluctance to carry it upstairs. Anita felt sure that if she had been droopier or prettier or older or younger they would have performed such a modest act of gallantry with enthusiasm. They dumped it roughly on the framework of her mother's bed, clattering downstairs before she could suggest they removed the plastic or put it square. The way they eyed her askance managed to suggest that they feared intimacy. The assumption that she might offer it, and the idea that they found the prospect unappetizing, seemed equally insulting.

Next morning the FIGHTBACK meeting was driven from Anita's mind completely. JoJo was ill. She came in to find he had not touched his previous evening's hay. The mixed feed still stood halfway up the bucket. The horse stood uneasily, as if apologetic for his own failing. His flanks were distended, and his breathing was laboured.

In the afternoon he seemed better; some of the hay and nuts had gone, and Anita rode him on the forest, up past Gill's Lap and on to King's Standing, describing a circle that brought her back into the lane as dusk was falling. JoJo had perked up when they were out, but she had kept him at no more than a leisurely walk. But back in his stable after she had rubbed him down he resumed the uneasy, tense posture of the morning, and his head hung down. She checked his hooves and ran her hand carefully along each leg, and when she went indoors she was worried and a little fearful.

In the evening he was worse. JoJo looked anything but the virile, powerful beast who responded to her every direction, whom she had been used to tending. She regarded him with an angry frown.

Next day, reluctantly, she called the vet.

Crossland idled along in the centre stream of the three crawling lanes of traffic reflecting with satisfaction on the arrival of the weekend.

A suspicion of a gap appeared as some dozy bastard hung back and Crossland pushed into the outside stream with a quick dab of the accelerator and swing of the wheel. A horn sounded a fanfare to his little victory. Alongside, he could see the resentful face of the driver of the Ford he had been following. He leant to hunt for a tape to insert in the player, and when he looked up his lane had speeded up, he was

19

fifteen yards behind the car in front and was barely in time to prevent that clever bitch sneaking back in front of *him*.

An hour. Bit less, if he was lucky. Sarah would already be putting tea together: one of those teas she knew he liked after a week on the road. Sarah, for all her faults, wasn't at all a bad cook. She'd have a tummy on him in a year or two. He summoned up the image he so often saw reflected in hotel bedroom mirrors and contemplated it complacently. No wonder really that the dolly birds proved so compliant. And not just the dollies either. That girl the other day, for instance, had proved to be a university graduate, even though she was working in a site office. Why, he'd joked, she'd probably been better educated than him! And she'd agreed, the cheeky bitch. But he had rather enjoyed the backchat. He liked being kept on his toes, and Sarah, poor cow, was not the world's most scintillating mistress of repartee.

He savoured the phrase as the traffic began to speed up a little. Soon a broken-down lorry appeared on the hard shoulder and the hold-up, miraculously, vanished and he was able to speed up, pushing at that woman in her Ford until she was forced to pull over, which put him in a good mood.

He'd done pretty well for himself, one way or another. And Sarah never let him down. He was not ashamed to be seen out with her, and it was not every woman of thirty-five you could say that about. He was never reluctant to go home at the end of the week, so she must be doing all right, mustn't she? Of course, it wasn't surprising she looked after him so well. She had a lot to be grateful about, hadn't she? The big house. Every gadget she asked for. The girls—ah, the girls, bless 'em. It wasn't every woman whose husband had given her a couple of little angels like his girls. She had her car, and her bit of music teaching to keep her occupied. He often brought little presents back from his travels—often as not a piece of lingerie that'd caught his eye and he'd enjoyed buying, chaffing the salesgirl; not that Sarah always appreciated them, she was a bit staid that way—and he rather regretted now that today he was returning empty-handed. But there were other ways of making it up to her. Well, he'd never been a dull lover. He'd treat her to something a little special in that line, something that piece had taught him the other night.

Just to show he didn't take her for granted.

'That'll do for today.'

The boy nodded obediently and began to gather up the music and push it into his school bag.

'Keep at that Mendelssohn. Try and get it as regular as you can. The feeling can come afterwards. Romantic doesn't mean you forget about technique.'

He grinned engagingly and shut the piano lid, even in that simple action conveying the feeling for the instrument that none of her other pupils possessed. He was the one who made it all worthwhile; the one who just might be a real musician one day. Or he would give it up next year to make more time for football or computers.

'See you next week, then, Mrs Crossland.'

'OK, Nick. And *don't* forget the practice.'

'I won't.'

After the boy had left, Sarah rose directly from the upright chair from which she supervised. It was four o'clock. The girls would be in in a minute, and Ken could return at any time after his long week away. So there was tea to get, and no time for self-indulgence.

As she moved about the kitchen, peeling potatoes, removing the plastic film from a pack of steak and kidney, turning on the oven, setting out the plates and dishes she would need, Sarah felt the cloud of oppression begin to settle over her spirits and knew her husband's imminent arrival was the cause. In recent weeks the cloud had become darker. She herself, of course, was growing older. Her thirty-fifth birthday, long a distant landmark barely visible on the horizon, had rushed up on her and swept past. She told herself that she had reached a time of life at which disenchantment set in; a time when the comforting illusion that she could alter things if she chose finally evaporated. She told herself that the oppression had nothing to do with Ken; and then derided the pretence.

She put the pastry lid on the pie and put the dish in the fan oven. She gathered up the saucepan and the used knives and added them to the breakfast and lunch things in the dishwasher and pressed the start button. Water began to swish into the machine. The convenience and cleanliness and gadgetry of this kitchen, of the whole house, had begun to grate on her. She had been quite happy to move here two years ago. It had been the show house on the estate, and the carpets, curtains and fittings came with it: classy, designer stuff, if a little on the fussy side.

So why were there times when she hankered for the make-shift, the second hand and the cramped—hankered for, say, a little terraced house? Because, she told herself starkly, when you visualize that little terraced house you visualize it with just one occupier. You visualize it comfortably lived-in, with books and records and furniture that sags, and a picture or two; not like this pristine marvel of spatial economy, in which the oldest thing was her upright piano, the only article of furniture which looked uncompromisingly *itself*. It was like an Edwardian front parlour in which nobody dared spill tea on the carpet or laugh out loud.

The front door slammed as the girls came in. Daddy's girls. He would be back soon, the good angel who appeared only at weekends bearing praise and treats, leaving her the everyday chores of nagging and reprimanding and generally forfeiting devotion. She reminded herself grudgingly that his working life was a demanding one. She herself couldn't have stood it. But Ken loved it. She presumed a good deal of all-boys-together went on in the evenings. Pubs, clubs. With other reps, or clients. Maybe that compensated. Maybe being away from her compensated, she told herself bleakly. And then there was the possibility of other company.

The depression deepened and the throb of pain over her temples became more insistent as it always did at this thought, which Sarah had increasingly forced herself to confront these last few months. She knew why she had been more and more out of sorts with the world. She knew why she was not much looking forward to Ken's return. She knew why Ken making love to her (even the way her mind phrased that was damning) had turned from a pleasure into a chore, and worse than a chore, a humiliation.

What made her angry was not the possibility that Ken was unfaithful, even habitually and persistently unfaithful, but that she herself had so long preferred blindness to sight. Of course he was unfaithful. He'd been unfaithful for years!

She heard the sound of the television going on in the living-room. One of the girls would come into the kitchen soon asking when tea would be ready. He'd been unfaithful for years—so what? So why now did it matter?

Because at last, she answered, I am no longer prepared to put up with it.

'I'll give you some stuff for him. Make up his feeds the way I said.'

The vet stowed his bag away in the back of the Volvo. He pulled a pad from his pocket, scribbled on it, tore off the sheet and handed it to Anita.

'Be ready this evening, if you want to call in. And we'll keep our fingers crossed, eh?'

He smiled sympathetically, the patronizing bastard. Just another bloody fee for him.

'I was sorry to hear about your mother,' he said.

'Thank you.' It was strange how people took her monosyllabic responses as proof that she was deeply affected by her mother's death. She supposed it was a convention: one of those hypocritical games people played, like pretending to the old and the young that sex does not exist. If not, Anita could only suppose they themselves had never known that rejuvenating stab of joy at the death of a tyrant.

All those years of tending flesh: ugly, leaking, pendulous, lard-like flesh: a world of servile nursing, emptying commodes, being forced to confront her own mother's nakedness, mopping her when she dribbled or spat food, changing her two or three times a day, two or three times a night, living her life day in and day out in the smell of soiled sheets and the monotonous howl of the washing-machine.

How it had disgusted her to do all those things for her mother. If she had been a shrivelled, wasted thing it would have been easier, but Anita's mother, even in her illness, had her daughter's doughty build, and at the end the sickness perversely blew her up like a hideous misshapen doll. It was JoJo who had kept Anita sane. The big gelding carried muscle like taut packing on his skeleton. She used to retreat from the sickroom to the stable and brush him for hours, over and over, until his sleek pelt glistened on the fine-toned muscles, and somehow that seemed to make it possible to return to the demeaning horrible intimacy with her mother's toneless flesh.

Now she had only the vacuum where those things had been. But she still had JoJo. If JoJo were to die . . .

In the long hours at night between closing her eyes and the access of sleep, Anita raged at her fate. That she, who had so long been deprived of her right to an ordinary social life, should have the odds stacked so high against her now that she was free to enjoy it! She had no friends of her own age closer than Ruth Samuels, with whom she had been at school, and who lived in Croydon, twenty-five miles away. And Ruth hadn't even been among those who got in touch after Anita's mother's death, though she must have seen the announcement in the paper. They shouldered her aside; they treated her as of no worth. They thought 'Oh, it's only Anita, she doesn't matter!'

Now the vet drove away up the lane. When the car had disappeared round the corner and the sound of its engine had given way to the wet drip from the trees Anita turned and buried her face in the horse's sagging neck. She supposed it would have horrified the vet if she had said out loud that JoJo claimed her love as her mother had not done. It was like the perversity of fate that death could not leave her alone once it had begun. Having taken her mother, tardily but with her joyful consent, it cast around for another victim and there was only this patient animal with whom Anita had meant to share so many good times now she was free.

The horse shifted its hooves restlessly and suddenly tossed its neck as if it wanted only to be left alone in its misery, not cosseted.

A shiver ran through its body and it pulled away from her to go and stand in the corner of the stable, head hanging, as it had stood all weekend. And Anita, tears of fury pricking her lids, shut the half-door, padlocked the tack-room next door, and made her way across the saturated grass to the empty house.

As Anita turned and kicked off her boots in the drab porch she knew in her heart that the horse would be dead by morning.

That evening, in Trenant, Wales, Hugh Lewis muttered with annoyance as he fished for his house key before he could let himself in at his own front door, and wondered where Tina was off gallivanting when she should have been at home starting to put tea on for Gwen to take over when she got back from work.

He called out, not expecting a reply, and received none. But when, climbing the stairs to shed his office suit and don jeans and a more comfortable shirt, he found the door of his daughter's room open, he was curious enough (not having seen inside for many months) to look inside.

Tina was lying still on the bed, staring up at the ceiling with bloodshot eyes. She wore her favourite Yale University sweatshirt and a pair of jeans. The jeans had been neatly cut up both legs to the waistband and turned back. He could see what had been used: his wife's nine-inch dressmaking scissors; because the same scissors had been used to cut Tina's body open and lay, in a dark puddle of blood that was so copious that it was still wet, between his daughter's wide-thrust legs.

3

The week after the killing of Tina Lewis the FIGHTBACK regional meetings took place.

They followed swiftly after the national launch of the movement, and the arrangements had obviously been made before Tina's death. Yet there was no doubt that the timing of Tina Lewis's killing was advantageous to the initial aims of FIGHTBACK. The television news showed a clip from a home video of Tina's sixteenth birthday earlier in the summer. How could you, seeing her smiling into the camera in the garden in Trenant, her life before her, help responding with loathing towards the monster who had killed her and then so brutally mutilated her young body? There were already calls for the reintroduction of the death penalty.

The meeting in Tunbridge Wells was one of a dozen all taking place in the same week in locations accessible to women with will and organizational potential—women with the self-confidence and leisure to rally to an eminently worthy cause, and with the background of law-abiding righteousness invaluable where militancy was on the agenda. The Carver's activities touched every woman in the country now, and with the death of a teenager those who had feared only for themselves feared more keenly now for their daughters. Who would be next? A pensioner? A child? There was a general compulsion to do something: to find some steps that could be taken to shift the danger from the Carver out of the realm of chance and into the realm of one's own determination. The time was propitious for the banding together of women in self-defence.

'All the same,' observed Alec Stainton, watching his wife gathering her things together before leaving for work, 'I'd like to know who's paying for this. And what they expect to gain from it. Are you sure it's going to be your cup of tea?'

'Lucy is very keen to go. The girls at school know all about FIGHTBACK. Not that I shall be allowed to sit by her, I don't suppose.'

'And you'd like to go anyway.'

Frances looked abashed. 'Sorry.'

'What on earth for? I've no objections.'

'Not that: for using Lucy as a pretext. All the time one thinks one has got this marriage business sewn up, and then one finds oneself behaving as if subterfuges were the only way to make it endurable.'

Alec said: 'I was on the train the other day. There were two schoolgirls in the seat behind me. About fourteen, I should judge. One of them turned to the other and said, "Do you really think *all* men are bastards like Vanessa says?" and the other replied, "Can you think of any who aren't?"'

'But there are real threats,' she reminded him. 'A real Carver, for example. Real women have died.'

He grunted. 'So why isn't it called Women's Defence? Why must it be FIGHTBACK? Do we really want to exist in armed camps, occasionally climbing out of the trenches like soldiers playing football on Christmas Day?'

'Is that the way,' Frances asked, 'that you view our marriage?'

'Oh!' he exclaimed exasperatedly. 'If we credited everything we are told, I am deluding myself about our marriage. You are seething with anger and resentment, and I am too typically blind to recognize the fact.'

'Are you sure, darling,' she asked, kissing the top of his head as he sat at the table, 'that I'm not?'

A moment later the deep rumble of her car passed the window, burbled down the short drive, and sharpened aggressively as she accelerated out on to the road.

*   *   *

27

Anita heard the clatter of the digger as it turned in from the lane, and when she went outside, there it stood, angular and masculine and brutal, rust streaking the scuffed yellow paint. Bert Parrish was sitting in the seat lighting his pipe. Only when entirely sure it was burning to his satisfaction did he jump down and come over.

'Nice day!'

Anita nodded. She saw the resigned twitch at the edge of his mouth at her coldness.

'In there, is he?' he asked, nodding towards the stables.

'Yes.'

He surveyed the narrow path, the gateway, the paddock. 'It'll make a mess, I'm afraid.'

'It doesn't matter.'

He looked back at her with rough understanding. 'You leave it to me, love. No need to watch. I can pick him out of there without a scratch. Just show me where you want the hole.'

So he appreciated her angry fear that even in death JoJo should be at risk of abuse. She had lain awake last night visualizing her horse's body being dragged across the harsh concrete by this machine as by some vicious yellow predator and swung casually aloft; had hunted vainly for some other practical way of burying half a ton of dead friend, living again the shiver of cold horror she had experienced when the vet—how could he?—had suggested as a matter of course that the knacker would collect JoJo, would even pay her for him. She showed Bert Parrish the corner of the paddock she had selected. The cherry saplings she had chosen with such care stood against the hedge in their black polythene. Then she took Parrish up to the stable and waited while he swung the door open. She saw his face screw up. The sweet smell reached her where she stood.

Parrish came back, looking rather less sympathetic. 'How long's he been dead?'

How long had it been? She thought about it and couldn't remember. Could only recall how she had churned the problem over and over in her mind, finally reaching a decision only when she saw Parrish's card in the newsagent's window advertising the hire of digger with driver, making the call quickly from the phone box by the Spar before she could change her mind.

'A few days.'

He looked at her appraisingly. Turned away muttering something about at least having no problem with rigor mortis. 'Leave it to me.' He threw the words over his shoulder as he went to open the gate into the paddock.

Had he no concept of how much she hated having to do just that?

Frances and her daughter drove in to Tunbridge Wells with one of Lucy's schoolfriends in the passenger seat and Lucy squeezed in the back. Someday, Frances thought, I'm going to have to grow out of this penchant for fast, unpractical, masculine cars. Masculine? Well, at any rate the cars I buy are never the ones I see other women in, even women who, like me, can indulge themselves. I choose the cars you see fat tomcats in—which is perhaps why so many men feel bound to challenge me by driving so aggressively, she told herself, keeping a wary eye on the Toyota in her mirror. On a brief straight stretch it came rushing needlessly past as Frances was already slowing for the 30 m.p.h. limit into Langton Green. One of the best things about driving a fast car was that it left you free of the need to assert yourself which so many road users seemed trapped in. You could enjoy a crisp, deft cross-country blind, or pootle along behind a pair of sight-seeing pensioners, with equal content. Someday she'd give up these indulgences. Someday.

There was no trouble parking at that time of the evening, but the town centre did seem busier than was usual for this time of night. People were climbing out of cars and locking doors and joining a noticeable flow of pedestrians down the hill.

The tide was not exclusively of women, but very largely so. Frances noticed with interest the expression on the faces of the few men. These were New Men, in their twenties and thirties, demonstrating political correctness. The women, by contrast, were of all ages. As they queued to get into the hall Frances observed that among the expected middle-class twenty- and thirty-somethings were a significant number of older women, in their fifties, sixties and even more. As if they had waited a long time for something like this. A long time for the news that society no longer required them to submit to male violence; a long time for the opportunity to do something about it. Perhaps (remembering her thoughts in the car) there were more important ways in which her own life was privileged than solely in the matter of material opportunities.

Anita did not take much notice of the types of people present. It would be more accurate to say that she did not see them. Her own world was too self-regarding. Since JoJo's death she seemed to be living more and more inside her head. The little contact she had in practice with other people reinforced the conviction that everything that mattered, the only things she could trust, were the things inside her head.

She did not even know why she had come to this meeting, except that when she found the sheet of newspaper among the pile of clutter on the kitchen sideboard she saw she had ringed it, and it was tonight, when the idea of sitting in Bracken Ghyll with the earth raw and yellow on JoJo's grave was intolerable. And she wanted someone to tell her a new way to run her life.

She was perplexed by what was said, though it excited her. The speakers told her that she must not be dictated to by men, and she could see that they themselves never would be. They told her it was time to turn the tables. Peaceful coexistence had been tried and had failed, allowing violence typified by the Carver to flourish unchecked. The future lay with those who fought back. Anita did not completely follow why a state of warfare was being proclaimed, but the encouragement she was given to take control struck a welcome chord. So far the relationship with JoJo was the only one which had given her complete satisfaction in her life. She cared for JoJo, grooming him, feeding him, seeing to his needs; and she taught him to respond to the control of fingers on the reins, toes in the stirrups. Big as he was, he was happy to obey her. But even JoJo had escaped from her control by dying.

'Was it what you expected?'

'Rather predictable. Mostly foundational stuff. Taking our destiny in our own hands. Forcing men to conform to our agenda now. But I was impressed, Alec. It was very professionally put across. The stage management was extremely competent, so much so that where there were flaws in the logic of what was said, the gloss concealed them.'

'What about defending yourselves against the Carver?'

'Well, you are useless for a start. The police, I mean.'

'So?'

'So we are going to capture the Carver for you.'

Back at home Anita made her preparations for bed—the *News at Ten* was long over—in a frame of mind more settled, if not exactly more happy, than she had known since JoJo's death. She leafed through her latest magazine idly. It was as if the evening's meeting had completed what the magazines had begun, allowing her to accept that she did not after all need men to hold her life together. Their role was not after all a dominant one; hers not after all a dependent one. Their most appropriate manifestation was within the pages of the magazine, where their smooth-muscled limbs and cheery, knowing faces were empty of deeper significance. They posed among the toys of masculinity, the cars, the boats, the microlight aircraft, like toys themselves, grinning but obviously totally amenable to control. Anita imagined what it would be like to be one of the women (she assumed without question that they would be women) behind the cameras, ordering the stripped men to adopt this or that pose according to whim. Anita thought of queen bees needing the drones merely as the occasional bearers of sexual organs. Anita knew all about bees. Dad had kept them. She remembered him saying how on the evening she was born he walked out into the field to give them the news. The winter after his death she had forgotten to feed them and they had perished. The queen only needed the drones' sexual organs because she had this drive to perpetuate the species. A drive which Anita had no intention of fulfilling; therefore there was nothing men could do for her that she could not do, and better, for herself. She leafed through the pages of the magazine again, but it was already too familiar. Tomorrow she would buy another.

She recalled something her father had told her about the queen bee: funny how she had never before realized its significance. When the queen bee copulated with the drone she castrated him. Which was swiftly followed by the drone's death.

FIGHTBACK, surely, would approve of that.

The first DEF/AID shop opened in Cheltenham. Within a week there was one in Tunbridge Wells. Alec had heard there was one in Croydon. And another in Guildford. The locations once again were the middle-class heartlands: further evidence that the guiding minds behind FIGHTBACK were shrewd, informed and experienced. He would rather have liked to know whose they were.

There was nothing illegal about the shops themselves. Such places could have been opened before, but perhaps never before would there have been the desire and the motivation to buy the things they sold in quite the way there was now, with the Carver striking where he would, and FIGHTBACK to tell women there were other roles open than that of victim. Perhaps, up to now, people would have had reservations about shops that existed to arm the combatants in the war between the sexes.

'Well, *someone's* got to help women protect themselves,' Lucy's friend Camilla protested hotly, when Lucy was lukewarm about them. 'They don't sell things for attacking anyone. Only for self-defence.'

'A stiletto is a weapon of self-defence in precisely the way that a tank is a weapon of self-defence,' Lucy pointed out didactically. 'Or a nuclear warhead, come to that.'

'That's different,' Camilla replied scornfully. 'And your father *would* say that, wouldn't he?'

'Why is it *women*'s defence supplies?' asked another girl, referring to the shops' subtitle.

'Because it's women who have to defend themselves,' Camilla said impatiently.

Lucy had been about to retort: 'He's not my father.' She walked away, confused and resentful.

4

'I hear Anita's mother's finally gone.'

'Gone? Died, you mean?'

Ruth's husband nodded. 'Died, passed away, gone to meet her maker.' He thought for a moment. 'I hope her maker's pleased to see her.'

'Poor Anita!'

'Poor Anita my foot. She's been a millstone round her neck for years.'

'Yes, but her mother!'

'Knowing Anita, I wouldn't have put it past her to give the old girl a helping hand along the way.'

'Alan! That's an awful thing to say!'

He looked at her thoughtfully. 'Well; I expect you're right. But you know how I feel about Anita. Maybe her mother's death will make a change for the better, anyway. I did wonder which was going to happen first, the old woman dying or Anita being certified.'

Ruth knew that it was her husband's hard view of her friend that determined her to seek Anita out, even at the risk of rebuff. Rebuffs there had been, in the past. There was no disputing that Anita was not an easy person to befriend and never had been. At school Ruth had been the only one who tried. Sometimes she was inclined to believe she was the only real friend Anita had ever had. Which made her all the more sorry for Anita now she was on her own.

Sometimes Ruth looked at her own life, with her stable marriage and her normal kids and her comfortable circumstances, and compared it with the turmoil which seemed to affect so many of her acquaintances, and felt guilty. What had she done, or who was she, to be so blessed? And along with the guilt went frustration that there was so little you could do to ease the lot of those caught up in marriage breakdown or unemployment or family troubles. How impossible it was really to get alongside anybody. Often you sat opposite people at a dinner party and weren't even aware of the tribulations engulfing them. People endured their misery in compartments, out of the public view, like abandoned pets shut in dark garden sheds, but with this difference: that the incarceration was in part self-inflicted. For a half-understood notion that science had left no room for God denied the comfort that in another generation would have been readily sought and gratefully accepted. If you couldn't trust God you were stuck, for in extremis only God is enough.

Telephone calls were never easy with Anita, so Ruth decided to write; but she ended her note with a definite invitation to Anita to ring her and come over or go out for a day together. Perhaps a day's shopping would be therapeutic, or an afternoon outing to Chartwell or Hever.

She reached to turn on the television. It was a few minutes before ten o'clock and the advertisements were beginning. There was a particularly witty one for a brand of north country beer which they laughed at. It was already noticeable that the majority of the advertisements were slanted towards Christmas and people buying presents. Was it really just illusion, or had the build-up started even earlier this year?

The music heralding the television news began and Ruth waited for the customary shot of the newsreaders in the studio. It didn't come. Instead the screen showed dayglo-jacketed policemen, white vehicles and flashing lights, orange police barrier tape, against a backcloth of unrecognizable woodland. The newsreader's solemn voice-over said: 'The murderer known as the Carver has struck again: this time in East Anglia.'

The sound of Big Ben tolling the first stroke of the hour rolled ominously over the ether.

*   *   *

East Anglia, yawned Liz Pink, feet up in front of her TV, slummily grasping a can of Guinness. That broke the pattern, anyway. The three previous killings had all been in the west country or Wales.

Back in March, workmen turning up to begin the day at a council highways depot in Gloucester found the corpse of thirty-five-year-old Sonia Wright stuffed into a skip. She had been strangled and her body mutilated in a way which made Liz's own lively body wriggle with imagined horror. The murder had gone unsolved, and the details of the attack had been kept from the general public so as to guard against copycat killings. Four months later Mandy Williams's body had been found in the yard of a builders' merchant in Wadebridge, in Cornwall. There was some dispute about whether she had taken part in some form of sexual activity. Though again not all the details had been made public, it was after that murder that the media gave the killer the name of the Carver.

Then the Carver had struck again in Trenant, Mid-Wales. This time a girl of just sixteen. Her father came home from work to find Tina Lewis prone on her bed, the marks of fingers still on her neck and the murderer's signature slashed through her flesh.

So far as victims went, this fourth murder told Liz nothing new. A woman again, of course. Julie Warren, the owner of a delicatessen in Wymondham. Thirty-three. Separated, lived on her own. It was speculated that the murderer had gone into the shop during the day and got chatting, as a result of which an assignation was made. She locked up the shop as normal at half-past five but never reopened it the next day. A farmer found her body in undergrowth on the edge of a disused airfield about twelve miles away. She had been hit on the head and then strangled. There was no doubt, from the nature of the other injuries inflicted, that the Carver had been at work again.

'What a lot of wallies,' observed Liz. 'Only half a dozen counties to search and they still can't catch him.'

The picture cut to the increasingly familiar logo of FIGHTBACK: a fleeing male, a pursuing woman, cleverly stylized into the outline of a clenched fist, and standing in front of it, the notorious Maria Tillotson. An interviewer asked her how FIGHTBACK proposed to extend their activities, showing a measure of respect which contrasted sharply with the accusatory tone of the questions fired at the harassed local CID chief earlier in the programme. Maria Tillotson, dressed in serge calf-length skirt, cashmere jersey and open white denim jacket, her hair clipped back, resembled a chatelaine photographed for *Country Life*. Liz pondered the usefulness of a change of wardrobe for manipulating the viewer's response to a man or woman on television. How long was it since Maria Tillotson, in off-shoulder T-shirt, torn jeans and dreadlocks had turned a TV chat into a gladiatorial arena, advocating the compulsory castration of another guest—even, to cheers from the studio audience, volunteering to carry it out?

'FIGHTBACK will not rest as long as men like this beast can terrorize women; as long as women go in fear of their lives, in fear of rape and violence. The government won't help women, so we want women to take their defence into their own hands. What this man has done to his victims sums up the whole problem of male violence against women.'

'It's generally believed that the Carver attacks his victims after they are already dead . . .'

'That's right.'

'. . . but there's been some speculation about the exact nature of the signature the Carver leaves on his victims' bodies. Some people have suggested that he carves his initials on them. There's even been a suggestion that he writes bizarre challenges to the police, similar to the notes Jack the Ripper sent to his pursuers.'

Perhaps they had agreed beforehand that the time was ripe. Speaking straight to the camera, Maria Tillotson told seven and a half million viewers in precise clinical detail exactly how, and where, the Carver left the wounds that were his signature.

'Damn!' Liz ejaculated. 'How the hell did she get hold of

that? Now we'll have every nutcase in the country executing murders and drawing crosses through his victims' genitals.' And then: 'A cross,' she muttered. 'How he must hate us.'

Maria Tillotson was pressing home her message, capitalizing on the free air time, while the interviewer smiled and nodded encouragingly. 'There's no way we intend to allow further women to be subjected to these attacks. We are implementing a five-point plan which starts tomorrow with the compiling of a register of men who can be cleared from suspicion. We shall be opening checkpoints in offices, village halls and special mobile units where men can voluntarily register, have their fingerprints taken and donate a specimen of blood. We have access to laboratory facilities which will enable us to exclude positively from the campaign men whose blood shows them to have been incapable of carrying out these attacks on women.'

Fine, Liz thought. Nothing like offering the Carver a challenge. And of course, out of twenty million men, he'll be the first in the queue. Glad you've got the money, too, gal, because it's going to cost you a mite. And when men don't come rushing to your self-incrimination clinics?

But that objection was already being met. 'These clinics will be entirely voluntary. We have no wish to force anyone to register. We have no powers to compel men to register if they don't want to. But we're envisaging an overwhelming response, and I would say to all women, tell your partner to come and register. And if he won't come, then I would say to every woman, ask yourself whether there might be a reason. Ask yourself—and ask him. This man who's attacking women is somebody's son, somebody's partner, somebody's dad. Don't think your man couldn't be the Carver. Somewhere, a woman may be unknowingly protecting him.'

'Don't you believe it,' Liz retorted. 'If he's got a wife, she knows all about it, and she's begging him not to give himself up because she won't know how to face the other mums when she picks her kids up from school.'

'He may be a managing director, a judge, a vicar. So I appeal to all women: help us catch the Carver. Make sure every man in your house, every man in your place of work comes to register with the special FIGHTBACK clinics. If the businesses you deal with have men on the staff, tell them you won't deal with them again until all the men have registered with FIGHTBACK. And if any man refuses—let us know. The time to catch this man is now. Before other innocent women are attacked. Next time, it could be you.'

'She's marvellous. They're really doing something, aren't they?'

Liz turned. 'Hi, Rosie. Come in. Like a drink?'

'Thanks, no—well, if you're making one. I'll just take a peek at Joy first.'

Liz realized with a guilty start that she had forgotten all about the baby asleep upstairs. 'She's been fine. Not a squeak,' she said honestly.

Liz and Rosie had first met before Liz had even moved in to the house. The day she had borrowed the key from the agents for a look round—the house was empty, repossessed by the building society, cheap—Rosie had knocked on the door, startling Liz, who was standing in the middle of the dusty carpet in the little living-room trying to visualize it warm and trim and hers.

Rosie had offered a cup of tea, coming right in to the house and having a good look around her as she did so, and remarking frankly at the state the departing occupants had left the place in. In fact, to Liz it didn't seem in too bad a condition at all, certainly without the ripping out of fixtures and wanton destruction some evicted owners indulged in out of impotent fury. She had already decided she would make a good offer, though even then something about Rosie's blatant curiosity made her uncharacteristically reticent about announcing as much.

Rosie's own house was the end one of the row, and slightly larger, with additional windows in the gable wall. Rosie was at that time heavily and happily pregnant with Joy. The evidence of her preoccupation with the imminent birth lay all around: the catalogues, the Mothercare bags, the shiny buggy folded under the stairs. Rosie in her maternity dunga-rees radiated right-on motherhood but Liz couldn't find it in herself to resent it.

'You're on your own, are you?' Rosie asked. 'Not that I mean to be nosey,' she added hastily.

'I'm a policewoman,' Liz had volunteered before the inevi-table next question. 'I work down at our headquarters.'

'I'd never have guessed.'

It was that simple reply that inclined Liz to feel she had gained a friend. Not only for the unintentional compliment, but for the matter-of-fact way Rosie went on, as if everything was equally significant or insignificant. 'Mike's at Glynde-bourne.'

'The opera place?'

'Right.' Rosie grinned again. 'He's a brickie.' Her face clouded. 'Well, that's not very fair. He's a sub-contractor. It's all being rebuilt.' She giggled. 'You thought I meant he was a singer or something. Wait till you see him. And I'm a primary school teacher. Except that I'm on maternity leave.'

Liz had not moved to quench the friendship since, though neither had she amended her initial reaction that it might be wise to commit less than her whole self into Rosie's hands.

Joy had been born five weeks later, and Liz visited the two of them in the Queen Vic. And only six weeks after the birth Liz was a little perturbed to be asked if she could babysit. The request came again the following week and showed signs of growing into an accepted service. Liz could appreciate that Rosie wanted to get out occasionally; but it seemed to square uneasily with the devotion Rosie otherwise showed.

Now Liz listened to Rosie's footsteps moving about over-head, and shortly she reappeared with Joy a barely visible scrap of flesh wrapped in crocheted blankets, and a tote bag of baby requisites over her shoulder. Liz tried not to notice that she stumbled on the last step and a sweet smell that might have been alcohol mingled with the smell of the baby's nappy.

Rosie proceeded to change Joy's nappy on the carpet. Liz

wondered whether she was being petty to resent so obvious and (as was apparent) necessary an operation being carried out on her admittedly bargain-price, but new, imitation Wilton, when Rosie's own house was not twenty paces away.

'There, sweetheart. That feels better, doesn't it?' Rosie rolled up the dirty nappy and disappeared into the kitchen with it. Liz met Joy's unfocused eye and shared a wry grimace with her.

'Really great evening,' Rosie volunteered, returning. 'We went to that new Thai restaurant on the London Road. You ought to try it.'

'I thought it was an NUT meeting,' Liz said.

'Yes, but we went on afterwards, of course. It was really great to catch up with the gossip. I can go back any time, of course. They're crying out for really good primary teachers.'

'But the idea was to take the longest you could for maternity leave.'

'Well, I know . . .' She picked Joy off the floor, sat down and began one-handedly tugging at her sweater and releasing her bra. Joy was thrust with casual brutality towards the ruck of clothing and seemed to latch on easily enough. Liz examined herself for symptoms of envy and cautiously concluded that she was immune for the time being. You couldn't imagine yourself doing it. Rosie seemed to be settling for a good chat. The study guides Liz had been conning for her promotion exam lay on the sofa beside her and she thought ruefully that it would have to be tomorrow night now. So much for Rosie being back by nine.

41

5

Sarah Crossland asked: 'Where is it this time?' hearing in her voice that tone which she had promised herself so often recently she would not allow: the flat, brittle tone which meant she was expecting a lie.

The girls looked up surreptitiously from where they sat in pyjamas, spooning cereal.

'New Forest. After that . . .' He let his voice rise to express the boundless possibilities. The neat suitcase stood at his feet as he tied his tie, containing the crisply ironed white shirts, the second pair of shoes; a suit in a carrying cover draped over it. Out of the kitchen window she could see the car waiting to carry him away—perhaps even to the New Forest—the back seat folded down; wellingtons, donkey jacket, white hard hat prominent. In the glove locker was the mobile phone which could reach him anywhere, ordering him to a fresh destination, an overnight stop hundreds of miles away, and with which he rang her from those glib, unverifiable locations to tell her that he would not be back for another night.

He checked the pockets of his jacket for his keys; a smart, competent-looking man with his fresh Monday morning shirt curving flawlessly over the incipient corpulence of his stomach, and smiled at her. That smile! What she had done for it. Where it had led her—to these two watching children, this pleasant, spacious house on the estate in Wilmslow, to this emptiness. It was a smile which knew its own power, and believed it was its own atonement.

He hadn't realized yet that she was tired of forgiving. That it was many months since she had begun to be disgusted with herself for responding to that smile.

Maturity had made him more handsome. The modest amount of extra weight lent him gravitas; the heavier features seriousness. At thirty-seven he was at his peak. The young could admire him, the middle-aged call on his understanding. The young women; the middle-aged women. Oh yes, physically he was a very commanding man. No question. Lucky Ken! As he kissed Beth and Amy he transmitted the illusion of dependability as glibly as a husband in a breakfast cereal advertisement. He bent towards her and she smelt his aftershave talc. He kissed her, as always, on the lips, not the cheek. A generous man.

' 'Bye, sweetheart.'

' 'Bye. Take care.'

He moved to the door.

'You'll ring me?' She hated the note of pleading in her voice.

He turned. 'Don't I always? Look after yourself, sweetheart.'

The children were intent on their cereal. She made herself smile, felt its shallowness, felt the knot in her stomach tighten.

Frozen at the window, she watched him open the rear door of the car to put his case in and hang up his jacket behind the driver's seat. Then he was doing up his seatbelt. The car door slammed. The starter cranked. The engine fired, raccd, slowed, receded as he backed out into the road. The horn pipped as he drove off. With a cheerful wave, as usual, no doubt, but she had shut her eyes so as not to give him her blessing as he drove away.

Off to a new week. New opportunities. Who knew what he would find in Fareham, Taunton or Felixstowe? Who knew?

I know, she told herself bitterly.

I know, you bastard.

In the Tunbridge Wells branch of DEF/AID Anita wandered round the displays bemused by the range of goods for sale.

There were personal alarms (some carrying the FIGHTBACK 'Seal of Approval'); self-defence manuals; aerosols of dye and unpleasant chemicals and even CS gas; windscreen stickers warning would-be attackers that 'this vehicle is equipped for the driver's protection' and cards to put in the window of your car if you broke down, warning your rescuer not to approach but to call the FIGHTBACK helpline number. Why had none of these things been available before? What women had been literally unable to think was unthinkable no longer.

Anita went back to the entrance and took up a wire basket and began a more systematic trawl of the display shelves. Calculating prices and comparing them with the state of her credit card account she added a knife to the contents of the basket. She had plenty of knives at home, of course, but real thought had been put into the design of these so that they could be worn without discomfort or risk of accidental self-injury and still be available in case of attack. Her back towards the checkout, she slipped the knife from its protective sheath and ran her thumb gently along the blade, watching her skin divide painlessly behind it and small drops of blood rise to lie like rubies on the exposed white flesh. Surreptitiously she fished for a tissue and pressed it to the wound.

Anita lingered, pondering the items in the basket, even tentatively putting them back and selecting others. Wasn't the knife an indulgence? If she did without it, she could take that pair of handcuffs, for example. The advertisement placard beside them showed an attacker hitched helplessly to iron railings while his putative victim indicated his plight scornfully to the crew of a squad car. The humiliation of the man, the pre-empting of the useless police, appealed to Anita. In the end she took both.

The girl at the checkout rang up Anita's purchases efficiently on an electronic till and tucked a couple of slips of paper into the carrier before she took Anita's proffered credit card.

'What are those?' Anita asked.

The assistant fed the card into the till and smiled. 'One's

an application form for FIGHTBACK. Members get a ten per cent discount on DEF/AID products. I've also put in a flysheet about some self-defence classes we're starting next week. The other's just a note we slip in saying goods are sold for defence only. We like to keep squeaky-clean with the law.'

'I thought this place was owned by FIGHTBACK.'

'It's not quite as simple as that,' the girl replied amiably. 'But you can certainly join here. You're not a member?'

'No.'

'I could process your application straightaway and you can pay your subscription by credit card if you like. In fact, I can deduct the ten per cent from the things you've just bought and it'll more or less have paid for the subscription.' She raised an eyebrow. 'Yes?'

'Yes!'

Anita walked out into Mount Pleasant not only a paid-up member of FIGHTBACK, but a fully equipped one too. She savoured the novel sensation of belonging. She felt the presence of ranks of unseen women up and down the country, women like her. Perhaps soon she would begin to meet some of them—at self-defence classes, for example. But for the moment, the knowledge that she was wanted was enough. She had not joined anything since she had ceased to be a child.

'Could I see inside your bag, please, miss? I have reason to believe you may be carrying an offensive weapon in a public place.'

Uniformed and bearded, his politeness a thin cover for scorn, the policeman barred her way to the car park. He reached for the DEF/AID carrier unbidden; and to Anita's humiliation she surrendered it and watched him riffling through its contents—her property.

He handed the bag back with a hard face. 'Carrying offensive weapons in a public place is a criminal offence,' he said.

'Why don't you arrest me, then?' she muttered.

'What's that? What was that?'

'I said, why don't you arrest me?'

'Believe me, love, there's nothing I'd like better. If those things weren't still in their packaging I'd run you in like a shot. You women ought to be warned: if you carry those things around loose you're as much a criminal as any young tearaway with a sawn-off shotgun.'

So if a man threatened a woman with a shotgun he was a tearaway, but if she carried a few items for self-defence she was a criminal!

The policeman warned nastily: 'If I stop you with any of those items loose on your person I'll run you in. And that applies to all you women, so pass it on to your sisters.'

He left her. Anita seethed, barely resisting the urge to snatch one of her new purchases from its packaging and run after him and assault him. She would have liked to hurt him: really make him cry. There in the car park for all to see. Demolish his arrogant, abhorrent machismo. It would have been worth what came afterwards: worth being beaten up in the cells and raped and framed. But she did nothing. That was the story of her life, wasn't it? Despite the contents of her carrier, despite the FIGHTBACK membership card in her purse, nothing had changed, and nothing ever would. Tears of anger and misery flooded her eyes, there in the middle of Tunbridge Wells; and her humiliation was complete.

The shut doors of the empty stable loomed starkly and faded again as the headlights swept past. Anita took her purchases inside, dumping the carrier of food in the back lobby and carrying the DEF/AID bag in to the dingy sitting-room. When she put on the light the windows gleamed blackly. Not yet four, and the winter night had closed in, presenting her with the long solitary hours so difficult to fill. But her mood was almost happy again as she took the purchases one by one from the bag and undid the packaging. The handcuffs gleamed with steely strength, and their action was sweet and sure. She read the instructions on the aerosol, took the cap off, placed her finger experimentally on the button and pointed the nozzle at an imaginary attacker. She slipped the knife from its sheath. Her finger, where she had tried the blade, ached dully now, a satisfying background throb. She drew the knife blade along the table and a neat V-shaped line appeared, clean-edged and precise. Not wanting to blunt the blade, she replaced it in its sheath and spent some time adjusting the fastenings to fit her waist.

By the time she had begun to tire of the new toys it was almost six, and she could put the television on and see what was on the news. She wanted to hear the Carver talked about. She would have liked to learn that he was nearby, so that she could with more foundation fantasize about encountering him. She almost hoped he had killed again. But there was quite a bit about the Norfolk killing for her to watch, and a brief shot of Maria Tillotson addressing a meeting in Harrogate. Anita left the set on when the weatherman appeared, and turned away moodily. The prospect of an unappetizing tea, and the dark, dingy hours waiting like cold greens she must eat before bedtime, oppressed her.

In her shopping bag, she remembered, she had a new copy of her magazine. She sat on the kitchen table turning the pages without much satisfaction, realizing that the house was cold. Eventually she extracted the centrefold pin-up and blue-tacked it to the larder door, where it grinned cockily back at her.

Crossing back into the sitting-room she fetched her knife. Studying the pin-up a moment, she placed the tip of the knife precisely on the spot, then leaned against the handle. The steel sank through the thin paper into the door. When she released it, it stood there. The model continued to grin back at her. 'Got you,' she said. She contemplated it with satisfaction and then turned away and forgot about it. She began to make tea.

The weather turned between Monday and Tuesday morning with a vengeance, the wind backing south-easterly and increasing to a blustery gale that rattled the rain against the windows and cut through the clothing when you went outside. All Tuesday it battered at buildings, lifting tiles, snapping branches that earlier storms had weakened. Then the wind

47

dropped and the sky turned leaden and the temperature fell fifteen degrees and there was talk of snow on high ground and people stiffened themselves for the winter, telling each other that it would be a hard one.

Nothing seemed able to eradicate the chill. Anita woke each morning to the condensation puddling on the window sills and black triangles of mould on the paper of the bedroom; and outside the window only white dank moisture, indistinguishable as mist or cloud or rain, a sort of aqueous ambience which seemed ill-suited for the survival of terrestrial creatures. The outbuildings were silent except for the drip of moisture from eaves; empty and cheerless since JoJo's death. The corner of the paddock where he lay was a wreck, moisture glistening on the clods of clay and gathering in the ruts left by the digger. The cherry trees which were supposed to be such life-enhancing mementos of her friend were dull damp sticks. Anita mooned around, standing in doorways contemplating decorating rooms, taking up a book and letting it fall, filling the morning with snacks and cups of coffee, gazing out of the upstairs window that looked towards the road, waiting for cars to pass.

Long before evening she knew that she must get out. Not in the hope of finding laughter and lights and happy company, but because she could not sit in the cold and damp waiting until she could go to bed. Food she cooked herself disgusted her. So: she should eat out. You did not need company to enjoy warmth and a meal cooked by more skilful hands than your own and more appetizingly presented. In her mind she built the forthcoming evening up as a major outing requiring long and careful preparation. Well, it would fill time. If only the self-defence classes had started. She was sure those would bring her the companionship she had been deprived of. But the first was not until next week.

Although she left early, shutting the door behind her when it was still barely six, Anita had had most of the afternoon to expend in getting ready. Earrings hung beside her cheeks and her lips and eyes, naïve statements in carmine and jet, struck through the mist like a carnival mask.

The car took a long while to start, but eventually it came grudgingly to life. She backed it out through the murk and started cautiously towards town.

Crossland held the phone in the palm of his hand and steered with his fingertips while he tapped out the numbers. The driver in front was observing the speed limit and Crossland kept his car close behind his offside wing, pushing him along, an eye open for a chance to overtake.

'Stephanie? Take this down, please, and get a fax off, will you, there's a darling.' He dictated quickly, not bothering about the punctuation and paragraphing—the girl was paid to look after details like that. Halfway through, the car in front slowed and the indicator flashed for a side turning and Crossland had to stamp on the brakes and swing out to avoid a collision. He dropped the phone to have a hand free to blare the horn as he rushed past. An oncoming van flashed its lights and Crossland swerved back into his own carriageway. The van driver raised two fingers.

'Stupid cunt, who does he think he is?' Crossland fumed, and his hand scrabbled for the phone on the seat beside him. 'Sorry, Steph. Bloody stupid drivers. Got that? Add the usual para and say I'll be on site next Friday. OK, I'm on my way to Lewes, and then I'll call it a day. What've you got for me tomorrow?'

Stephanie, in the office in Stockport, listed the requests that had come in. A bulldozer that had shed its track on a site in Winchester; in Stratford a site manager demanding action because the gearbox in one of his graders had seized; in Northamptonshire a digger tipped into a ditch and damaged in the getting out. Stephanie had arranged all three calls for the following day. Crossland's Audi was less than a year old, and the mileage was already nudging seventy thousand.

Crossland rang off and reached for a tape. The van driver's insult had put him in a bad mood. It had been a long day and he still had to get to Lewes, where he knew the site manager was stubbornly unresponsive to blandishment; a gloomy sod if ever there was one who would never say thank you. Crossland felt the need for a scapegoat to whom he could pass on his frustrations, and whom he could belittle when other people, perversely declining to respond to his bonhomie, belittled him. It would be nice if he spent a bit more time in the office, if it weren't for the bust-up with Steph. Stuck-up cow. He turned over in his mind ways in which he might get rid of her in favour of a more compliant secretary.

As for tonight, he felt the urge to find a woman; one he could impose his will on and from whom he could demand and receive the respect he needed to maintain his ego. He felt his body stiffen in anticipation. He needed—what? Not a kid, tonight: not some little feather-brained dolly bird impressed by his car and his suit and his man-of-the-world air. He was jaded with easy conquests, bored with the unsatisfying adulation of girls whose experience was too limited to give their admiration substance. He needed a woman tonight. His mind filled with images of more mature womanhood. Someone who could give as well as take, who knew a few tricks and who would not be averse to leaving the thoroughfares of sex for a sortie down one of the murkier side alleys. He had a very good idea of the sort of woman he was looking for, and as soon as he had seen this miserable sod in Lewes he'd set about finding her.

Back in Stockport, Stephanie dealt efficiently with the dictated letter and faxed it to its destination, working steadily until ten-to five. Then she took out her bag and ran over her make-up and banged the drawers to and donned her coat, and on the dot of the hour closed the office door behind her. She never failed to feel a weight lift as she did this. The people she worked for—the men—were such pains in the arse. So laddish: and Crossland the worst offender of all. Fortunately he spent his time mostly on the road. Steph had a feeling that when the weather clamped down on the construction sites and he was more often in the office, she might have to look round for another job. The prospect didn't worry her. It was, however, annoying to have brought it on herself. If she had never, stupidly, accepted Crossland's overtures she would never have had to suffer his peevish resentment when she ceased to sleep with him. Going to bed with Crossland had not been one of the more uplifting experiences of a girl's life, but it had been stupid to tell him so.

Steph put all that behind her as she drove out of the car park and headed home to her flat. She turned her mind instead to the much more edifying prospect of the evening's activity. There was a FIGHTBACK meeting tonight in Macclesfield. She looked forward to it with interest. Eight months as Crossland's secretary had made her quite susceptible to the aims of FIGHTBACK.

Crossland, looking round the lounge bar as he entered, stale and tired from driving in the dark and the drizzle, saw at once that she was the only possibility. She was sitting alone at a small table out of the main light, eating slowly, and she had that resentful keep-your-distance hauteur which in Crossland's experience betokened the professional. He noted the heavy eyebrows, the harsh make-up, the gingery hair made nothing of, the tawdry jewellery hanging from her ears as she slowly chewed. He wondered if she was on her first night, somebody's wife, driven to desperation by financial necessity. He thought about moving on, driving somewhere else, but it was all too much effort. She wasn't much, poor cow, but she looked cheap, and she'd do.

He reached for the bar menu and ordered.

He startled her, looming into her vision and settling himself immovably at the table. Flustered, she nevertheless drank in with her eyes his strong, paunchy bulk and his confident smooth face and the beginnings of fleshiness round his neck and imagined him at once lying on top of her; and saw cocksure certainty in his eyes that that was precisely what was going to happen.

Now he was winking at her lecherously, intimating that

51

she would know a thing or two that they could explore together, and she thought of the virgin mattress waiting on her mother's double bed, and knew that this was the night, and she could no more turn aside from what was to be than she could fly.

As they were leaving the hotel she was trembling. His arm round her shoulder slipped down and he squeezed her breast crudely. She smelt the fruity musk of his aftershave. Her breast hurt and the discomfort was reassuring: this was what she expected.

'All right, darling?'

She looked up into his lazy, self-confident face and he smiled down at what he took for her expression of salaciousness. Her voice shook with what certainly sounded like professional insincerity as she answered him: 'I can't wait.'

Sarah Crossland tucked her elder daughter into the bed-clothes and kissed her good night.

'When will Dad be back?'

'Soon.'

'Where is he?'

He's somewhere snug and comfortable, you can bet your life on that, thought Sarah, and a woman will warm him before the night is out. But she said, 'He's somewhere safe, probably having his tea.'

'Is he going to come back?'

'Of course he is. Now that's enough. Go to sleep.'

'How do you know, if you don't know where he is?'

'Just believe me, will you?' Sarah heard her voice suddenly loud and high with strain. How could the child not pick up the truth of her anxiety? 'Dad'll be back soon.' She made herself say it gently and convincingly as if she could still be the source of adult verities. 'I promise.'

Downstairs, she thought: I'm going out of my mind. It was three days since he had rung her. Perhaps this time he would announce that he was leaving her. Or was that only what she hoped he was going to say? She reviewed her resources.

She could support the children and run the house. It would be tight, but she could do it. He would contest that. He would want the girls, and he would try to prove that she was incapable of supporting them.

But most of all she feared that a different scenario would be played out. Ken would return to his comfortable home in Wilmslow, and her dutifully there running it, with no intention of throwing up a life that suited him so well. And she would not have the strength to resist.

I'll get the locks changed, was her first thought. I won't give him a chance to get in and start talking, because if he gets in and starts talking I can't trust myself. He will be good-natured, plausible, considerate. He will have brought me a bunch of flowers or a new nightie. And if I press him he will have a story about where he has been, and if I lose my temper he will be hurt. And if ever I have positive proof that he has been cuckolding me—she repeated the word in her mind, trying it out, pleased with the idea that it was no longer the preserve of males to be cuckolded—if I ever have proof, he will be abjectly penitent and promise whatever I demand. He will even cry.

Before she knew it she was sitting at the table in the dining area with a note-pad and a ballpoint, listing the things she must do. She marvelled at herself. Sitting at home, with her children upstairs, planning how she was going to end her marriage! End it, she repeated to herself; and on *my* terms. For a moment she let herself survey those fifteen years with a wistful eye. They had been years which contained much that was good. But her resolution, far from weakening, was reinforced. Fifteen years of deceit were not lightly to be forgiven. She didn't know exactly how long Ken had been cuckolding her. It didn't matter. Whether it was a year, five years, or ten made no difference: the fact sullied every moment of their time together.

In the small desk in the dining-room was a drawer where all the Christmas things were kept: spare cards and lists of cards received, gift tags and a few decorations. It was where Sarah slipped any small thing that was personal: a letter she did not choose to submit to Ken's scrutiny; a photo or two which he might have jeered at.

And her own, as opposed to their joint, address book.

Next morning she dropped the girls at school and took a train into the city centre. Anne had given her the solicitor's name eagerly; Anne who had herself just emerged from a protracted and messy divorce. Anne whom Ken thought hard and brassy. Sarah remembered his outrage when they learnt that Anne was to stay in the big Victorian semi while Chas moved out; Anne keep the Rover; Anne have custody of the children.

'But *she* was the one who divorced *him*,' Ken protested.

'Take the bastard for every penny you can get. It's your right. Why should he have it all?' Anne had said last night.

But Sarah didn't want to take him for everything she could. She'd settle for just taking the girls, so long as she could be free of Ken. She wanted the girls—oh, how she wanted to keep them. If the solicitor told her she might lose *them*, she didn't know whether even now she could go through with it . . . Everything else she was prepared to lose. With the girls starting secondary school she could go back to work and pay the mortgage on a starter home or a terrace in one of the inner suburbs. She would have despised herself if she thought she was tied to Ken by addiction to the material comforts he provided.

When she reached the solicitors' office and the young woman Anne had recommended began ticking off what sounded outrageous claims, she felt overwhelmed.

'Wouldn't it be better if I moved out first? I mean, this is all bound to take some time.'

The woman looked as if she couldn't believe what she was hearing. 'God, no! Don't do that! Whatever for?'

'I just . . . I don't care about how we settle it all. I simply feel I can't live with him another day. Another night,' she added quietly.

'No one's asking you to. God, no, Sarah.' Incredulity that

such dangerous innocence existed shone from her earnest face.

And in the end, Sarah capitulated; and the solicitor listed everything that was going to happen and Sarah acquiesced, thinking in her heart that it was going to be a blow Ken would never recover from. And then she thought of the more gradual but no less sure way he had humiliated her over the years. No doubt even now he was picking up some compliant little tart in readiness for the night, some artful tight-jeaned brazen thing for him to fuck on his hotel bed. And the thought, and the use of the forthright word even behind the curtains of her own mind, stiffened her resolve.

'Well, I think that's all. Don't you worry, Sarah. All you have to do is ring the locksmith as soon as you get home—' she handed Sarah a card with a phone number on; it seemed they had people who were used to just this sort of urgent call-out—'and leave the rest to us. If he gets nasty, you ring me first and then the police, but say nothing at all to him. Let him stew in his own juice. OK, Sarah?' She smiled. 'Don't worry. And don't feel too sorry for him. He owes you.'

And Sarah, thinking of the way she had connived at her own humiliation all these years, said, 'I suppose so,' and drove home rather less contentedly than she had expected.

The locksmith came that afternoon. Now, Sarah thought, even if he comes home tonight he'll be too late.

But he didn't come.

6

The roads were slick with the night's rain and with the last leaves that drifted from the trees, swirling in the paths of the oncoming cars like lithe dancers, whirling into the gutters to become in a moment lifeless and sodden.

The two men stood looking at the red Audi estate with the neat hole smashed in the side window.

'Been here how long?'

'It was here on Friday,' said the ranger.

The policeman noted the drift of fallen leaves against the wheels, the dark stains of bird-droppings on the windows. He walked back to his car and reached for the microphone of the radio.

'Take a few minutes,' he observed, leaning against the roof. The ranger nodded. The policeman bent closer to the window as a distorted voice spilled from the radio.

'Roger, er, vehicle looks like it's been here a day or two . . .'

He listened again, then slipped the microphone back and ambled over. 'Making their minds up what to do.'

'Is it stolen?'

'Not reported.' He bent to squint through the windows, tried the door which opened, peered inside. 'Registered to a company up north. No need for you to stay if you're busy.'

'That's all right.' The ranger had the normal ration of curiosity about police business, and anything that happened within the boundaries of Ashdown Forest could be regarded as within his remit, so he had no conscience about staying.

By unspoken agreement they drifted a few yards from the red Audi.

'Nice spot,' the policeman said, looking out across the cricket pitch. He produced a bag of toffees. 'Want one?' The ranger took one, and at that moment the squawk of the radio called the policeman back to his car.

'Sending someone out from CID,' he reported, returning.

'Something important, then?'

The policeman jeered. 'Nah. They just fancy a ride out as a change from sitting on their bums.'

Detective-Constable Johnson found the ranger and the uniformed constable had discovered a mutual interest in fishing and were swapping details of good beats. Johnson walked round the car, peered in the window, then opened the door and sat inside looking round. Apart from a hole in the dashboard where the radio had been it was not much marked. The plastic cover to the steering column was unbroken, from which it was an obvious deduction that the car had been driven to its present spot legitimately, not hot-wired by joy-riders and then dumped. And it had been here at least since Friday, since when it had survived the weekend. Johnson reflected on the affluent society, where a car like this was too much trouble to steal; then climbed out and joined the other two men.

'It's a wonder it's still here.'

'Stan here says he surprised some kids who ran off.'

Johnson nodded to the ranger in a friendly sort of way. It was decidedly pleasant out here, even on a chilly winter's day. 'Get a look at them?'

'Not so's to swear to them. Forest Row kids.'

'Yeah?'

'Pretty sure.' He spelt out the names, and Johnson wrote them down in his notebook.

'Ah well,' the beat constable said reluctantly, 'I'd better be moving on.'

He drove away. Johnson used the time while they waited for a tow truck to turn up to take the ranger's statement.

'We'll give it a go for prints back at the pound,' he said. A couple of girls came by on horseback, with whom the ranger passed the time of day, while Johnson watched them appreciatively. He continued to watch as they rode off, backs supple, buttocks moving easily in the saddle to the rhythm of the horses' gait. Presently the truck chugged up the lane, the Audi was winched on to the flatbed and strapped down, and it drove off. Johnson arranged for the ranger to call in to the police station to sign his statement, and the two men parted. There were worse ways, Johnson thought, of spending a morning. Crisp sunshine, leaves rustling under foot, and a simple crime against property with no blood, no drugs and no nastiness.

'Where's the motor now?'

'In the pound. Registered keeper's a company up north.'

'Fair enough. Get on to them and see who was using it, where and when, and try and get a photo, last-seen, all the usual.' Liz picked the papers out of the in-tray and shuffled through them while Johnson watched her.

She dropped the papers back and angled her head to see what he was working on. Then, with a nod, she turned to go. At the door she said, 'If you want to stay a constable, Johnson . . .'

'Yes?'

'Just go on spelling "appreciation" with one p.'

Johnson subsided with a grimace.

'Where's Dad?'

Sarah turned away to the oven where the casserole was cooking, aware of her daughter's accusatory stare at her back.

'He's had to stay over,' she said. 'I told you! How many more times?'

'But he was going to take me ice skating at the weekend. He promised!'

'I said I'll take you tomorrow if I can.'

'But Dad always takes me.'

58

'Well, you'll have to make do with me. But I can't take you until I've finished my lesson.'

Amy muttered under her breath, 'Sod your lesson!'

Sarah bent her head until it touched the metal of the oven. It was warm and reassuring. She made herself pretend not to hear the remark. What was the point? What could she say? In her own heart she was cursing more systematically than Amy. Why couldn't the bastard even let me know?

And yet it was ridiculous! She'd changed the locks against him, on the expectation that he'd be coming back. And now she was worrying because he hadn't come.

She wondered again whether she should report it. Report what? A man of thirty-seven doesn't come home. What were the police going to say beyond the obvious, that he was probably with a woman? She couldn't face being the object of their patronizing pity. She'd had enough of that from his firm. She wouldn't have rung them, because she would have feared to hear that Ken was working just as usual, from some other address. But they had rung her, several times at first, angry at the trail of unkept appointments. When they grasped that she really had no idea where he was they became pruriently sympathetic. Then with frightening abruptness they lost interest. She presumed someone else had been hired to do Ken's work. She knew she should check the contents of the bank accounts, but she was afraid, lest she find they'd been cleared out, that she had nothing to live on.

'Mum?'

Amy was at her side; an arm raised tentatively, as if she might venture to place it round her mother's neck.

'He'll be all right. Don't worry, Mum. He'll be all right. Don't cry.' Crying herself, big childhood tears at seeing an adult weep.

Curse him, Sarah shouted silently, curse him for doing this to us. For making me lie to my child. I'm not crying because he might be hurt, my daughter. I'm weeping because I want the bastard dead!

*   *   *

Frances arched her back until her body seemed to describe one smooth contour from the tip of her chin to the sharp crease at the top of her thighs where she knelt on the bed. Her nipples and the points of her collar bones, like steeples and hills on a distant horizon, served only to emphasize the smoothness of the overall shape. Her fine, fair hair hung back from her head and her eyes were closed.

'Bored?'

She opened her eyes suddenly, jerking her head forwards. 'To death.'

With a toe, Alec tickled her thigh. Mid-week. Mid-afternoon. Scandalous, to be in bed. Outside it was still light, except that light was too emphatic a word for the condition, thickened by the mist of drizzle which had once again closed in, that prevailed beyond the undrawn curtains and rain-streaked window. From the floor below came the sound of rock, not so much heard as felt through the structure of the house: Lucy back from school. Lazy afternoon, nearly at the end of a fortnight's holiday from work. Holiday from sordid violence, mean theft, callous brutality, avaricious thieving, sophisticated fraud.

'A week never used to be long enough because I never managed to unwind before it was time to go back. Now it's worse because you help me relax so completely. Monday's going to be hard.'

'Monday may never come.'

'It always does. Sooner or later.'

'One day it won't.'

He blinked. 'What is this? A sudden obsession with death? That's twice you've alluded to it.'

'How many men,' she teased, 'would use the word "alluded" in bed?'

'Keep to the point.'

'Oh, the point? Is there a point?'

'Isn't there? You, of all people, believe so.'

'Hence my readiness to *allude* to death. In the midst of life . . . In the midst of life we spend an afternoon bringing each other to the little death.'

'The little . . . ? Oh, I see.'

'Isn't that what people call it? I die! Oh . . . h . . .' She mimicked orgasm histrionically. Alec's body roused even as he savoured the happy thought that you never knew quite where you were with Frances. She was perfectly serious even as she uttered apparently flippant remarks, and then she could clown outrageously in a way that anybody who knew only her public face would flatly refuse to credit. And now she was bending forward over his body, serious again, losing herself in the pursuit of his pleasure.

'Monday will be just what it should be,' she broke off to predict. 'A welcome return to work after two weeks' idleness, a welcome return to colleagues after two weeks' wife and daughter. You will come home a happy man. And Liz Pink, who has no doubt enjoyed having you away but has probably had enough of sitting like the little Dutch boy with her finger in the dyke, will go home a happy woman. Not,' Frances said, as, satisfied with her preliminary work, she straddled him, 'as happy as she would be if she could be here doing this in my place, but happy none the less.'

His eyes opened very wide. 'For heaven's sake, Frances. You do say the most extraordinary things sometimes.'

She lowered her body carefully, all the time watching his expression intently. 'You don't believe me? Perhaps that's as well, after all. I've been practising,' she continued, 'using Eastern techniques to create the most astonishing sensations for you, just by moving a few muscles.'

'You have?'

'And I've decided I can't do it.' Instead, she began to move gently and rhythmically, still watching him with that teasing appraisal. Alec, somewhere among all the other things his body was doing and trying to do, began to laugh.

Downstairs, somebody turned the music up.

The police officers from Greater Manchester Constabulary called just as Sarah was sitting the girls down to their tea. Sarah's first reaction was guilt. She had wished Ken dead, hadn't she? Now they had come to arrest her for his murder.

They asked if they could come in, avoiding volunteering what they were there for. The woman started making cheery talk with Beth and Amy. There were not enough chairs in the kitchen. The male officer suggested perhaps he and Sarah could go through into the living-room.

'What it is,' he said in his friendly local accent, 'there's not been no accident or anything, but it's just about your husband's car. Your husband's not in, I suppose?'

'No. He's away. His work.'

'Been away long?'

'Since last week. What about his car?'

'Do you happen to know what make it is, like?'

'Audi 80 estate. Red.'

'Don't happen to know the number, do you, love?'

She gave it.

'What it is,' he said helpfully, 'we've had a call from another force, and they've found a car answering to that description parked in a place called Ashdown Forest. Never heard of it meself, seems it's in Sussex. Your husband down in that part of the world, is he?'

'I don't know. He travels around.'

'He does, does he? You don't know what he might have been doing in Sussex? Only, the car had been there a couple of days. Nothing to be worried about, but they'd like to locate him. Travels a lot, does he?'

'He works for a construction machinery firm. Trouble-shooting. Firms hire excavators and dump trucks and whatnot when they get a contract to build a by-pass. If the machine breaks down, part of the deal is that Ken goes along and sorts it out. Gets it mended, or orders a replacement. They're all on bonuses for early completion, so if the machines break down they risk losing a good deal of money.'

'Is that so? I never knew that. So he could be anywhere, like? Matter of fact, I've got to call on his employers. They'd know his movements?'

'They ring him on the mobile phone and tell him what his schedule is. Sometimes I don't see him all week.'

The policeman was looking at her speculatively, and she

realized she was not showing very much concern. Presumably he expected her to be terrorstruck, hearing of Ken's car found abandoned. Sod it. Let them guess.

They left her then, after offering a few conventional warnings about not jumping to conclusions, a few conventional assurances that there was nothing to worry about. And the man gave her a look which seemed to say: We'll keep an eye on you.

'Nice life,' observed Liz, scanning the fax. Crossland's employers, she noted, could not say what his schedule might have been until they had done some checking. Nice life indeed. She handed it back to Johnson. 'Fancy a job like that, do you? Always travelling around, away from under the missus's eye, no one taking too much notice if you shack up for a night or two and you'd still claim subsistence for the hotel room, wouldn't you?'

'Not me, skipper,' Johnson replied self-righteously.

'Today's Thursday,' Liz mused. 'Car'd been there since last Friday morning at any rate.'

She looked out of the window at the trees dripping drearily. The rooflines further off were vague in the chilly mist which so often prevails over Sussex in winter. Easy for some city type to wander off into the forest in his city shoes, his light suit, and become disorientated and unable to find his way back to his warm metal cocoon. The forest was crisscrossed with roads; if you walked long enough in a straight line you'd hit one. But if you twisted your ankle in a rabbit hole, if the unaccustomed exercise triggered a heart attack, or if you simply succumbed to the unforgiving elements, you could lie a long time unnoticed in the forest's six thousand acres. And she wouldn't give much for his chances.

'He'll show by the weekend, skipper.'

'I sure hope so, sunshine.' She nodded towards the window, down which the sleety drizzle streaked hazy patterns which blurred the dismal outlook. 'This is no weather to have a manhunt on our hands.'

7

The chief super's 'garden parties' every second Friday at nine-thirty were officially senior and divisional officers' plenary sessions. They were garden parties only behind Oaks's back, and because prevailing CID wisdom regarded the chief as fussy and a trifle matronly. They took place in the larger of the two conference rooms on the top floor of the headquarters building where Liz worked, and every divisional or specialist DCI and above was required to be present in person or by proxy. While muttering mutinously about them as a waste of case time, most of those who had to attend conceded the need for some such forum for the exchange of information in an age of increasingly compartmentalized policing.

Liz was deputizing for Alec Stainton and likely to be the most junior present. She timed her arrival for maximum unobtrusiveness, slipping into the room when most of the chairs were already occupied and there was a general hum of conversation. Nevertheless, several heads turned at the sound of the door opening, and some of the younger and more human of those present gestured to empty seats beside them. Liz headed for a place halfway along one side of the table where it should not be too difficult to avoid Detective Chief Superintendent Oaks's eye; but Detective-Superintendent Blackett ordered loudly from his seat at the foot of the table: 'Come and sit by me.'

Liz altered course as Blackett obligingly shifted his chair. Taking her seat, Liz found herself gazing up the length of the conference table directly at DCS Oaks. One of the younger DCIs caught her eye and winked sympathetically. Liz kept the calm competent expression she had stitched on to her face in place and began to read the agenda paper, all dutiful attentiveness. Beside her, Blackett loomed, breathing stertorously. She caught the scent of the mint he sucked. She was not the only woman in the room, but the other two, an inspector and a chief inspector, were severely buttoned into their power suits, obligatory cream blouses clasped with brooches (one garnet, one diamanté) at the neck, hair close-cropped or tightly drawn back. In their presence Liz tended to feel as if the hem of her slip was hanging down, and now their disapproval seeped down the table like bad breath. She leaned her elbows on the table, deepening the cleavage visible in the open neck of her shirt. She heard the muffled crack of the mint fracturing between Blackett's teeth and smiled to herself. Who said she had no aptitude for diplomacy?

The moment the hand of the clock clicked to the vertical, Oaks tapped his pen unnecessarily on the polished table and called the meeting to order.

Having attended once before with Stainton, Liz knew the form. DIs and DCIs reported bits of information which might have a bearing on others' cases; then Blackett briefed them on matters of import at Force CID level; finally Oaks ran through a digest of briefings from other forces which might impinge on their own operations.

Liz sat quietly, took notes and, in preparation for her future meteoric rise to senior level, observed who was going where and how fast, and who had already reached their plateau. Oaks himself was hard to assess. He had never been much of a case officer. He was a manager. Coppers at the 'sharp end' referred to him disparagingly as Dumb Arthur ever since a musically literate recruit had first made the pun on the Dumbarton Oaks Suite; just as they nicknamed his beloved plenary sessions garden parties. Still, managers were the people who seemed to be taking over the world. Not a man to offend. And not a man to write off too hastily, either. He wasn't head of CID because he was a numbskull, and despite his exasperating style and petty official pomposity he got the job done, and done well.

Blackett, of course, was a star on the wane. He was not very far off retirement, though Liz sometimes wondered if he would ever reach it: she had a feeling that Blackett would die—in that grim phrase beloved of civil servants—in harness. He would remain a force to be reckoned with to the end, and he might be around to help her up the next step of the ladder. He had, after all, given Alec Stainton the odd discreet bunk up on the way to chief inspector. Of course, she reminded herself, he respected Alec Stainton's potential and appreciated his style. He liked her figure; but that was by no means the same thing.

Liz eyed the two power-suited inspectors surreptitiously and wondered if they knew something about Dumb Arthur's proclivities that she didn't.

'Detective-Sergeant Pink?'

Liz snatched her attention back hastily. Her report was all ready, typed on a sheet in front of her. It was the fruit of a long morning's labour; neither too cursory ('This officer is inclined to underestimate the complexity of CID work') nor too verbose, and would last precisely four minutes. Two ongoing sagas had been nicely tied up just before Alec Stainton went on leave and one, to her intense gratification, had been resolved in the last week. The car found on the forest did not rate a mention in this company. She concluded with a report about a vigilante group on a notorious housing estate, and sat back demurely. Blackett grunted approvingly.

Oaks as usual invited questions. Marjorie Weston leant forward. 'You mentioned the availability of weapons via the DEF/AID shops. Have you any evidence that the goods on sale are finding their way into hands other than those of women for self-defence?'

'No evidence, but it seemed a reasonable assumption that if they haven't yet, they will.'

'Have you taken any steps to corroborate this supposition?'

'None. Not yet. No.'

Marjorie Weston sat back as if satisfied. 'Thank you.'

Thank you, sister, Liz thought. She smiled innocently.

Blackett cleared his throat with the rumble of a great battleship going down the slipway. 'I don't think it's very helpful to speculate at this stage. I'm keeping an eye on it.'

'No more questions?' Oaks gathered the meeting together. Heads shook. 'Then perhaps . . .'

Blackett swallowed his latest mint and ran through a list of current operations at great speed. Pens scribbled hastily in diaries and on scratch-pads. The point of this was to ensure nobody who fouled up one of Blackett's major operations could later plead ignorance. Liz was especially diligent with her note-taking. The double wrath of her governor and Blackett, should she put them at loggerheads, would be awful to endure.

Then it was Oaks's turn. Everybody sat back and looked more relaxed. News of other forces was always received with interest. Often there was the pleasant prospect of another force making idiots of themselves. Very gratifying.

'Only three matters,' he informed them. 'First: Lothian and Borders have been tracking a drugs ring for the past eight or nine months, and there's some indication things are coming to a head.'

There was murmuring, some of it amused.

'I know.' Oaks raised a hand deprecatingly. 'But it's places like that, rural and isolated, where these people operate, as we know. More immediately to the point, the trail passes through our own patch. As part of their winding-up operation they're sending two detectives to sew up this end of things. The ACC's cleared it, and they'll be in touch next week. Marjorie, it's your country and I'd like you to give them every facility.'

Marjorie Weston nodded and made a note on her pad. Liz hoped Lothian and Borders were sending people who could stand up for themselves.

'Secondly,' Oaks continued, 'you'll have seen speculation in the media about these homicides. The "Carver" killings.' The quotation marks were expressively audible. Oaks had a love–hate relationship with the media, because, Liz was inclined to think, he didn't really understand them. He objected frequently and testily to their unhelpful complication of cases, but, required by his position to give press conferences, journalists' briefings and the like, he relished the spotlight. There was a certain innocence about Oaks sometimes which was curiously attractive; as if at heart he was dazzled by the limelight and seduced by the romance of the greasepaint. 'I mention it not because I expect any of you to go about the countryside spotting psychopaths; but because if or when a fifth murder takes place the force in whose patch it occurs will suddenly find themselves wishing they'd taken up needlework instead.' Mouths twitched obediently at the weak joke.

'Are there any grounds,' asked a DI on Liz's left, 'to believe a psychopath is responsible?'

Blackett forestalled Oaks's reply. 'When the same person kills four times,' he said with heavy irony, 'you'll generally find we call him a psychopath. The real question is, are these killings all by the same person? The answer is, yes they are.'

'So far as is known,' concluded Oaks, hastening to resume control. 'And lastly, we've mentioned two matters I find extremely disturbing: the Ross Mill vigilantes and these, ah, DEF/AID shops. Chief Superintendent Wilson is setting up a committee to report on vigilante movements in general.' He smiled sourly. 'They seem to be something of a growth industry just at present. Meanwhile, any operations which may touch on such groups are to be cleared with me.'

'Does that,' asked Marjorie Weston, 'include FIGHT-BACK?'

'Yes,' Oaks replied shortly. 'It does.'

On Monday, Alec found Frances's prediction fulfilled. As he drove in to work he felt refreshed and invigorated by his fortnight's leave and ready to get things done. The wind had changed again, lowering the temperature still further but dispersing the mist, and although the forecast showed formidable fronts building up over the continent, for a brief interlude the air was clear. But there was no mistaking that autumn was over. The trees stood suddenly stark, the light had the pearly hardness that presaged winter proper, and the air temperature dispelled illusions.

By half-past nine Alec and Liz were conducting their own, less formal, version of Oaks's garden party; Alec ensconced behind his desk, Liz in her customary position with one elbow on the filing cabinet. Considering her with the clarified appreciation with which one greets an intimate (some days, after all, he saw more of her than of his wife) after a period of separation, he relished afresh all the idiosyncrasies of her person that familiarity normally rendered invisible—all that made her *her*: the round good-humoured face; the rebellious dark hair gathered back today in a ribbon from which strands were already escaping to dangle round her cheeks; the un-fashionably ebullient figure confined (not without threat of escape) in well-cut skirt and smart blouse generously open at the neck. The money she spent on clothes she was learning to spend well, but there was always a happy unpredictability about her, as if the conflict between discipline and impetuos-ity which lent her personality its attractive frank nature found its correlative in her outward appearance. He counted himself extraordinarily fortunate to work so closely with someone he actually liked. That could bring its own prob-lems. It is not always easy to discipline someone who is an occasional guest in your house. But today, when everything about his work glowed with the favourable light available only to one returning reinvigorated from a happy holiday, Liz Pink seemed one of the more substantial blessings for which to be thankful.

Now he was culling the news: that invaluable mixture of hard fact, gossip and reading between the lines which would put him back in the swim.

'Right,' said Alec. 'What's next?'

Liz turned to matters of more immediate local interest. 'You saw,' she said modestly, 'we had a piece of luck about the betting shops while you were away?'

'Luck, was it?'

Liz blushed. Might have known mock humility would get short shrift, she reproved herself.

'I've glanced through the papers,' he continued. He was not smiling, but there was a glint to his eye which told her he was in indulgent mood. 'What else?'

'We're getting our collective knickers in a twist about FIGHTBACK. Reading between the lines, Oaks wants the DEF/AID shops closed down. We're cracking down hard on vigilante groups in general, but nobody's rushing to grasp the nettle where FIGHTBACK is concerned.'

'It's a uniform problem. Not our pigeon.'

'Wilson is chairing a group to look into it,' Liz agreed. 'But Oaks has seen the future, and it's populated by beefy women wielding baseball bats and he doesn't like it.'

Alec's mouth twitched. Auto-thefts on their local bane, the Ross Mill estate, had fallen dramatically since, during the summer, a self-styled watch committee had organized regular dusk-to-dawn patrols of young, fit men. The 'citizens' patrols', as they were known, carried no arms except baseball bats. So far, there had been no reports of any clashes with would-be criminals, and no injuries. But now beat officers were beginning to be unwilling to patrol Ross Mill. There were, it seemed, two faces to self-help.

And if vigilante activity to protect possessions was becoming commoner and thus insidiously more acceptable, how many voices were likely to be raised against those who took similar action to protect life itself? With a Carver at large, anyone who complained when FIGHTBACK mobilized against male aggression was going to be badly out of tune. Where did that leave the police, the despised but at least legitimate bastion of law and order?

'What's the policy on the DEF/AID shops in the meantime?'

'Counsel's opinion apparently is that so long as nothing is advertised as an offensive weapon and the shops display a prominent notice to the effect that carrying a weapon in a public place is an offence, we can do nothing except under the Shops Act or Health and Safety legislation. All of which

70

they comply with meticulously. Business rate paid, planning permissions all correct, washbasins spotless, the lot.'

'And in any event,' Alec observed, 'any infringement would take months to come to court.'

'If you are telling me they'll have caught the Carver before then, I'd be grateful if you'd put it in writing. Anyway, uniform branch have put out a standing order that women carrying DEF/AID bags are not to be stopped and searched any more, so someone's showing a glimmer of sense.'

Sense, if not logic, Liz added to herself. You allowed a bunch of would-be vigilantes to walk round the streets carrying CS gas and knuckledusters and knives and did nothing about it just because they were women. Belonging to the great sisterhood did not make women, as far as Liz's experience went, noticeably less prone to make a pig's ear of things than if they had been men.

'That's about it. I've got a bit of a watch going for a missing bod. Found his car abandoned on the forest. Wife hasn't seen him for a week.'

'What have you done?'

'Had a chat with the uniformed mob. Issued some photos.'

Alec nodded. 'Come and chat if you need to. OK, on your way out will you see if Ken Taylor's around and let him know I'd like a word?'

'Right you are, guv.'

'Looks as if we might have something, Liz.'

Waving the uniformed sergeant to a seat, Liz perched herself against the desk.

'Last Thursday week there was a bloke in the Brambletye who might have been Crossland.'

'How much might have been?'

'Well, young Sampson went in about a security matter.' Sampson was Crime Prevention Officer. 'He called in about half-eleven, and the bar staff were just coming on for the lunch-time stint. So being a bright lad, he took the opportunity to show round the photo of Crossland.'

'And?'

71

'One of the barmaids reckons she remembers him. She got a good look at the chap, because she took his order for food and served him his meal, and she noticed him specially because she watched him pick up a bird. She's given Sampson a description of the bird, but it could be anyone. But she's sure they left together.'

'Ah ha. What d'you know?'

'She didn't recognize the woman, and she's been working there a couple of months. Said she looked happy enough going out with the bloke.'

'On the game?'

'Could be, though you know the Brambletye—it's not that kind of place at all. I didn't put it to the waitress—she's only a kid. Hate to destroy her faith in human nature.'

'You slay me, Bill. I take it this bird hasn't been in since?'

'The girl can't say. She doesn't usually work evenings; seems that day she was doing an extra shift for a friend.' Liz felt a tiny shiver of apprehension ripple down her spine.

'Thanks, Bill. Tell the lad good work.'

'Tell him yourself. Make his day.'

'I'll do that. Then I think I might mosey on down to the Brambletye.'

So it was probably a woman after all, she told herself, following the road between the bare trees and brown bracken back from the hotel.

And it need not follow that she was a remarkable woman merely because the cost of taking up with her was likely to prove so high. He had abandoned both his car and his business appointments and by all accounts that had already cost him his job. Then, if he'd run off with a bird, his wife would want a divorce. The kids were girls, who would probably elect to stay with their mother. She'd keep the house—if the building society didn't repossess it; either way, he'd seen the last of it—and he'd find himself paying maintenance to keep the life he'd abandoned running. Yet people left their spouses every day for no better reason than that (as Liz had recently heard one acquaintance put it) they 'had found someone they liked better'. Crossland was a fool. By their actions shall ye know them, and perhaps he was one of those men whose brains are located between their legs.

Yet . . .

Yet the link with the woman at the Brambletye worried Liz. Back at the office, she spread the thin file with its scanty entries before her and nagged away at them, trying to persuade herself that she was content to wrap the case up.

No entry on the Police National Computer, so he was unlikely to be engaged in anything criminal, because he was in his late thirties and mature students are rare in the world of crime. At his age he'd have got himself on the computer somewhere if he was bent.

Anything spooky? Well, if there is, Liz told herself, I'll be the last to know; but the fact that we haven't been told to lay off the case suggests that if he is of any interest to any organization with an ex-directory telephone number they don't know it themselves yet. She smiled at her own tortuous logic; but no warning bells rang, and anyway, as a working hypothesis it was not very practical.

What about the car? Crossland seemed to have amassed a large number of penalty points on his licence, though without quite being disqualified. His insurance premium must be horrific, but of course the firm had paid that, and his generous salary and bonuses already told her that he had been worth a good deal to them. The fingerprint expert had given it a cursory once-over, and Liz abstracted his short report from the papers in the file even though she knew it almost by heart. It hadn't rated an examination by the bods from the forensic science laboratory; but Liz had been out to have a look at it for herself. No bumps or knocks, and anyway she'd already checked that no hit-and-runs had been reported. Just the smashed window-glass where thieves had forced an entry. What had there been in the car before it was rifled? Donkey jacket and wellingtons for muddy construction sites, and electronic diagnostic gizmos to do with his work, possibly. Suitcase? Clothes? Wallet and cheque book and credit cards? The car had a high mileage. Liz noted that it was less than a year old and amended that: an astronomical mileage. Deduction: Ken Crossland spent much of his working week on the road. Well done, Sergeant, please accept this commendation and promotion to chief superintendent.

Liz stood up and walked round the room. It was nearly five-thirty. Outside it was properly dark, throwing her reflection back at her from the black window. She should be calling it a day, going home, making tea in her new cookeryware in her new kitchen. But she preferred to stay here, beating her brain into a mousse as she grappled with the disappearance of a machinery rep who sounded, it had to be admitted, better lost.

How had he left the Coleman's Hatch cricket ground? Had someone else driven him away in another car? Had he, a stranger from a couple of hundred miles away, walked either along the forest roads or cross-country? On the other hand, the bus passed Coleman's Hatch church, half a mile away, and it would have carried him to the station. Mini-cab? Three avenues for exploration, but exploration could not be justified.

In the end, Liz went home, putting the mystery of Crossland's whereabouts from her mind before the swing doors of the building had sighed to behind her.

'Perhaps I'll call,' Ruth said on Saturday.

The postman had already been, and the post lay on the table beside the marmalade pot; buff official envelopes, and arresting coloured ones enclosing free offers. No letter addressed in Anita's remembered obsessive, miniature hand.

'She hasn't replied, then?' Alan said without surprise.

'She never was very good at that. Sometimes it feels as if I'm the only person in all our friendships who tries to keep in touch. I wrote to the Thomases with our Christmas card last year, and the Pratts, and we never heard a peep from either of them. I hate the idea that I'm bludgeoning people into keeping up a friendship against their will.'

Alan glanced at her, then came over and placed an arm

carefully round her shoulder. 'Most people can't be bothered, and then regret it. You can be bothered. It's one of the things I love you for.'

'If I rang Anita and asked her over . . .' She looked up at him tentatively.

'Sure.'

'She might only be able to come over in the evening. She may have a job now her mother's dead.'

'Don't worry. I won't refuse to let her in.'

'You could have an evening out. Andy's always badgering you to go karting. She does need friendship so much, I'm sure she does.'

He gave her a wry grin expressive of his view of Anita and his love for his wife's compassion. 'Do it.'

Alec was out when Lucy came home from Croydon with a dye-spray and a high-decibel alarm. She submitted the DEF/AID carrier to her mother's inspection in mutinous silence. Frances handed it back and regarded her daughter doubtfully.

'This is all you bought, isn't it, Lucy?'

'What's the matter? Scared I might embarrass you with Alec?'

'You do know, Lucy, that someone who used a knife on an attacker could find themselves on a murder charge. And it's so easy for accidents to happen. Something someone does is misinterpreted . . .'

'You think that's what the Carver's victims did? You want me to be attacked, do you? I'm supposed to turn the other cheek because I'm a policeman's . . . but I'm not a policeman's daughter. My mother just happens to have married one.'

Frances flinched. This too was the Carver's doing, she told herself bitterly. In addition to taking lives, he was blighting so many more. She watched Lucy go, wishing she could be free of the corrosive presence of suspicion.

Up in her room, Lucy shut the door and dumped the carrier on her bed. Then with a thrill of excitement she pulled her jersey up and fingered the handle of the short knife, its blade only three inches long, held by a quick catch in its rigid plastic sheath horizontally across her stomach.

Liz was at her desk at eight on Monday morning, but out of fairness made herself wait until half-past nine before she rang the fingerprint officer. He was out at a house that had been burgled overnight. At half-past eleven she learnt that if she had rung five minutes before she'd have caught him, but as it was he'd been and gone again, this time to a car which may or may not have been involved in a break-in.

It was well into the afternoon before she pinned him down, and he was in a bad mood, only grudgingly agreeing to see her, and then not until the next morning. The divisional station was on her own way to work, except that he wouldn't see her before eleven. So she'd have to drive all the way over to the office, and then all the way back again, virtually passing her front door both ways.

She did, however, manage a mutually rewarding conversation with Crossland's secretary Steffie in the office in Stockport, which left them both with a good deal of food for thought.

'I'm just not convinced. It's too obvious.'

Alec Stainton said: 'The obvious solution is usually the correct one.'

'Frequently. Not usually.'

He shrugged. 'Why not in this instance?'

'Why now? Why should he leave his wife, his job, now? He meets women every day. Picks them up all the time. If a bloke runs off with another woman, isn't it usually because he doesn't meet many, and when he finds one who at all responds to him he goes overboard?'

Alec considered that as a proposition. It was perhaps true that men who were easy in the company of women, and accustomed to it, were less likely to deceive themselves that they had 'fallen in love' than men to whom holding a serious conversation with a woman other than their wife had the shock of novelty. True only insofar as generalizations ever were true.

The real trouble with the 'other woman' assumption was that it depended on the idea that Crossland, having met someone in the Brambletye with whom he struck up sufficient acquaintance for a one-night stand, became so infatuated during the course of that night that he failed to keep his next morning's appointments and simply buried himself in his new-found illicit bliss. That sort of romantic infatuation did not seem to accord with the sexual sophistication, or facility rather, of a man like Crossland.

Eventually he said: 'Get on to Greater Manchester again. See if you can speak to someone trustworthy and ask them to have another word with Mrs Crossland. We can't waste time on this one, Liz. There's nothing to investigate, is there?'

'People disappear on the forest, guv. We find them, wrapped in plastic binliners, we excavate their limbs from shallow graves where the foxes have started our work for us.'

'But we don't dig the place up every week on the off-chance that there may be another corpse there.'

'I wonder what we would find, if we did that? What's your guess, guv? A dozen? A hundred?'

'I suppose. Anyway, we can't do it. We don't know where to look, and we've no reason to suppose Crossland's corpse is there. We might find him in some little cottage with roses round the door, that I grant you. Or more likely in some mansion solacing some fading blonde while hubby's on a business trip abroad.'

'Crossland wouldn't do that, though, would he? I mean, he'd do the solacing; but not at the cost of his job and his children. Not unless it was going to be a permanent arrangement, and how could he have decided that so soon?'

'The car?'

'I'm seeing Arthur Thorpe tomorrow morning. See what he found, try and persuade him to give it the works.'

'He won't do it. Why should he? On the other hand, it

might be a wise precaution to arrange for it to be taken to the forensic lab and put under cover. If anything comes of this, we can ask them to have a proper look at it. I'll think about having a word with Mr Blackett when you've talked to Thorpe and got word back from Manchester. This woman Crossland picked up: it'd be a great help if we knew who she was.'

'I'll work on that.'

'It'd be a comfort to know just where she is.'

Liz looked at him long and thoughtfully, realizing that he had fetched out into the open a vague idea that had been floating at the back of her mind. 'Yes,' she said slowly. 'I think that's right.'

8

It was not the morning, but the afternoon, with wasted hours behind her, wasted largely on chasing after Thorpe. The roads were busy. Mums returning from the school run with cars full of kids overlapped with the first home-going office workers.

Liz was not optimistic about the outcome of her journey. After twenty not very scintillating years in which he had worked his way up to sergeant in the CID Thorpe had been given his niche as fingerprint officer and guarded it jealously. He did his work as he had throughout his career: adequately, ensuring nobody would ever be able to say he had failed to comply with the letter of his job description. Keenness, however, was to Thorpe not merely an alien but a dangerous concept. Keenness was for rookies and dummies—and he never grasped how little he was liked in consequence. Everybody knew he never went the extra mile—never the extra yard, come to that; never put in that little extra effort at his own expense or in his own time. And, because he fulfilled the letter of his contract, he presented a barrier of hostile affront to any querying of his work. He handed out the results of his examinations as if granting a personal favour, with the clear implication that you took what was given and were grateful. Even senior officers found themselves in the position of supplicants when they dealt with Thorpe and, like their juniors, dealt with him in consequence as little as possible.

'What's all this about?' he asked rudely as she tapped on his door and entered the small office which was his empire.

'Afternoon, Arth. I won't keep you. It's this motor that was found out at Coleman's Hatch.'

'What about it? You've had my report.'

'Yes, thanks, Arth. I've brought it with me. I wondered if we could have a little chat about it.'

'What's wrong with it?'

'Nothing's wrong with it, Arthur.' She fished the flimsy out of her document case. It ran to less than one side of A4. She set it on the desk between them and ran a finger down the lines of text. 'You took prints off the door handle, door frame and steering wheel.'

'I've said so in that report.' And they were the right places to take them from. A thief forced the door; held it open; sat inside and even if only reaching for the radio steadied himself by grasping the wheel. Quite adequate for the purposes of investigating auto-theft.

'Arth, I'd like you to go over the car properly.'

He snorted. 'You would, would you?' He spoke habitually with a long-suffering timbre very irritating to endure, as of a man who deals with idiots. He made no attempt to mask his contempt and Liz, who could take any amount of back-chat, found his downright rudeness, as always, hateful. It valued the recipient at nothing; the verbal equivalent of the callous blow that doesn't care how it wounds.

'Please. I'm speaking for DCI Stainton, actually,' she answered.

'Oh? And has DCI Stainton deigned to give me one good reason?'

They argued it tersely, the semblance of courtesy becoming more tattered, mutual contempt more naked with every minute. In the end, Liz said, 'I'm putting in a request for the forensic lab to have it and give it the works.'

'For a stolen radio? You're out of your mind. Run along and play with your dolls,' he dismissed scornfully. 'Come back when you're dry behind the ears.'

Liz stood. She felt perfectly clear-headed, even calm, but she knew she was going to say something foolish, and couldn't stop herself.

'The advantage of the forensic lab,' she said sweetly, 'is that at least I'll have some confidence that if there are prints, they'll find them.'

She saw the red spots appear on his cheeks and spread into hot angry stains.

'If you were my daughter,' Thorpe said slowly, 'I'd put you over my knee and belt you.'

'Try it.'

She smiled at him, enjoying his mounting fury. For a long minute they stared at each other in mutual dislike.

Liz said: 'Shall I tell DCI Stainton you refuse to do what he's requesting, or will you?'

'Tell DCI Stainton—if he's got anything to do with this— that I shall do it if I receive a proper request through the proper channels. I certainly won't do it because he chooses to send his latest fancy piece to throw names at me. Now run away and find yourself something better to do than waste my time. Tell him to send a real police officer next time, if he's too scared to come himself. Now get out.'

Liz looked him in the face. 'You know, Arth, I never really believed you could be such a turd as people said. Shows how wrong a girl can be, doesn't it?' And she left the room, leaving the door open.

As she walked through the CID room on her way out every head was studiously bent and the room was preternaturally quiet. Liz was well aware that every word she and Thorpe had exchanged had been overheard. Oh, hell! And she was going to have to explain to the governor, too!

Crossing to her car she heard a clock chime in town and checked her watch. It was half an hour's drive back to the office. She would arrive in time to do ten minutes' work before knocking-off time. Home, on the other hand, was but a few minutes away, and she could stop off in town for a couple of pairs of badly-needed tights.

She climbed into the car, turned out of the car park and pointed the nose, as she had known she would, back towards work. You idiot, she told herself. Not one person in a hundred has a conscience so perversely sensitive. But you couldn't change the way you were. It was yourself you had to live with, and you just had to make the best of it.

At the junction there was a queue of traffic on the main road, but a man in a Mercedes stopped and waved her through. Perhaps it wasn't such a bad world.

Alec sensed that there was an edge of need in Frances tonight, and characteristically she broached the anxiety herself without waiting to have it wheedled out of her. He listened as the story of Lucy's DEF/AID purchases was related to him.

'I suppose,' Frances concluded with a self-deprecating turn of the mouth, 'the real problem is that I can't adjust to her growing up. They know so much. And most of the time they seem able to handle it, but sometimes . . . We were innocents, by comparison. Was that really such a bad way to be?'

But in today's world such innocence would be vulnerable. Twenty years earlier, when Frances had been a teenager, there had been child molesters, there had been murderers and rapists and abductors. Fewer, perhaps. Less remorselessly publicized, so that people could live in ignorance much of the time; and being in ignorance, were not made wary and suspicious by knowledge.

'I'm afraid she'll do something silly.'

'With a dye-spray and a personal alarm?' He smiled affectionately.

'I keep wondering what else she bought.'

And the fear that your daughter told you a lie, he thought, is sharper than the fear that she bought a stiletto or a CS canister.

She put a CD of Gregorian chant on the player, and came and sat by Alec and took him in her arms. He said: 'If she has anything to tell you, I don't think she'll keep it to herself for long. Better to show trust.'

'Better, but harder.' He heard the hint of mockery, felt the fractional relaxation. After a while he began to tell her about

82

Liz's encounter with Arthur Thorpe, filling in with shrewd guesses the lacunae she had tactfully left in her confession that afternoon. Frances recounted the trivia of her day at the office. They kissed, and began to make love.

The monks sang on unperturbed.

After four hours' solid study Liz retired to bed with her sense of virtue restored and fell quickly asleep. When it came, the relentless summons of the bell reached her brain only dimly through a vast depth of unconsciousness. A dream flashed through her mind in which a telephone was ringing. She came up on to a shallower level and her consciousness admitted the bell as a real sound, but insisted it had no relation to herself. Arguing the point, she groped for her alarm clock. The luminous hands read twenty-past one or five-past four, she couldn't be sure which. Finally, her mind struggling into some sort of wakefulness while her body still yielded to the tug of slumber, she realized that it was the front doorbell calling, on and on and on, and leaped out of bed, reaching for her jeans.

Her first thought was that someone had died; then that some terrible thing had happened at work. The Carver had killed again; he was holed up with a hostage and a gun. But it would have been the phone, not the doorbell that summoned her then. But if it was not work or bereavement, then whoever it was had chosen a hell of a time of night to haul her out of bed.

And if it was not bereavement or work . . .

Despite her certainty that the bell was about to stop she diverted to the kitchen and seized her new rolling-pin out of the pottery utensils jar in which it resided. Only then did she switch on all the lights and unbolt the door.

'Rosie!'

'I'm sorry, Liz! God, I thought you'd never come.'

'What's wrong? Come in. Have you got . . .' She saw the bundled clothing wrapped in a crocheted blanket, and a wisp of fine hair. Rosie's breath whirled on the frosty air. What could have brought her out at such an hour with her baby?

As Rosie crossed the threshold, Joy started crying. Liz hurried into the kitchen and punched the central heating advance. The boiler lit with a welcome thud. Thank God for a small house which heated up quickly.

Rosie sat down without invitation. She seemed in a daze. She began unwrapping her coat. Beneath she was wearing only a garish blouse and tight jeans as if she too had dressed hastily in the first things to hand. She began to unbutton the blouse, her hands clumsy with cold, as if to feed Joy. But she undid all the buttons one by one until the garment hung open, then turned her head and watched herself pull it off her shoulder.

'Oh, God, Rosie!'

The bruises were dark, reddish purple. Four of them, in an unmistakable hand print arcing round beneath the collar bone and over the top of the breast just above the tough cloth of the nursing bra.

'Not . . . Mike?'

She looked up at Liz but didn't meet her eye. 'I know it's a lot to ask but . . .'

'Yes, of course,' said Liz with a sinking heart.

'Just for tonight. At least . . .'

'Let's not make promises for the future. I'll go and make up a bed. Of sorts.' She grimaced. 'It's no palace.' And it would seem so small with two—no, three. Joy whimpered and Rosie unhooked her bra and offered the baby the breast—of them here. How long could it last? If there were serious problems between Rosie and Mike, the last thing she wanted was to be caught in the middle. And now, of all times, when she had to devote all her spare time to study! Why, oh why did she attract lame ducks?

Her last image before she went upstairs to get things ready was of Rosie sitting contentedly at the table, the pain, indignity and ill-omen of her experiences displaced by a simple biological function, serenely suckling Joy.

It seemed a little too cosy for comfort.

9

Alec raised the question of Crossland at Friday's garden party.

Oaks sat back in his chair. 'Are you telling us, Alec,' he asked in the reasonable civil servant's manner which could be so maddening, 'that you have decided this man is the *Carver*?' His voice rose incredulously on the final word.

'No; I'm not saying that. I'm merely suggesting that at this time, when the activities of the Carver are at the forefront of media attention, it would be prudent to insure ourselves against the remote contingency that we could later be judged to have taken the possibility insufficiently seriously.' The cumbrous sentence was not unintentional. It was the style of reasoning most likely to appeal to Oaks's defensive cast of thought.

'There's one good reason for believing the Carver might be on the forest,' Blackett interjected.

'Indeed?' Oaks permitted himself a thin smile as he sat with his eyes closed. You could not call them merely two approaches to policing, Alec mused: they are two generations. And is Oaks, the manager *par excellence*, any more the policeman of the future than Blackett, the seat-of-the-pants man? Or will the head of CID in twenty years' time be Sally Field, sitting in a room surrounded by VDUs on which the location of every known criminal in the country is continuously monitored?

'It's a good one, mind,' Blackett replied. 'And it's this: nobody's got sod-all idea where else he is.'

'*Could* Crossland have committed the other killings?' Oaks

asked the room at large; and then focused on Alec. 'I suppose you have checked that?'

'There are certainly construction sites at or near all the locations,' Alec replied. 'The Norwich by-pass; the Wadebridge by-pass. The Second Severn Crossing. The Trenant relief road.'

'And did he in fact visit them?'

'We're checking,' Alec said. 'It's difficult. Crossland's own diary was in his car, and is presumed stolen. His secretary keeps a diary of his appointments, but it's not a reliable guide to his movements: he slots in additional visits, and sometimes site managers contact him direct. His travel claims are the best guide, but he makes them up in arrears. Months in arrears. We know he was at Wadebridge. That's the only one we're sure of at this point.'

'I hope you haven't made any enquiries that might lead anyone to jump to conclusions, Alec.'

'No, but I'll have to speak to the HOLMES staff,' Alec warned. Officers from the Norfolk, Devon and Cornwall, Gloucestershire and Dyfed/Powys constabularies were all working on the Carver case. The investigations were being coordinated under HOLMES, the Home Office Large Major Enquiry System, although reading between the lines of the scant reports Alec understood that the hunt for the Carver was stalled for lack of data.

'I think I'd rather you didn't, just at present. If, for the sake of, um, regard for the future, we were to elect to devote some resources to looking for this man Crossland, what do you suggest?'

Alec outlined the course of action which he and Blackett had discussed as the best provisional way forward. No out and out search for the time being, and no public indication that the Carver was thought to be in Sussex. Every effort would be made to identify and trace the woman Crossland had met in the Brambletye, and Crossland's firm would be asked as a matter of urgency to account for every hour of his schedule over the time since the first Carver killing. Greater Manchester Police should be asked to interview Sarah

Crossland more searchingly. If this low-profile approach produced no results by the end of a fortnight, if Crossland had not been otherwise eliminated, and if no developments in the Carver case had occurred elsewhere in the country, then they would meet again to discuss the desirability of a full-scale combing of the forest, with the media attention that would attract. There was a few minutes of general discussion, in which it became apparent that those who favoured Alec, those who favoured Blackett, and those who liked needling Oaks, combined to a larger total than the opposition. It was clear the sense of the meeting was for going ahead on the lines Alec had suggested.

'All right,' Oaks said. His manner made it plain that he was acceding to a majority decision while his own judgement remained uncommitted. 'I'd rather we spoke to Mrs Crossland ourselves, though. The fewer people in the know the better.'

'We'd have to give a reason for going there. We'd end up telling them one way or the other; or they'd end up guessing.'

Oaks frowned. And then he surprised Alec by saying: 'If we're going to take any steps, there's no sense in half measures. I'd like this man searched for, actively. You'd better draft me something with the requirements for manpower.'

He's rattled, Alec thought. He sees a murder on our ground and the press getting wind of us knowing about Crossland and doing nothing. But I don't believe Crossland is the Carver—do I? I just want him found so that I can sleep at night without a nagging feeling that something no good has happened to him.

'Sod him,' said Blackett as Alec strode at his side towards the stairs. 'Clever Dick. Now let's get down to work.'

Liz said bluntly: 'What do we get?'

'He's asking uniformed branch for eight constables and a sergeant.'

'Twenty would be more like it,' Liz observed tartly. 'I'm not Paul Daniels.'

'Take it or leave it.'

'I'll take it. Thanks, governor.' She knew how much he hated asking Oaks for favours. 'Starting when?'

'Nine o'clock Monday morning. Get your skates on.'

Liz risked a look of long-suffering. 'No problem.'

Once she had been given the green light, Liz wasted no time. Experience told her that unless she moved fast, some other task would come to light which had a higher priority, and the resources made available to her would dematerialize quicker than mist on a summer's morning.

A phone call to the Ordnance Survey confirmed that they would have the maps she wanted available for collection that afternoon. The scale Liz had asked for would show not only every building but every hedge, fence, stile, stable and outside privy. No; Liz mentally corrected herself: this was a part of the world where even the horses had en suite bathrooms. And yet . . . Ashdown Forest was a queer place; still, in parts, anachronistically cryptic. There was more than one community inhabiting its clearings and hamlets. Sure, there was the visible community of the middle class, who provided the Volvos and Mercedes on the roads, the neat, orderly children in their private school uniforms, the horses in the paddocks; who seemed, to some, and indeed to themselves, to be the only community. But living as it were in parallel, in the spaces in between, like a race of full-size Borrowers, was an ancient society not much changed by the coming of the car or the electricity or even the coming of the middle-class hordes. Men who subsisted by doing building jobs and tree-felling and dealing in eggs and vegetables. Women who would no more think of working in an office than of flying; who cooked on solid fuel ranges which they rose at six to light; who kept a handful of Buff Orpingtons and a vegetable plot; who went in and 'did' in those big houses with the three, four or five bathrooms; old men and women retired from service; even kids, still, who scamped through the village schools much as their grandfathers had done, until they could leave and buy a motorbike.

That was the community, unobtrusive and easily over-looked, where, if Crossland had gone to earth, he could be literally unfindable.

There was something restful about spending Saturday morn-ing cutting up maps in the deserted CID room. Despite the fact that crime has a seven-day working week, Saturday and Sunday still felt different, with fewer staff around and a generally more relaxed atmosphere. And—Liz acknowledged unsparingly—it was easier to run away, today, when other-wise there would have been the prospect of a day at home with Rosie and Joy's presence only too unavoidable. During the week it had not been impossible—Liz was out in the mornings before Rosie surfaced, and the evenings had largely been spent swotting for her promotion exams while Joy slept angelically upstairs and Rosie was out somewhere, to return at bedtime or even (she had asked for a key, to save dis-turbing Liz) later. It's myself I distrust, Liz told herself, if we have to endure too much proximity in my little house. Better to be unavoidably absent . . .

She began by dividing Ashdown Forest into sectors, and then subdivided the sectors into individual beats based on postcodes. Now she took a purposeful pair of scissors to the expensive maps, cutting them up so as to furnish each of the house-to-house team with the relevant extract.

At eleven, there was a light step in the corridor and Sally Field came in, looking if anything even more elegant and poised in her off duty sweatshirt and jeans than she did in her weekday plain clothes.

'What're you doing here, Fieldy?'

'Want a hand?'

'Fieldy, today is Saturday.'

The other girl shrugged. 'I hadn't anything planned.' She hunted in desk drawers until she found another pair of scissors and reached for the pile of maps. Liz grinned to herself and felt happy.

After a while she gave Sally Field a sidelong look. 'Toby playing away?' she enquired innocently.

'At home against Old Dunstonians, as it happens.' Sally Field's bent head did not reveal any emotion. Liz nodded sagely to herself.

Sally Field attracted men. Juicy men with City salaries untouched by the recession; men with new 'nineties money who fully intended to be occupying a modest manor house by thirty-five. Men able to afford the best and who, as a precaution against not getting it, looked for the goods with the highest price tag. Fieldy slightly despised them all; for their jejune aspirations, for regarding girlfriends as probationary wives, for requiring their presence on touchlines or in corporate hospitality tents, auditioning, as it were, for a more permanent job. Sally ran them for a month or so— about the time it took them to realize she had no intention of falling into anybody else's design for her life. Then she traded them in. Some went with a good grace; some begrudgingly; but they were all discarded sooner or later. Thus Toby.

One set of maps went on the wall of the CID room.

'Our very own incident room, Fieldy,' observed Liz, standing back. 'What you've always wanted.'

It was a vast area they had to search. Seeing it delineated on the maps, Liz realized just how vast; and how intricate. From Haywards Heath to Uckfield; Uckfield to Tunbridge Wells; Tunbridge Wells to East Grinstead, and over to the A23 and down to Haywards Heath. A great . . . 'What d'you call this shape, Fieldy?' Liz sketched it with a wave of her arm.

'Rhomboid,' replied the other girl, after studying it for a moment.

'Right. Just testing.'

'You're looking,' Liz said, 'for any evidence that Ken Crossland is, or ever has been, within the boundaries of this rhomboid here.' She indicated it on the map. Alec Stainton was sitting quietly in the back row, and she tried to forget the reference he would soon be writing for her confidential file if—when—she succeeded in her promotion exams. 'Dead or alive,' Liz said, 'but preferably alive. He could be shacked up. He could have *been* shacked up and moved on. You've all got your packs? In the pack is a pix sheet.'

Most of them had the sheet out already; the others pulled it out and studied it; an A4 sheet with four photographs on it: Crossland head-on in business suit and in casuals; Crossland left profile, laughing; Crossland right profile, his arm round his daughter.

'There's also a pic of the car, and a list of things that were in it when he left home. They may be with him, or they may have been nicked from the car either before or after it was abandoned. Some of them may have turned up on a pub table. Somebody may have been offered them. Somebody may have seen the car.' She paused, and swept the room with a schoolmistressly eye. 'I know the routine: knock on the door, wait ten seconds, tick the sheet and off to the next; if there's a reply, quick flash of the mug shot and "Sorry for troubling you, madam" and off down the path.' She looked round the assembled faces sternly. Some were grinning. 'That won't do for me. I'm an old-fashioned type. If it's worth doing, it's worth doing well. If there's someone there, get yourself invited in. Accept the tea, even if it means drinking fifty cups and stopping behind every hedge. Get chatting. Pass the pix and give them time for a good look. If there's no one in, take a gander round the outbuildings, peer through the windows. You're all in uniform, you can swing from the weather vane and nobody's going to mind. And if there's no one in, you go back later. Or next day.'

'Skipper, it'll take till Christmas.'

'Which one?' grunted someone *sotto voce.*

Liz said: 'OK. But I'll tell you this. You're going to spend the next few days looking for this bloke the easy way. Cars. Warm houses. If we don't find him this way, maybe we're going to be out on that forest in our wellies for a month examining every bit of bracken and every blade of grass. Some of you have done that before. Mick, you have. Tell them.'

The constable shrugged, and nodded his agreement. 'All right in August . . .' he let it tail off expressively.

Someone said: 'You're pretty certain he's on the forest.'

'That's right.' She wasn't, of course. Say, eighty per cent sure, and half of that was just a feeling under her diaphragm. But if she showed doubt, she wouldn't get the commitment or the diligence. 'He's here, or he's been here. It shouldn't be beyond the wit of you lot to find some trace of him.'

They shambled out, leafing through their packs of addresses, map sections, photographs and other data. She had organized the search into runs, so that one constable with a car could take three others out and drop them off to cover their own sectors, collecting them later from a different point. Liz herself was to spend this first day roving across the area, not only keeping up morale but collecting completed sheets. With luck, there would soon be information to analyse. It would be her task to analyse it and make any follow-up visits that were necessary.

Liz wondered whether she should have gingered them up with talk of Crossland being the Carver. She knew why she hadn't. A morbid fear she had had since childhood of counting her chickens. If you raised no expectations, success—if it came—was if anything sweeter. And failure far, far less bitter.

The girls had barely set out for school and Sarah Crossland was washing up the breakfast things when the car drew up. From the kitchen window she watched the two men climb out and walk up the drive and knew at once they were policemen in plain clothes.

They were distantly formal when she opened the door to their ring. Both looked to be in their thirties: close to her own age. They told her names and ranks. She didn't really take it in; just that the thin, balding one was the senior of the two. The hall seemed very crowded with the three of them in it and the other man—the heavy, dark-jowled one—suggested they go through. They made Sarah feel like a stranger in her own house as she led the way. They sat forward confidently in the chairs in the lounge. Sarah subsided gingerly on to the sofa, waiting for she knew not quite what: the revelation of the threat.

'Your husband is Kenneth John Crossland,' the heavy man began, reading the name out of a notebook and glancing up at her for confirmation. She nodded.

'And he's away. How long has he been away, Mrs Crossland?'

'Three weeks. Three weeks yesterday.'

'Three weeks. That's a long time.'

'He's often away several days at a time. A week, anyway . . . Look, we've been over and over this.'

'Right. And he works for a firm called Construction Technology International.'

She sighed. 'He sorts out problems. When something breaks down on site.'

The thin man was inspecting his shoe, moving it this way and that against the light, as if testing the shine. 'Could you tell me, Mrs Crossland, what his schedule was for any particular week?'

'No. I mean, it doesn't work like that. He doesn't know in advance. Only his first appointment.'

'What was his first appointment that Monday when he left here?'

'The New Forest, I think. That's what he said.'

'Don't you believe what he said?'

'I . . . Yes . . .'

'It sounds to me as if most of the time you have no idea, Mrs Crossland, where your husband is when he is travelling around the country on business.'

'No. The company . . .'

'Yes. Does he tell you afterwards where he's been?'

'Sometimes.'

'Aren't you curious?'

'No. Well . . . no.'

The thin man said, without looking up from his shoes, 'Aren't you curious about what he gets up to in the evenings?'

Sarah Crossland lifted her head and jutted her chin. 'Not any more, no.'

He looked up at that, scrutinizing her carefully with a steady, slightly hostile gaze. 'Why not, Mrs Crossland? Why not *any more*?'

She didn't answer. What could you answer to a question like that? Easier to let the silence tell them what they wanted to know.

The thin man said, 'When did you stop being curious, Mrs Crossland? Most wives would be.'

She said nothing, but sensed the increase of his hostility.

She didn't see the sign between them, but the big man took over, reeling off a list of place names and asking her if they meant anything to her.

She looked at him disparagingly. 'They're places in England. So what?'

'Trenant isn't in England, Mrs Crossland.'

'England and Wales, then.'

'Notice anything else about them?'

'I didn't hear . . .'

He repeated the list.

'No. They're all in the south and west. Is that what you mean?'

'Did your husband cover the whole country, Mrs Crossland?'

She had answered—his area had been the Midlands, East Anglia, Wales, the south and west—before the words he had chosen reached her consciousness. Not: Does he, but: Did he . . . Did he . . .

The thin man spoke conversationally to his companion. 'Lot of names there, Tom. Perhaps Mrs Crossland didn't take them all in. Suppose we slim the list down a bit.'

'Right.' He paused, as if assessing her, then said deliberately, 'Trenant. Norwich. Wadebridge. Gloucester.'

Sarah Crossland stared at him, bemused. What was this all supposed to mean? Why were their questions suddenly accusations? The names echoed in a jumble of meaningless sounds in her brain. Wadebridge? Norwich? Everybody was talking of Norwich. Why, even on the television the other night there were pictures of the place. Something to do with a woman killed nearby . . . A woman. Killed. By the man they were calling the Carver, because he . . .

The big man judged the moment, then asked casually, 'You are quite sure Mr Crossland hasn't been back here in the last three weeks, Mrs Crossland?'

'Of course I am.'

'We'd rather like to meet him, Mrs Crossland. If he turns up, or if he rings, you will let us know, won't you?'

They rose to go. The thin man explained, 'There are some questions we'd like to ask him, Mrs Crossland.'

Then they were gone. As simply, as meaninglessly as they had come. And Sarah Crossland found herself back in the lounge, desperately plumping the cushions and shifting the chairs, as if she could erase the traces of their presence, as if somehow she could project herself back to that moment before their car drew up outside, keep herself forever in the world in which she had lived before she realized that Ken, with whom she had lived intimately for fifteen years, was the Carver.

10

'Alec? It's Chris.'

'Chris, hi.'

'Got a moment?'

'Sure.' Alec laid down his pen and pushed his chair aslant the desk, settling the telephone properly to his ear. And told himself that it was ridiculous to feel foreboding on the basis of six words. Even from the force's press officer. 'What can I do for you?'

'I've had a bloke called Martin on the phone. You won't know him, probably. His real name's Michael—at least, that's his byline, but everyone calls him Muddy. If I tell you he's a staffer for the *Globe* you can probably guess the reason.'

So it might be irrational, that feeling of foreboding, but once again it was about to be justified. What curious turn of voice had communicated trouble so unerringly?

'He's asking how the hunt for the Carver's going,' Chris Roberts continued. He paused expressively. 'We don't have a hunt for the Carver. Or do we?'

Alec's first reaction was anger; but it was useless to speculate where the leak had occurred, or whether accidental or malicious. 'What did you tell him?'

'He's one bloke I can't afford to run around, I'm afraid, Alec. I said I'd find out. He's ringing back in an hour.'

Alec said nothing while he thought. At the other end of the line, Roberts said eventually, 'It's a question of whether we can play it our way, Alec. He'll get there whether or no, but if we play straight we can call a few of the shots, maybe.

I get the feeling he's had a tip-off from another force. Could that be right? I'm assuming there's something in it?'

Alec made his mind up. 'When did he ring?'

'Ten minutes ago. I didn't think this was one for wasting time on.'

'Thanks, Chris. I'll get back to you before the hour's up.'

'OK, thanks, Alec.' He paused. 'Had I better clear my desk?'

Alec mouthed a smile Roberts couldn't see. 'Do that. You're about to earn your salary, Chris.'

They held a full press briefing the following morning, as Alec had known they would; and he conducted it, and he had known that too. Oaks's ostensible reason for asking him to do it was that to have a more senior officer in evidence would be to give credence to the belief that the man they were looking for really was the Carver. Alec, Oaks and Blackett had thrashed out the substance of the briefing late the previous afternoon, after the immediate task of providing Muddy Martin with his exclusive had been dealt with. The *Globe* had been on Alec's desk when he came in this morning, and he read Martin's article with wry appreciation. There was a lot in it that had not been in Chris Roberts's low-key revelations. Having secured confirmation of the Crossland/ Carver projected link, Martin had drawn on much more extensive sources of information. Alec would rather have liked to know just what those sources—those uncomfortably accurate sources—were. Angry CID officers from other forces had already been on the phone asking what the hell was going on.

The *Globe* article ensured that the press briefing would be widely attended; and tough. Alec doubted whether the damage-limitation exercise they had mapped out would succeed. One thing he was sure of: they would not be able to continue the Crossland hunt as at present constituted. The cat was out of the bag. The media did not deal in tentative suggestions of possible identifications: from today, the force would be hunting 'the man believed to be the Carver', and they would have to be seen to be hunting him with the determination and the resources the pursuit of the Carver warranted. Unless and until attention was drawn off by some development elsewhere, the Carver hunt was here. Alec was instructed to play down the Carver dimension as much as he could; but in his top-floor office, Detective Chief Superintendent Oaks was closeted with the Chief Constable, one of the ACCs and the divisional Chief Supers, planning the management of the role the media had without warning thrust upon them, of Hunters of the Carver. One thing was for sure: Liz wouldn't long have to be content with her eight-bobbies-and-a-sergeant door-to-door.

Ah, well. Tomorrow someone would report the Carver in Lincolnshire or Cardiff or Lundy Island, and the spotlight would drift away from them again. The briefing would take an hour or so, he supposed. Be done well in time to clear his desk and leave work promptly. There'd be long days aplenty ahead; and it was his turn to do the shopping on the way home.

A vaporous winter mist covered the south of England, moist and clinging, depositing pearlescent drops on woollen scarves, car door handles and the manes of horses snorting morosely in muddy fields. The mist was rendered more noxious by the exhaust fumes of the cars and lorries, which there was no breath of air to disperse. Vehicles loomed out of opacity, the headlamps surrounded by auras like distant moons, ground cautiously by, and receded into obscurity. Pedestrians ventured out muffled and suspicious into this alien environment where familiar landmarks seemed mysteriously displaced as if they had been moved by perverse beings out of a malicious humour to confound. People who could remember them spoke of the smogs of the 'fifties.

It was lethal weather for some, and good weather for death in general. Good weather for disposing of a corpse, if that was what you happened to want to do; as someone did, near Petworth. Not elegantly, and with no care for the disarrayed clothing or for what it revealed—but what has elegance to do with death? Any quiet lane, any field gateway or farm turning will do to lug the guts from car boot to sodden, beaded grass, when there are only the dully dripping trees to look on.

The autumn dusk began to fall soon after three, darkening the mist that had enshrouded the forest all day, and by five it was inky night, and the temperature dropping fast. At half-past, as Detective Chief Inspector Alec Stainton drove away from police headquarters, in a lane between Hartfield and Forest Row a dozen or so miles away Constable Webster placed another neat tick by torchlight and turned over the sheet on his clipboard. The photocopied Ordnance Survey extract was beneath it and he held it up to the light and peered at the grid lines. Only two more properties to go and then the blessed relief of the station where he could put his notes in order in the warmth and light with a cup of tea by his side. He flicked the light off and plodded off along the silent lane.

The barn came first: isolated in a field carved out of the forest, beneath dripping naked branches. Webster turned up his collar and blessed his wellingtons. The grass was rank and wet, and the air heavily damp. It was Webster's twentieth building. He was a conscientious young man and he tried to search it as thoroughly as the first, even though his torch was waning. He left the barn only when he was sure it contained nothing but hay, and that the hay showed no evidence of intrusion. No stray cans or bottles, no food cartons, no damp mud on the floor. He trudged back to the road and placed another tick on the sheet. Just one to go: a house. He debated whether to accept a cup of tea if it was offered. Depended who offered it, of course.

Even though he was on foot he almost missed Bracken Ghyll. With the darkness thickened by the gauze curtain of mist, visibility was negligible and from the road the only indication of the house was a flattening of the verge where a track led off, crossed by a raggedy wire fence. An oil drum had been tied up and crudely painted POST. The pressure of the trees round him was almost tangible, as if men and women had barely hacked their settlements out of the forest, or all but lost them again to the encroaching undergrowth. The only sounds were the elusive echoes of the mist itself: the drip of moisture, the slow decay of sodden timber. If there was any life nearby, the sound of it was swallowed up in the saturated air.

Webster pushed down on the wire until he could step carefully over it, alert to the barbs. Now he became aware of denser patches of darkness. From the house itself there was no sound; and only the glint of rain on the windows of an upstairs room distinguished it from the two or three other shadowy masses ahead and to one side which must be out-buildings. He sensed abandonment heavy in the wet night like the odour of dry rot. Duty was still arguing with incli-nation when the radio crackled his call-sign and he reached for the handset to reply.

'Three-two.'

'Control. Three-two, report position and current activity.'

'Three-two. I'm on the Marsh Green/Chuck Hatch un-classified on building check for missing person.'

'Control. How many to go, over?'

'Three-two. I'm on the last one now.'

'Control. Wait.'

He waited. A minute passed. Two. The steady drip of damp and decay continued.

'Control. Three-two, leave that task, proceed to pick-up point at—' she read out a grid reference.

'Three-two, wilco. What's up, love?'

The machine-like voice became for an instant human and urgent.

'There's been a homicide.'

'Three-two. I'm on my way.'

Constable Webster hastily added a tick to the sheet along-side Bracken Ghyll, tucked the clipboard under his arm, stepped back over the wire and set off at a brisk trot for the rendezvous. Before he got there he saw the headlights of the patrol car gleaming between the hedges. They pinned him to the darkness like an insect to a board and it pulled up sharply. The other three were already in it. He passed back his clipboard to be added to the heap on the back shelf and clutched for the seatbelt as the driver spun the wheels on the damp tarmac.

The Carver had emerged from cover.

11

Alec heard the news on the car radio as he sat in the queue for the car park. Frances was working late: he had undertaken to do the supermarket shopping on his way home. Behind in the mirror, he could see at least five sets of lights; ahead there were still three cars between himself and the ticket kiosk. Either side were foot-high kerbs; beyond them, bollards. Once you were in the queue, you were deemed to have made your choice. There was no way out except forwards. He swore. And the mobile phone in the glove locker began to warble.

Liz was struggling with a recalcitrant lace, foot up on the changing room bench. Sally Field was already knocking up: Liz could hear the hollow slap of the cold squash ball echoing from the court across the way. Just as Liz got the ends equal, the door opened and a girl she half knew came in and dumped a sports bag on the bench.

'He's struck again,' she said. 'Have you heard?'

Liz froze. There could only be one 'he'. 'Where?'

'Petworth.' The girl shivered. 'Getting a bit too close.'

Liz ran across to the court, thumped on the door and in defiance of the rules shoved it open. 'Sal! Sal!'

Sally Field glanced round sharply, racket poised.

'Forget it,' Liz said briefly. 'Come and get your togs on.'

'Why?'

'Work.'

Sally saw it in her eyes. 'Oh, no!'

There were already reporters and camera crews in the yard when Alec reached headquarters, and they were out for blood. They turned as Alec's car lights appeared, and they were on him in a mob before he had locked the car.

'This afternoon you told us that Ken Crossland was being sought to eliminate him from enquiries. Have you any comment to make on the fact that the Carver's been able to kill a fifth victim?'

'Why . . .'

'In the light of . . .'

'No comment at the moment.' Alec pushed tight-lipped through the jostling crowd. Another car turned in and the media pack turned to see if it offered better prey. Alec glimpsed Liz and Sally Field; but at that moment more headlights appeared, someone shouted that it was Oaks, and the pack was off at a run like looters on the rampage. Alec took advantage of the diversion to stride gladly for the entrance. Let Oaks deal with them, since he loved them so dearly.

Inside, the atmosphere reeked of adrenalin, and shock was only beginning to settle to productive bustle. It took time to piece together the facts.

The body had been found just after four by a man walking his dog in scrub woodland on the edge of a village in the very furthest corner of the furthest division of the force. It had been dumped in the undergrowth where a footpath left a little-used lane. There had been no serious attempt to prevent its discovery—just as there had not been in any of the other murders. Just as in the other murders, the victim was a woman: this one was in her mid-thirties. Her name was Sandra Allen, and she was the mother of toddlers.

It took until a quarter-past five before news of the killing reached the force's headquarters because it happened to be the day the local sergeant was at his divisional station having his annual review, and the assessing officer was the only senior officer in the building and had left instructions that they were not to be disturbed for any reason. Moreover, all the police surgeons were attending a course in Maidstone so that an ordinary GP had to be found and called out to certify death. It was close to an hour and a half after the body had been discovered before the normal procedures of investigation rocked back on to their accustomed track. Well before that time, the jungle drums had rumbled to good effect and the bare facts of the death were on the press agency tape machines. Muddy Martin beat the news to headquarters by ten minutes, exploiting his advantage to glean a damning reaction of bewilderment from Chris Roberts in the press office. The killing was a late item on the television news, and headlined the radio bulletin at six o'clock, when Alec was sitting in the car park queue in East Grinstead.

It was a major, if fortuitous, botch-up to begin their personal association with the Carver, and the electricity in the air at headquarters sparked to a higher voltage for the awareness that heads would roll.

The chief held a conference at seven-thirty. By then the building felt like a fortress under siege, with the press camped out on the steps, and the atmosphere in the room was sober. Alec wondered if he was the only one holding himself back from saying 'if only'. In everyone's minds were the additional steps which, following the *Globe*'s revelations, were to have been put in hand tomorrow: the cordon round the forest; the painstaking searches that had been authorized, building by isolated building, all predicated on the assumption that the killer could not be far away; that impressive-sounding word 'containment'. When in fact the killer had slipped through the net—if he ever was in it—with laughable ease to choose another victim fifty miles away and rob a husband of his wife, children of their mother, a woman of her life. Alec could not rid his mind of the horrible thought that the woman must have known, in those terrible last minutes about which she would never tell, that the hands round her neck were those of the Carver. He hoped, with all his heart, that the pathologist would be able to confirm that her death took place before her dreadful mutilation.

'I've ordered an immediate investigation into why the press knew before we did. I can give you my assurance that it won't happen again.' The chief just nodded, a little irritably.

Did he feel the same stab of scorn for Oaks at his pompous worst? Did Oaks really believe that the credibility of the force mattered more than the failure to prevent another tragedy?

Sitting in the conference room, the air heavy with the acknowledgment of failure, it was as if Alec could feel the weight of fear pressing round him: the fear of all those unknown women haunted and perplexed by the knowledge that the Carver was still free.

It was late when Alec got home; almost ten.

'Have you eaten?'

'No. You heard?'

'The news has been full of nothing else. I've some soup I've been keeping in the freezer for emergencies, and after that one of those little pizzas. I think there's one left.'

'I didn't get to the supermarket, I'm afraid. We're just about out of everything, aren't we? Damn, damn, damn.'

Frances brushed a gentle hand over his cheek as she crossed to the utility room.

'It cost me forty pence for the privilege of driving straight through the car park and out of the exit,' he said. It seemed to sum up the evening: indignity and futile expenditure of effort. 'Lucy in bed?'

'She's out at Cynthia's.'

'Dammit, Frances, she shouldn't be out late like this! How's she getting back? Anything could happen to her!'

Frances turned to him, matching his anger. 'Must life stop?' she demanded.

He opened his mouth, saw the anxiety in the tension of the skin across his wife's cheek, the dark shadows beneath her eyes; shut it again. Must life stop for Lucy because a woman had been killed fifty miles away? Must it stop for Frances herself, for all their women friends, for his female colleagues, his friends' wives, every person in the kingdom who was neither male, an infant nor senile?

'Cynthia's mother's bringing her home.' Frances lanced the boil of worry. 'I telephoned earlier in the evening.'

She stirred the thick, meaty soup until it bubbled then

poured it into a bowl. Alec felt an almost visceral protectiveness towards her as she placed the bowl before him. How would he cope if she suffered? Suppose the Carver picked her? Suppose she, Frances, were to feel those hands around her neck, that smooth, loved neck, squeezing out her life? Or suppose the Carver changed his style of killing? Suppose he began to rape before he murdered? If he could not face the thought of Frances dead, could he—harder, more damning question—cope with Frances raped, but alive? And must it be impossible to cease to be self-regarding? Must one always care only how it would affect *oneself*?

Just to think of the threat to her churned his guts. But logically, it was infinitesimally greater tonight than it had been a month ago; possibly even slightly less today than yesterday, now that the Carver had for the moment found his victim. But what part had rationality in the fear of a lawless killer? The fear and the terror would continue until the Carver was captured or killed. For preference, killed. The proper end for the Carver was extermination.

Maria Tillotson was on the *Today* programme as Alec drove in to work, calling for changes in the Carver investigation, an increased role for FIGHTBACK, and for their voluntary registration scheme to be made compulsory. She also demanded that Sandra Allen's post-mortem examination be carried out by a woman.

'That'll please Ransome,' Alec muttered to himself. FIGHTBACK would themselves supply a woman pathologist, Maria Tillotson declared. For anyone else to carry out the autopsy would constitute a second violation of the dead woman's body, almost, Alec understood cynically, eclipsing her murder.

It happened that the post-mortem was in fact being conducted that afternoon, and Alec arrived at the hospital to find Ransome hopping from foot to foot with anger.

'Do you know this woman they want to use?' Alec asked.

'I know her. Dammit, she's not even accredited! That'd be misguided but I'd have some sympathy. But no, they want a girl from Bristol who I happen to know has twice failed to gain accreditation for the simple reason that she is a bloody awful pathologist. These bloody women! You'd have thought they'd appreciate that finding this girl's killer is showing her a sight more respect than using her death to make political capital for nutcases and anarchists.'

'They probably don't even know how the system works.'

'Pah! They know precisely how it works. It works bloody well, which is no doubt why they want to change it. And the hell of it is that this bloody government is quite likely to give in to crackpot pressure groups if they shout loudly enough.'

All this time Ransome had been changing and scrubbing up. Now they went into the autopsy room itself, Ransome through the 'clean' path, Alec, who was in his ordinary clothes, via the 'dirty' route to the little viewing gallery to join the coroner's officer. The mortuary assistant had the body already set out on the table and had completed the preliminaries.

'Is this bloody thing switched on?' Ransome demanded, gesturing to the microphone of the tape recorder; and began dictating with total dispassion as he turned his meticulous attention to the unresponsive shell that only yesterday had been Sandra Allen.

It was four nights since Sarah had slept. Not since the two hard policemen had invaded her home and infected her mind irremediably with the knowledge—she wished she could say notion, but self-deception had never been her strong point— that Ken had been murdering women across the country for the last nine months.

She had not told the solicitor about Ken's being missing. She could not bring herself to inform her of this latest development. But she felt cheated. It was so wildly unfair that at last, when she had nerved herself to do what she should have done years before, Ken should put this unanswerable spoke in her wheel. If she went on with the divorce now it would seem it was only because of the suspicions against

Ken. If he was guilty, she would be the woman who did not stand by her man. If he was (could he be?) unjustly accused, she would stand revealed as even more vindictive. Even by his simple absence he had thwarted her, for how could the action proceed until he was found?

She did not, literally, know what to do, and therefore the hours and even the days passed locked in inactivity.

Inevitably, overnight Crossland became the undisputed candidate for the role of Carver. It was a progression of policy that Alec recognized was not wholly rational, but which had its own momentum which would not be deflected. Indeed, as soon as the media had published the name of the man the police were seeking, it could be said that other avenues of investigation were closed until that man had been found, so strong was public feeling. And after all, that man was missing, a man reported to have some skill in survival techniques, and if it was possible that he had gone to ground intentionally, then one had to speculate why he had chosen to do so. And even the remote possibility that it might be because he was a serial killer entering a new phase in his madness excused a certain amount of hysteria. If Crossland—and the media had seized on the significance of his name so that there was scarcely an infant or a senile pensioner who was not aware that it was a cross which the killer carved on his victims—was innocent, then why had he not, in the face of the blazoning of his name and features around the country, come forward to clear himself?

That strand of the argument remained valid; but it was open to question whether Crossland ever had gone to ground on the forest at all, since the death of Sandra Allen had taken place fifty miles away from the location where his car had been found. Was the abandoning of the car a blind? It was the one fact which to Alec's way of thinking rather lessened the probability of Crossland being the Carver. Hitherto the killings seemed to have maintained a pattern; whereas, if Crossland were the murderer, *his* pattern had been decisively broken when he abandoned his car, his wife and his job.

In the end this sort of speculation was bootless. Direction of the Crossland/Carver hunt was way out of Alec's hands, up at ACC level, and it was for others to weigh the probabilities and assess the congruences and decide policy. Now the Carver had killed in their area, Alec's duties were prescribed and easy to follow. He was a reporting officer for the purposes of HOLMES, and much of his time was going to be taken up with administration. Just one of a team. So be it. There was relief in being, even as a chief inspector, occasionally a mere cog in a machine.

Liz did not think she would have minded her investigation into Crossland's whereabouts being subsumed into the wider Carver enquiry. But she was piqued when it was ignored altogether. OK, more senior hands had grabbed the reins now, but the efficient little hunt on which she personally had worked so diligently could have formed the foundation of the larger case: instead of which it was shunted decisively into a siding and left to rot.

'What do I do now?' she complained to Alec. 'Am I on the Carver enquiry or am I not? Do I go on with finding Crossland or do I assume that that is now the job of the chief supers and above?'

'Now,' Alec replied, 'you are demoted to the status of face-less helper.'

'From governor to squaddie in four days.'

'There is still the normal work. And while everybody else is rushing about like bees round an upturned hive you could be catching up with your swotting for your exams. Have you passed on the results of your house-to-house to Marjorie Weston?'

'She had me in this morning to go through what we'd covered so far,' Liz admitted grudgingly.

'There you are, then.'

'She told me we'd done a really professional job,' replied Liz with a moue. 'It was only not wanting to see her crack her make-up that prevented me saying a very rude word. I offered to leave the file with her.'

'And didn't you?'

'She didn't think that would be necessary.' She mimicked DCI Marjorie Weston cruelly.

'So long as the data's available it'll probably come into its own in due course.'

The heavy grey mist still enveloped the town. Even within the air felt dank and heavy with moisture: outside it was chill, too, with a penetrating malice that seemed to reach into joints and pierce to the marrow. 'I still think he's there, you know, guv. On the forest.'

'The Carver? Or Crossland? Are they one person, or two?'

She shook her head. 'I don't know, guv, I just don't know.'

'Well, the chances are, even if he isn't the Carver, we'll find Crossland before long.' Now the bandwagon was well and truly on the road, Crossland's name and face were in every newspaper, outside every police station. Tomorrow the *Crimewatch* programme would be screened, with a reconstruction of Sandra Allen's last known movements and heavy advertisement of the search for Crossland. Already the extra phone lines were being set up to deal with the expected flood of response from the public.

'I just wish we'd been allowed to finish. We'd made a good start. I could show you on a map, but roughly we'd covered everything within a radius of five miles of where the car was found.'

'It'll be hard for him to stay under cover now, if he's hiding up.'

'I don't know, guv. If this weather continues and if he is out of doors, we're going to be looking for his corpse.'

'That's not for her to worry about,' Detective Chief Superintendent Oaks responded tartly when Alec mentioned the conversation later in the day. 'I'd like you to get to work on building up a picture of the dead girl. Have a word with Wilcox. He was the local bobby in the village where she was brought up. Her family still live there. Wilcox is a bit antediluvian, but use your charm on him and see if he can come up with anything. After that, I've arranged for you to go down to see a forensic psychiatrist at the university; a Dr Carey. He's agreed to help us build up a profile of the Carver.'

'We can get information about Crossland from his friends and associates. Greater Manchester are working on it. Building up a pattern of his activities and movements.'

'Carey's going to help us approach this the other way, from the Carver end.'

Chief Superintendent Oaks was, to Alec's mind rather unfortunately, of the view that enthusiasm for the latest trends in crime detection demonstrated that one was not hidebound; and was also an enthusiast for all things American, fond of quoting from what he had seen on attachment to the Chicago Police Department a year or two before. When electronic tagging of convicted offenders came in, or satellite surveillance of the entire population, come to that, Oaks would be first in the queue of senior officers anxious to demonstrate that they had the new techniques at their fingertips. It had often occurred to Alec that Oaks saw the pinnacle of his career not in being a future ACC (Crime) or a Chief, but in becoming one of those *éminences grises* who advise governments, safely distanced from the messy business of daily crime.

Alec himself was enthusiastic about the development of technological aids to policing, but he did not welcome their automatic and indiscriminate implementation. They were just aids, after all; no more. Had he been running the Carver enquiry (and he thanked his stars he was not; it did not seem to him that anyone was going to come out of this with a quick arrest and press plaudits) he would have concentrated first on eliminating Crossland from the enquiry altogether by giving Blackett his head, using traditional painstaking methods to continue Liz's grid search of the forest and locate the woman Crossland had picked up in the Brambletye. Instead, he was instructed to recruit this psychiatrist who was supposed to tell them what sort of man the Carver was, as if, having learnt that he liked lager and hated his mother they were going to be any closer to finding him.

*   *   *

Wilcox was due, Alec knew, to retire in the spring. He was working out his final year in a desk job two floors below, but most of his career had been spent within five miles of the scene of Sandra Allen's death. The last of the country bobbies, maybe; the last of a breed of men with less thought for promotion than for the communities where sometimes they spent their whole working lives. Wilcox had accompanied the detectives from the Carver enquiry who had conducted the first interviews with the dead girl's family.

'Have a seat.'

'Thank you, sir.' A spare, wizened man, he spoke little, but with a marked Sussex accent, not dissimilar to the casual ear to the tones of London, but softer and with a burr.

'I've been reading these transcripts,' Alec said. 'You won't have seen the post-mortem report, I don't suppose.' He passed it over. Wilcox took it in his big hands and read it steadily and carefully. He took rather a long time about it. 'You knew the family, of course. Did you know Sandra?'

'They moved in 'bout twenty years ago,' Wilcox informed him. 'Makes 'em pretty near oldest inhabitants. This Sandra woulder bin fourteen or fifteen then. Priddy gal. Bit wild at first, settled down, had a lodder boys around her. Nice gal.'

'That's what puzzles me,' Alec said. 'How the Carver could ever have got her in a position where he could kill her, when every woman in the country knows there is a serial killer at large. Any ideas?'

'It puzzles me, too, sir, I tells you straight. I know it's a different world now, but I'd'er sworn she just wasn't that kinder gal.' Wilcox's face wore a troubled expression.

'I'm not sure that's quite the right way of putting it. You can see there were no indications of sexual intercourse.'

'I suppose there's no doubt about that, sir? It seems a bit peculiar to me, this Carver being so vicious and that, yet he never interferes with them.'

'We don't know what sexual satisfaction he gets. Perhaps killing them gives him his thrills.'

Wilcox rubbed a hand over his chin. 'That's true. I'm sorry not to be more help, but it's a mystery ter me, sir, and that's the truth. I know these days it's rash ter say as much, but I'd'er sworn Sandra Allen warn't the sort to let herself be picked up by a stranger outer the blue. I did wonder, sir, could they all 'ave known him, like? That's the only thing I can think of.'

'Five victims now,' Alec reminded him. 'Their address books have been gone through with a fine-tooth comb.'

'I'm at a loss then, sir, I'm afraid.'

Join the crowd, Alec told himself glumly.

While Liz waited for Alec Stainton, she sat on the edge of a desk in the CID room and asked Sally Field the same question. What did she think she was doing? 'Was she just stupid or what?'

'Perhaps he spins some tale. Says he's a talent scout, promises them modelling assignments.'

'That one's got whiskers on.'

'It doesn't seem to stop poor idiots falling for it.'

'But with four women already dead . . .'

'And now she's the fifth.'

Liz looked at her watch and wondered where the governor had got to. She said: 'Unless she knew him. We've got five women, all strangled, each one sexually mutilated but no sign that they'd had sex before they were killed. For four of them, nobody outside the investigation knew exactly what he did with his knife after he strangled them, so we could be pretty sure that the killings were all carried out by the same man.'

'You think they all knew him. Not very likely is it?'

'Nobody said anything about it being likely.'

'And if they did, it probably wasn't Crossland.'

Liz sighed. Because the whole basis of the Crossland theory was that he was in a position to commit opportunist crimes all over the country. If there was a *plan* to the choice of victims, that opened a whole new field, virtually limitless.

'Trenant,' Sally pondered. 'Wadebridge. Gloucester. Norwich. Sussex.'

'That means nothing these days. I was born thirty miles from where I live, and these days that's close.'

'They weren't all the same age.'

'Four of them were fairly close. In their mid-thirties.'

'Like Crossland.'

'Mm.'

'So he's going round bumping off his old girlfriends?'

They heard Alec Stainton's door open and close, and Wilcox's figure passed along the corridor. Liz swung herself off the desk.

'The bright sparks latched on to that possibility yonks ago, of course. But there must be some link. The trouble is the lack of data. The women aren't around to ask for it.'

Liz spent most of the journey pondering what lay at the end of it.

It was partly the fact of their destination that prompted her unease. 'Used to be the poly,' she grumbled when Stainton told her where they were to go. And that led her to reflect on the changed order of things since she left school, and her place in it. Used to living on her wits and fighting her corner with a tough mix of humour, worldly wisdom and verbal quickness, Liz was not quite sure where developments in her job were going to leave her.

'Tell me, governor,' she said, 'when you were at school, did you do all this computing business?'

He grinned. 'We did have a computer, yes.'

'You did?'

'It occupied a room—and I mean a room—on the maths corridor and worked on punched cards. I never got to use it: only favoured acolytes were allowed in. It had been donated by ICI or someone, as surplus to requirements. For all it taught me, it might as well have been an abacus.' He glanced at her again. 'You have one advantage over me, Liz.'

'I have?'

'You're still young enough to learn.'

She thought: and that means he thinks I'm bright enough too . . .

114

'By the way,' Alec remarked, 'there's a sergeant coming up from Trenant to help us put our picture together. He's also supposed to be something of an outdoor survival expert. Name of Pritchard. He'll be sharing your room, Liz.' Liz groaned. 'Go easy on him.'

She stared. Do what? For heaven's sake, she wasn't some kind of piranha, was she? She opened her mouth to protest, then said instead: 'Is it true Mr Oaks has asked for help from the SAS?'

Liz felt rather than saw Stainton's saturnine grimace. 'Some equipment has been found at Crossland's house which suggests he may know something about survival techniques. If he's living rough and he knows what he's doing, he might hide out for months. I didn't think any decision had been made yet.'

'I heard it on the morning news.'

A pregnant silence ensued.

That just about sums it up, Liz thought. It was on the tip of her tongue to suggest that they should just leave the little matter of finding the Carver to the press, since they seemed to be first in the field with everything so far. But she left the quip unuttered. It wasn't very funny, after all.

12

Liz considered Detective-Sergeant Geoffrey Pritchard with a sinking heart. He was sitting at her desk—on the visitors' side, not in her chair—studying a file, and when she came in he stood up, in his tweed jacket, pressed grey trousers, white shirt and tie, and waited politely for her to say something.

Oh God, Liz thought. They've sent us their prize prune. No wonder Oaks foisted him off on us.

She went forward and he turned to keep her before him as she crossed to the desk.

'Liz Pink,' she said without much hope. 'DS.'

The prune nodded and said seriously, 'I'm Detective-Sergeant Pritchard.'

He was still standing. Liz slumped into her chair and he sat as if plucked down by a spring. A performing seal, Liz thought. She looked at his tie, beautifully knotted. The cuffs of his shirt showed dazzlingly beneath the sleeves of his jacket. For heaven's sake, they had cufflinks in them.

He was following dutifully a pace or two behind her like a poodle, but somehow, as they came to the doors, he had eeled past and was holding them open for her.

'You want to watch that,' Liz said seriously. 'You could get blood on that clean white shirt, doing a thing like that these days.'

'Oh dear. Do you really think so?'

She glanced at him as she overtook him again. His face

was empty except for a trace of anxiety. She pushed down a sudden urge to say something really cruel.

Johnson and Simms and Sally Field were in the canteen, and when they had had their trays filled Liz led the way to the table next to them and introduced Pritchard. Simms and Johnson looked him over in a puzzled sort of way. Sally Field turned her calm enigmatic gaze on him and said hello.

'Good afternoon,' Pritchard replied respectfully. Johnson's eyes widened a fraction. Liz bit her lip and sighed inwardly.

Duty done, she let herself join in the general conversation and gossip. Pritchard ate neatly, without saying anything. Once she thought she caught him casting a doubtful glance at her. Perhaps in Powys or wherever he came from sergeants were so near the top of the tree they ate in silence off special plates while an exquisitely uniformed probationer read out extracts from the Police and Criminal Evidence Act. When Johnson, in the course of a racy anecdote, used a naughty word, she could swear Pritchard winced.

The only thing, Ruth decided, as Anita would not answer her letters and the phone was such an awkward instrument for delicate matters, was just to call. She shied away from it; but reminded herself sternly that you had to make a bigger effort with just those friends who were least responsive. Didn't Anita, precisely because of her spiky awkwardness, precisely because the death of her mother would have left her disorientated and defensive, need friendship uncomplicatedly offered, much more than Ruth's other friends, whose lives were disturbed by nothing more serious than debates over the merits of rival schools for the children?

She planned carefully, so as to call at a time when Anita would be free of any obligation to invite her to stay for a meal; and in daylight, to be less threatening; and she arranged a truthful reason for being in the vicinity, remembering that an old schoolteacher was in a retirement home in Forest Row and should be visited. She should have visited her ages ago; so that would be one positive thing achieved, though Ruth felt a pang of guilt at calling only as part of a plan aimed at another object altogether. Stimulated by the idea, she took out her diary and flicked through to see when would be best to go.

'So the Carver is mad,' Frances said quietly as she and Alec sat sharing the remnants of a bottle of wine, after Lucy had gone to bed. 'But can we expect him to be recognizably mad, or will he only be seen to be mad in retrospect?'

Alec said wryly, 'It's the old syllogism that only madmen commit murders, so if we catch this killer, however sane he seems, the murders prove he's really mad.'

'Frightening to think of him living an ordinary decent life as a loving husband and fond father. Isn't it true that schizophrenia, for instance, tends to affect people of higher levels of intelligence?'

'Your average non-mad homicide tends to be pretty low down the educational scale. I don't think it means the Carver is necessarily a member of MENSA.'

'There's something I don't understand, Alec. Here is a killer preying on women. I take it I'm not being naïve in talking about a sexual element—even calling these sex killings?'

Alec hesitated, weighing his words. 'We have a series of homicides, and, yes, associated with the homicides are mutilations of a sexual nature. I'm sorry. It sounds like cavilling, but . . .'

'You mean, suppose you find an empty wallet beside a corpse. Was robbery the motive for the murder? Or did the murderer opportunistically help himself to what was on the body?'

Alec nodded. 'I've been puzzling over it myself. Why none of these killings have involved any plainly sexual acts. No rape, no interference of that sort after death. No signs of sexual gratification. Yet this obsession with the women's sexual organs. In one case they were all but shorn off.'

'The *Globe*'s suggesting he's impotent.' Psychiatry being even better than physical medicine for offering opportunities for speculation, a number of 'experts' had been given air- and page-space in recent days. The *Globe* had recruited an astrologer to predict the identity of the Carver, and a 'sexologist' to ruminate pruriently about the significance of his awful signature.

'Overlooking the fact that Crossland has two daughters. OK. First: yes, it is possible that the killer is impotent. But Carey down at the university reckons it's unlikely. The ease with which he has been able to get alongside all his victims and win their trust suggests a measure of social facility usually associated with promiscuous lifestyle. But according to Carey, the satisfaction the Carver gains from killing may be separate from sexual gratification altogether.

'And we don't know that he obtains no sexual gratification. There's been no rape, no semen stains—but those are negative factors which don't prove anything, and anyway, four of the five killings took place away from the location where the body was found. Without more extensive evidence, we aren't in a position to do more than speculate.'

Frances said: 'He's going to do worse things, isn't he?'

Alec acknowledged the likelihood with a pessimistic turn of the mouth. 'It's part of a sort of challenge offered by the killer to the law enforcement agencies.'

Privately, Alec expected more killings, more daring and more eccentric. They'd find the Carver leaving messages to the police, perhaps. They'd also find that the things done to the bodies became more outrageous. Necrophilia. Cannibalism. Almost certainly the killer was following his own career in the media. With great gratification, probably. He was famous. He was feared. He had achieved a sort of fulfilment. But he had to maintain his credibility as an object of the public's hate. His mouth twitched sourly. 'He has to keep the price of his autobiography up,' he said. In short, he thought, we probably ain't seen nothing yet.

They sat in the car at the viewpoint, and the reservoir stretched away ahead of them, turning in and out of wooded inlets artfully landscaped. Mid-week, and December. No other cars: a bleak prospect and, despite the warmth lingering from the heater, bleakness inside the car too.

*'I don't know. Somehow I don't seem to have made a great
success of things. When we were seventeen . . . The whole future.
All the ambitions. I don't seem to have achieved any of them.
Redundant. Failed marriage. I didn't tell you I've . . .'*

'Yes?'

*'Well, if you must know, I've been in prison. Nothing awful.
Well, I suppose it must seem awful to you . . .'*

'Would it help to tell me all about it?'

'You won't want to hear.'

*'Oh, but I do. I'm glad we came. And I'm glad you've been so
honest. If you hadn't, I'd have gone on thinking you were just like
. . . Well, anyway.'*

'Just like who?'

'Just like the others.'

'The others?'

'Is he a violent lover, Mrs Crossland? When you make love,
Mrs Crossland, does he ever put his hands round your
throat? Well?'

'No. Maybe. I don't know. We've been married fifteen
years, Inspector.' And with a flash of venom, 'Have *you* never
put your hands round your wife's throat?'

'I'm not married.'

She drew in a deep shuddering breath. How was she meant
to bear this? The day the newspapers first named Ken
Crossland as the man the police wished to interview in connection with the Carver killings Sarah had hidden the papers
and disconnected the television aerial. But the girls had been
taunted at school and had come home in tears, and that night
there had been wet beds from Beth for the first time in years.
She told them no one thought their father was the Carver,
and hated herself for the lie, even as she recognized its futility, for the reaction of their schoolfellows would accurately
reflect public feeling, which was that the Carver had been
identified and it was just a matter of time before he was
caught. She thought of keeping the girls home, but told herself they must learn to take it before worse came. The truth

was that she could not bear having them at home, and feared for her sanity.

Sarah herself believed her husband was the Carver. She only wondered that she could have been so blind for so long. A phrase she recalled from school English lessons ran round and round her brain: 'A man may smile and smile, and be a villain.' She looked at her own body in the mirror as if the touch of his hands should have left stains on her flesh. She imagined it, like theirs, his victims', lifeless. Her own body had become repugnant to her, and it was not hard to imagine those she met looking at her with repulsion and telling themselves that this was the woman who had shared a bed with the Carver; had probably connived with him to carry out his crimes.

She felt herself to be—and these policemen barely bothered to try and conceal that they viewed her this way too—a sexual pervert; a killer by proxy. Everybody believed that the wife of a serial killer or multiple rapist was 'in on it'.

And she had been doubly cheated. For she had not managed to make an appointment to see a solicitor before the story broke, and now it was trebly difficult to do so. Who would believe that she had been on the point of seeking a divorce? Who would believe she was not trying to run now that the truth was out, trying to sever her ties to Ken and leave him to face the music alone? Who would believe mercenary considerations were not uppermost? Already two envelopes sat in the desk in the sitting-room, shameful even unopened: national newspapers offering her money if she would let them tell her story.

The police had ransacked the house. Looking for blood—Ken's blood. To analyse the type and match against the traces he would—must—leave at the scenes of his crimes. The brutal fundamentality of it disgusted her and was another cruel twist of the knife for the girls: forcing them into the world where the things that mattered were not what was for tea or the evening's television programmes, but whether blood taken from their father's razor would prove to contain the same genetic components as body fluids spilt by a murderer.

But they had found no blood. Ken shaved with an electric razor, which had been in the case stolen from his car. They pulled out all his clothes and bundled them into plastic bin-liners, pushing perfunctory receipts into her unwilling hand. They took the sheets off the bed. She watched them do it, and couldn't believe it was happening. They took the sheets off the bed—her bed—as if they might never have been washed in the weeks since Ken left. A policewoman asked her whether she had any underwear with Ken's semen on, and Sarah felt the vomit rise in her throat and didn't know whether it was nausea at Ken, or the policewoman, or herself.

Once they found the camping things they quizzed her about Ken's interest in survival. I didn't know he had one, she said. But they took the gear just the same, took a couple of books she didn't know he'd got, invaded the attic and the garage and the suitcases on the top of the wardrobes, holding up for each other's approbation the walking boots they found amongst Ken's shoes, the Bowie knife, the gas stove and the billy cans and the bivouac sheet they'd once, before the children, used for a summer's break in the Lake District, when she was young and without a care. But he left these things behind, she cried; and they had looked at her derisively as if that only proved that he had bought more and was living rough and was a murderer of women.

With the sudden change in status of Ken Crossland from outside chance to front runner, the evidence contained in his abandoned car at last received concentrated attention. Liz heard early on that the car had been rescued from the yard at the forensic laboratory and subjected to detailed scrutiny. Her resentment at this belated acknowledgment of her earlier diligence was somewhat assuaged when Alec Stainton told her he was driving over that morning to speak to the scientist principally involved and asked if she would like to come too.

To her disgust, Pritchard made a third; and to her greater disgust, Stainton and the Welshman engaged in a discussion of the prospects for the Five Nations Rugby Championship which lasted almost the entire journey while she, isolated in the back seat, was neither invited nor readily able to make any contribution.

The scientist was cockily pleased. 'Go on: say it.'

Pritchard obliged. 'I thought you couldn't get prints off something like that.'

He gestured with his head and they followed him into a side room. A machine on a stand occupied much of the space. A double eyepiece projected from it like a seaside peepshow.

'Take a look,' he invited. They did. Stainton first; then Pritchard; Liz last. She saw a circle of lurid light and the ghostly image of an unmistakable fingerprint.

Behind her, Pritchard was asking admiringly: 'How's it done?'

'Glue. The print's fixed by putting it in a cabinet and letting it seethe in glue fumes; when we take it out, any prints can be revealed by putting it in that box of tricks behind you.'

Liz took a last look and turned back to the men. She said: 'Just plastic?'

'No. All sorts of things we couldn't take prints off before. Wallets. Handbags. The plastic round steering columns—the thieves break it off to get at the steering lock and usually just leave it lying on the carpet. We can get an excellent print off that. More's the pity,' he added. Liz didn't need to ask why. Every detective who heard of this magic trick would be sending in plastic steering column shrouds by the van load.

'And you're satisfied,' Stainton said, 'that you have every print?'

The scientist turned away and led them through into the main office where he perched on the edge of a bench. 'I'm sorry. Believe me, we've done our damnedest. Given the circumstances—'

Yes. The circumstances. The car dumped in the pound after

Johnson and the local plod and half the kids in Sussex had swanned all over it. The fingerprint man rubbishing her. The bloody circumstances which were somehow her fault.

'—We were quite pleased to get what we did. I'm just sorry they none of them fit the bill.'

Liz said to Pritchard in an undertone, 'Am I supposed to know what the hell's going on?'

Pritchard said: 'They none of them correspond to the prints of the dead women. And Crossland's prints can't be linked with any of the bodies.'

Liz stared straight ahead. This clown knew what was going on. Nobody bothered to tell her. She was reduced to tagging on at the back of the queue. What had she done? Or not done? Apart from being the bright spark who first fingered Crossland for the Carver. Was that what she'd done wrong?

The governor was talking about other things found in the car. A second scientist was summoned. Was there anything they couldn't have learnt from the written reports? Was the governor covering every base? From where she stood, it looked to Liz as if what he was doing was running round like the rest of them sniffing at the ground in the sure and certain knowledge that he was totally and absolutely lost. She listened restlessly as they covered the ground. Fibres. Hairs. Various types of mud. She was mildly interested to learn that Crossland had apparently spent a good deal of his waking hours having it off on the back seat of his motor, but as he had apparently done so with every woman in the country except the dead ones, she turned away, suddenly overtaken by lassitude and distaste. Pritchard had an eager look switched on his face, like a puppy that hopes for great things in the obedience classes.

As they crossed the gravel forecourt to the car, Liz asked, 'What was all that about, guv?'

The numbers of pressmen could no longer be contained in the conference room and they were using the Methodist hall for briefings now. Chief Superintendent Oaks was in buoyant mood as the journalists and correspondents took their seats.

124

He loves it, Alec realized, as the technicians jockeyed lights and cameramen hoisted video recorders on to their shoulders and tested angles, and Oaks stood below the dais chatting to a personable woman in a smart blue suit whom Alec recognized as a detective-superintendent from Devon and Cornwall. The colours of her outfit were shrewdly calculated to show true on screen, her make-up just that shade heavier than she would wear if cameras were not present. She and Oaks both wore competent, serious expressions as the pressmen took trial shots, neither of them innocent enough to let the press sneak pictures of the officers in charge of a multi-murder enquiry laughing.

Oaks looked at his watch, and then up at the wall clock, and moved to the side aisle, holding open for his visitor the door which led backstage. Alec fell in behind. At precisely eleven-thirty Oaks led the way up the little stairway to the wings and they emerged in front of the curtain and took their seats at the long table, draped with the cloth with the constabulary insignia.

'Ladies and gentlemen. The purpose of this briefing is to provide you with up-to-the-minute information on the progress of the investigation into the so-called Carver killings. I am happy to say that we have a very positive development to tell you about, but first I am going to ask Detective Chief Inspector Alec Stainton to bring you up to date with the events of the last forty-eight hours.'

Alec rose to his feet and, knowing perfectly well that his role was to be the warm-up man before the big act, began. It took him fifteen minutes to detail what had been done over the two days since the last briefing by the police of four counties, and ten to deal with questions. These were easy: the correspondents were waiting for Oak's revelations, keeping their powder dry.

At the end of his twenty-five minutes, Alec resumed his seat. There was a buzz of conversation in the hall, which Oaks skilfully allowed to run for a full minute. Then, looking to Alec's prejudiced eye like a chairman about to divert shareholders' attention from the non-payment of dividend by announcing an order from Saudi Arabia, Oaks stood, and the hall fell still.

As Oaks revealed his 'positive development', making public those parts of Dr Carey's predictions he wanted widely known, it all sounded, as it always did, rather obvious. Somehow one expected a magic prophecy, and what one got was a series of deductions of greater or lesser banality. They were looking, it seemed, for a man who hated women. Indeed, Alec reflected, one might fancy a degree of hate present in a man who had killed five of them so viciously. The psychiatrist speculated that the hate might be disguised beneath a superficial attraction to them. Oaks concluded with a grim warning.

'This man is dangerous. He has killed five times and he will not hesitate to kill again. All the signs are that he is friendly, sociable, easy to approach, good company. But I cannot emphasize too strongly that this man is a killer. We are confident we can catch him, but in the meantime I must warn all women to be on their guard. Don't take chances with strangers.'

The best reporters scribbled busily; the cameras probed for the best angle to catch Chief Superintendent Oaks's sober features. Alec allowed himself a fractional, private grimace. Oaks was confident they would catch the Carver. Alec wished he could be quite so sure. There were a lot of women out there.

The killing of Sandra Allen, the Carver's fifth victim, was the event which finally catapulted FIGHTBACK into the forefront of popular consciousness. As FIGHTBACK took centre stage, so, despite Oaks's press briefings, the tone of reporting the official investigation became brutally disparaging. 'Police,' reported the News at Ten's man, posed in front of the incised granite name-stone outside force headquarters, 'still don't know whether . . .' 'Senior officers still won't say . . .' 'Police sources say senior officers are divided about whether the crimes are the work of one man . . .'

Perhaps because of the critical nature of the reporting of

the police investigation, or perhaps because FIGHTBACK had opened an information hotline of their own; at any rate, the highly-publicized police hotlines were a good deal less busy than they normally were on an investigation of this type. Before the end of the week the collators entering information under the various headings on to the computer database were reduced by half, the surplus reallocated to other areas of the investigation. Alec, hearing the gossip and seeing the occasional transcript, wondered whether FIGHTBACK had indeed managed to attract any serious callers, or whether this rump of maniacs and mischievous nuisance-mongers was all there was. In the heat of the investigation the existence of FIGHTBACK further heightened the odds stacked against the law enforcers, but there was little time to consider what, if anything, should be the official response.

They were storing up trouble for themselves, Alec told himself unhappily. Next time there was an investigation into attacks on women, FIGHTBACK would be there in strength with their 'voluntary' data bank and their demands for the dead victims' 'rights': established and consolidated and accepted. Was it paranoid to see anarchy in the hazy, but possibly not too distant, future? At any rate, he reflected in his more philosophical moments, it was not what the government had had in mind when talking of the privatization of the police.

On a more intimate level, he was worried about Liz Pink and the visiting Detective-Sergeant Geoffrey Pritchard from Trenant. He had thought it an obvious move to put Pritchard in Liz's room. She would welcome him with her cheery good humour and they would form an instant and productive team.

It was not looking as if it would turn out that way. He knew, from the best part of five years' experience, that when storm-clouds did build in Liz Pink's sunny landscape they tended to result in a more than usually violent tempest. His own contacts with Pritchard had been completely favourable. The man was intelligent and painstaking, with the equable temperament so invaluable for routine police work but the ability to keep a strong analytical faculty alive through the tedium. Moreover, he was about Liz's age or a little older. It was difficult to guess what might have set them at odds. Perhaps it had started with something as small as Pritchard invading Liz's space in her office—for which he himself was responsible. Perhaps Pritchard had attempted to patronize Liz. Perhaps he had made advances—or perhaps the trouble was that he hadn't. The fact remained that ominous shadows darkened the horizon. Meanwhile, Pritchard produced good work. And the quality of Liz's declined.

Liz drove home jaded and listless. Her head felt thick and her limbs ached and she hadn't the energy to work out whether it was 'flu or merely the onset of her period. It was raining, a fine curtain of drizzle out of which the headlights of oncoming cars bored relentlessly. The traffic seemed heavier and the speeding drivers more boorish. Once Liz had to swerve to avoid a van cutting a corner and felt something clang ominously against the underneath of the car as her nearside wheels brushed the verge. When she got home she found the decorative circle out of the centre of one wheel was missing. Wearily she drove back to the place where she had heard it go, pulled off into a farm track and walked back on the verge with her torch, the traffic swishing derisively by. She found the wheel embellisher after ten minutes' damp hunt, but something had driven over it. She tossed it angrily in the ditch, then made herself fish it out because she despised people who littered the roadside with debris.

Back home yet again, she threw the useless plastic in the bin, stuffed her muddy skirt into the wash basket and propped her sodden shoes on the doormat.

Bloody Pritchard! Even as she damned him she knew she was using him unfairly as a peg on which to hang her anger. But why not?—she needed one. And how the man did get on her wick, with his intolerable bloody politeness that suggested he was sneering at them all behind their backs and his patronizing courtesy to everything in a skirt. Perhaps they still treated women like china dolls down in his benighted part of the world, but that made it no less insufferable that every time she looked up from her desk she saw his bland features and his *tie*, for God's sake, its neat little knot in his smart ironed shirt. He looked more like a milksop curate than a copper; and then she checked herself, because she had known some bloody good clergymen and she didn't want to slander curates.

Rosie came in then, humping Joy on one hip and tugging at the pushchair which caught against the door frame. Quite how and where Rosie spent her days was a mystery to Liz; she seemed to live an attractive sort of life, never putting in an appearance before Liz had left for work, coming in after dark, often with purchases from the town's boutiques which she would try on before the hall mirror, turning and preening like a model on a catwalk. Later on, the new tops and pants would make an appearance as attire for the night out, complemented by striking make-up: there was no doubting that Rosie had a talent for making herself look good—as well she might, given the time expended on preparation; time during which the bathroom was inaccessible.

Liz could sympathize with the need to get out and live her own life. It must be hard, being bound by a baby's repetitive needs, feeling oneself prematurely condemned to the role of matron. Yet . . . yet it was so short a time since Rosie and Mike had been apparently such a happy couple. Liz couldn't help feeling that she herself would not so soon have given up on the past, nor so blatantly gone out night after night like an unattached teenager, had hers been the marriage tragically come to grief. Grief—surely there should be time for a little of that?

Rosie was in a good mood, jaunty and looking forward to the evening. She made herself a meal and ate it with an appetite, at the same time offering spoonfuls of prepared baby food to Joy and informing Liz that Joy would soon be properly on to mixed feeds and not before time, she was looking forward to being able to fit back into an ordinary bra. She was vain about her figure, highly critical of girls not so blessed; and Liz tried not to read any personal application in her disparaging references to women with big udders.

While Rosie was putting Joy to bed and getting ready for the evening, Liz tried to work; but the living-room was open-plan, and what she had meant as a study was now Rosie and Joy's bedroom; and one way and another it was difficult to settle. She would not watch TV to while away the time, she told herself; but she ended up washing the dishes from Rosie's meal instead, as a means of filling in the space until she could have the house to herself. She set the washing-machine to deal with her muddy skirt and read through the mail to learn that she could win a million pounds, but in actual fact owed the electricity board what seemed an outrageous sum.

Rosie went out just after eight, glamorous and eager, throwing reassurances about Joy over her departing shoulder: fast asleep; she'll be no trouble. Until she wakes, Liz thought.

Liz burnt her tea and ate it without pleasure. At nine she at last set to, only to discover she had left at work the one vital book she needed to study for her forthcoming examination. She fished out her sewing machine from under the stairs, made a mess of turning up a new pair of jeans, and gave the day up as a bad job, running herself a bath. The water, because of the washing-machine, was lukewarm.

13

It was well after half-past five when Liz stumped into Alec Stainton's office. The uncurtained windows threw back a black reflection of herself. Seated at his desk, Stainton seemed to be working within a sort of aquarium, the outside world isolated beyond sheets of glass.

He looked up and took in her stormy eyes and the tension of her limbs. 'What is it, Liz?'

'It's that bloody Welshman,' she said before she could stop herself. 'He'll have to go!'

She knew it was the wrong approach before the last word had left her mouth. Demanding, unreasonable, self-important. A little irreverence, a little cheekiness she knew Stainton liked in her. This forthright bolshieness was the unacceptable extension. His expression cooled.

'I'm sorry, sir. But he's getting right up my nose. The man's a total disaster.'

The temperature dropped a fraction further. 'In what way is Detective-Sergeant Pritchard's work disastrous?'

'In what way?' she echoed, as if it was self-evident. That sobered her up and she thought quickly. She had obviously caught the governor at a time when he was not going to be sympathetic to any little personal frictions between her and Pritchard. More: his question clearly indicated that unless she had any allegations to make directly touching Pritchard's competence, she had better forget it. If she stood on her dignity all she would get back would be a tart lecture on the seriousness of the task overruling fancied personal slights. 'He's just dim, sir.' Not the most incisive analysis, but the best

131

she could do. 'Absolutely without imagination, and totally without a sense of humour. I mean, apart from making him a bit of a pain to work with, it means he just doesn't have a contribution to make. He's a passenger.'

Stainton lifted the papers he had been studying an inch off the desk. 'This,' he said unsmiling, 'is an analysis prepared by Detective-Sergeant Pritchard of the post-mortem reports on the killings. The analysis I asked you to prepare four days ago. Pritchard completed it at my request this afternoon. I have to say that not only has he done it as requested and without delay, but he has done it better than you would have done. It is entirely lucid, cogent and suggests one or two lines of enquiry that could be very productive.'

The governor was hateful when this mood was upon him. He rarely indulged it; that he was doing so now was an indication that she had angered him very much indeed.

'Are you saying that you will find it difficult to work with Detective-Sergeant Pritchard?' he concluded.

She drew back from the pit opening at her feet just in time and drew in a deep unsteady breath. 'No, sir.'

'You had better say now. I shan't listen to such nonsense again.' This was a different man from the one with whom she had raked autumn leaves not six weeks ago, joshing happily as they fuelled the bonfire together.

'Quite sure, sir.' What must she do? Kneel on the carpet? Beg for a penance?

He looked at her severely, and nodded. It was a dismissal. Liz swallowed and left. Now she knew exactly which of them Stainton valued more. Just occasionally, perhaps, it was as well to remember that the governor was steel all the way under the nondescript appearance.

By the time she reached her room Liz's humiliation had translated into anger looking for a scapegoat. Pritchard was still there, at the second desk, and looked up with bland concern.

'I was afraid it wasn't very wise,' he said mildly.

'Don't you begin to tell me what's wise and what isn't. Who do you think you are, you sanctimonious Welsh bastard? You deliberately set me up! Why the fuck didn't you tell me about that post-mortem analysis? Oh, yes, your report was a little model of perfection. They may not teach you much in whatever godforsaken hole you crawled out of, but they teach you arse-licking and they teach you back-stabbing, that's for sure!'

'Could we at least avoid the racism, do you think?'

Liz's eyes blazed. Why, why did she always put herself in the wrong like this? How was it that even this priggish git could succeed in making her feel a heel?

Pritchard watched her with a mixture of regret and admiration, neither of which showed in his expression. He said placatingly, 'We do have to work together, after all.'

'Yes,' Liz retorted. 'That's been made ultra crystal clear to me. Well done for really screwing me up with my governor. We'd better change seats tomorrow. Yours is the permanent one, behind the big desk. Mine is the makeshift effort, so long as I'm a good girl. God, I hate you, Pritchard. I'm going home. You can stay here impressing the governor with your bloody diligence till the bloody morning, if you like.'

'Diligence,' he said, amused. 'That's a long word, Eliz . . .'

But with a slam of the door that echoed like a rifle shot down the stairwell, Liz was gone, cursing as hard as she could to make sure she got to the car before she blubbed.

Detective-Sergeant Pritchard sat on thoughtfully for a while, not working. Then, with a sigh, he reached his coat off the stand and went out to his car and drove home to his digs.

Alec Stainton heard the thunder of the door's slam and knew it was Liz. He hoped she'd calm down before morning. What had Pritchard done that she had gone off her head like that? They had to work together—he couldn't spare either of them. Despite what he had said to Liz, there was no question of her having to go. But in the longer term, if she couldn't master herself, was all her natural ability and engaging manner going to carry her much further up the ladder?

By tomorrow she'd be herself again: he'd never known her storms last long. He regretted being so severe with Liz.

He shouldn't have allowed his own strains to find their outlet in vindictiveness.

By half-past nine Liz had reached some sort of inner resolution of her anger. She had convinced herself that Stainton would move her without a qualm if she insisted in behaving like a spoilt child. The best—the only—thing to do was make sure her work was impeccable—how the hell had she come to neglect that report on the post-mortems like that? It was because she was so busy following up her pet theory about the women all knowing the Carver—and conduct relations with Pritchard as correctly as the job demanded.

She took a long time over her meal, easing herself down from the foolish peak of her anger, placing a carefully-chosen CD in the player and drawing half a glass of wine from the box she had bought for the store cupboard. After she had eaten and washed up she kept the television off, choosing a book instead, consciously soothing her psyche back into equilibrium. Rosie came in about ten, but mercifully went straight upstairs with Joy, taking the Aspirin out of the kitchen drawer and muttering about migraine.

When the front doorbell rang twenty minutes later it broke Liz's hard-won serenity jarringly. She glanced at her watch. She didn't have friends here who just dropped in, apart from Rosie; and Rosie was an established resident now, upstairs in Liz's spare bedroom.

The bell pealed again and Liz jumped up quickly. She put all the lights on in the hall before flinging the door wide.

The step was empty. She stood there foolishly looking out across the estate to the backs of the next block fifty yards away. A car engine started away down at the parking spaces, and the glow of lights swept briefly over a wall as someone drove off. Liz was about to shut the door when she saw that something wrapped in white paper had fallen forwards on to the mat; she dimly remembered a rustle as she opened the door.

She reached down with a terrible premonition and gathered it into her arms, shutting the door and turning off the lights. Then she walked through into the kitchen, put the knife down, laid the bundle on the worktop, and unfurled the white paper.

Chrysanthemums: gold, shell-pink, purple, brown: the unemphatic autumn colours a man would choose.

She looked for the card. There must be a card. She hunted grimly, finding it finally between the paper and the cellophane wrapper.

The ink had run a little, but the lettering was, of course, orderly, and the one-word message still legible. *Sorry.* And the name at the bottom: *Geoffrey Pritchard.*

'You bastard!' Liz bellowed. 'You bastard, Pritchard!'

A long, thin wail issued from upstairs, strengthening and splintering into a volley of sharp cries. Liz heard Rosie's footsteps, and waited for them to move towards the stairs. But mercifully they stayed over the kitchen, and the wails stopped too.

So his name was Geoffrey.

You stupid berk, she berated herself angrily. You stupid, stupid berk. You never even bothered to ask.

Liz planned carefully for her meeting with Pritchard next day, rehearsing her lines as she drove through the back roads to work. But when she arrived the desk was clear. Johnson informed her that Pritchard had been called back to Wales.

'Thought you'd like to know. I like to spread a little happiness.' He paused as if expecting a reaction that wasn't forthcoming. 'He's coming back, though,' he concluded. 'Tough luck.'

Pritchard returned from Trenant forty-eight hours later. Liz Pink, turning away from the counter of the canteen with her tray of shepherd's pie, saw him sitting alone over by a window. She ate fast, and as he stacked his things neatly on the tray she was ready to gulp the last mouthful of coffee and follow him. She found him just settling at his desk: he looked up and as he saw who it was, so a reserve shadowed his eyes, as if cautioning her not to say anything irrevocable.

'Pritch,' she said at once, 'Pritch, if we're going to work together, there's something you ought to know about me.' Determinedly, she continued. 'I'm a bloody fool. Speak first and think after. If at all.'

'It's all right. We've both—'

'No, we haven't both anything,' she cut him off forth-rightly. 'Since you came I've been prancing around like a spoilt toddler. So, I mean what I want to say is, I'll try not to do it any more.' She took a deep breath, and managed the words that stuck so tightly in the throat: 'I'm sorry.' She met his eye and twisted her lips ruefully. 'The chrysanths were lovely.'

'*I'm* sorry,' Geoffrey Pritchard replied. 'I've been teasing you. Very rude, when we don't really know each other.'

Liz felt a knife of remorse twist in her gut. He was more or less saying he'd treated her as one would treat a friend, and she'd been too dense, or too stuck-up, to take it.

She became aware of the atmosphere in the room: thick with intimacy like incense hanging in the air. Apologies offered and received by both sides.

She said brightly: 'Well, thank God that's out of the way, I've been practising my speech all morning.' She turned away, and the pregnant heaviness of the air evaporated; the walls opened out again into the normal world, where type-writers clacked from adjacent rooms, footsteps pounded in the corridor, phones rang and snatches of voices carried as constables chaffed each other in the CID room nearby.

Perhaps it was the new confidence that she and Pritch could work together, and a desire to put it to the proof, that turned Liz's thoughts more and more to the Trenant murder. Before, it had seemed the most remote of the killings—another country, even, since Trenant was in Wales—and the least interesting, since it was surmised that the Carver had killed the girl, Tina Lewis, by mistake or necessity rather than by choice. But with her new, heightened sensitivity towards her room-mate (the knowledge that he had been teasing her when she had thought him strait-laced made her wonder what else she had missed) she gradually became aware that for Detective-Sergeant Pritchard, what counted most about the whole enquiry was that it should result in catching the killer of Tina Lewis. Trenant, she realized, was probably not big—no bigger than a large home counties village. Nothing could happen that did not involve everyone. Send not to know for whom the bell tolls, she thought idly.

'Pritch?'

DS Pritchard sat back in his chair and contemplated her seriously. 'Yes?'

She looked back at him, studying him, trying to read behind the bland amiable unremarkable face. 'Tina Lewis. You feel a good deal about her death, don't you?'

He said: 'Everybody does, round our way. We don't have murders, you see. It's as simple as that. We have crime, certainly. We have hooliganism and young tearaways and domestic affrays, but killing other people is not much in our line.'

Time will put that right, Liz thought. Time and 'progress' that homogenizes cultures, bringing the few benefits and the many evils of civilization to the farthest-flung communities, and doing so at a faster and faster rate. Progress will bring you murders soon enough, you'll see, along with superstores and more roads and golf courses on your sheep farms and children not daring to walk along a country lane. Was it innocence on Pritch's face, that lent it that frustrating blandness? Or did he know that all these things were in store, and only hope to do his best to mitigate their effects when they arrived?

Aloud, she said: 'She breaks the pattern.'

'You don't get much pattern with five murders. But go on.'

'Well, what characterizes the victims?'

'All women,' he said slowly. 'All white. All middle class. Otherwise . . . two blondes, one redhead, one brown, one black. One tall, others middle height. Geographically very spread. Four in their thirties, and . . . one, Tina Lewis, sixteen.'

'Precisely. You know my methods, Watson.'

'Tina Lewis,' Pritchard resumed, 'is also the only one killed in her own house. Supposedly, the murderer was invited in. She was on the bed when she was discovered, when her father came home. It was the only one where prints were found. Prints which aren't, as we now know, Crossland's. Because of the different MO, there is doubt in some quarters whether Tina really was killed by the Carver.'

'Do you doubt it, Pritch?'

'No.'

'And the wounds were the same, weren't they?'

'She was cut across the pubic region,' he said unemotionally. 'In the shape of an X.'

Liz said curiously, 'Did you see her, Pritch?'

He said: 'I was the one who went, when the call came in. My governor was fifty miles away. Ours is a big patch.'

She resisted the urge to proffer banal comfort. 'You arrested Tina's boyfriend.'

'And let him go again.'

Liz pulled a bitter face. 'Poor kid.' She thought about that for a moment. What would have been done to the boy's life before he was released. 'But supposing Tina was killed by the Carver.'

'We still have the question of why should he break out of his MO?'

Liz said: 'Supposing he didn't.'

'But he did.'

'I mean, supposing he hadn't intended to.'

He regarded her dubiously still. 'What's on your mind?'

'The main reason for thinking Tina's murderer couldn't have been the Carver is her age, isn't it?'

'She's sixteen.'

Liz said simply: 'How old's her mother?'

Pritchard let his breath out in a long thoughtful stream, staring at her. He's not so bad, Liz thought, when you get to know him. I wonder why I thought he was dim? He's just rather . . . private. Certainly there's a brain there ticking over pretty briskly.

'So,' he said, 'you're casting your lot with those who

reckon that the victims all have a link to the Carver. If only we could find it.'

'Victims, or intended victims.'

Alec found himself regarding Detective Chief Superintendent Arthur Oaks with a certain amount of sympathy, which was a novel sensation.

In the days since the death of Sandra Allen, Oaks had gained a harassed, harried look as if constantly expecting a pack of reporters to materialize at his shoulder. Alec realized that Oaks had actually been pleased to be drawn in to the Carver enquiry in the first instance. Presumably he had regarded it as the chance he had been waiting for for so long to shine in a media spotlight. Possibly he had never considered that the enquiry could degenerate into this waking nightmare of public failure. Two Sunday papers had run major features on the Carver hunt at the weekend. In each case the investigation had been dissected with an accuracy that suggested inside information. In each case the conclusion had been that provincial forces were incapable of mounting a successful investigation on a countrywide basis. Sideswipes, also of disconcerting accuracy, had hit the tender spot of Oaks's lack of operational command experience. Coordination of the enquiry should be allocated, the articles decided, to a commander from the Metropolitan Police. It was a solution with a comfortable nostalgic ring that would appeal to the papers' conservative readership. Send for Scotland Yard!

Alec happened to think they were wrong, even though the reasoning was not totally unsound. Oaks was not the ideal man for the job. But, even discounting natural umbrage at the suggestion that the country had two classes of police force—the Met, and the provincial hicks—Alec believed that switching horses now would be counter-productive. And what was Oaks? The figurehead, certainly; but not so very much more than that. There were shrewd enough men and women working on this investigation, and enough of them, to neutralize the shortcomings of any one man, however senior. Alec was confident of catching the Carver. He would only have liked to be as confident they would do so before he killed again.

But this morning's meeting was not directly concerned with strategy. It had been called in strictest secrecy—and limited to the minimum participants—to consider one specific gall on the collective elbow: FIGHTBACK.

Marjorie Weston, one of the two women present, was in no doubt that the official forces should now acknowledge a common cause with the irregulars. 'It's time we stopped looking down our noses at them. They're getting a long way with their testing of men. Further than we ever should.'

'I take leave to doubt that.' That was Blackett, with the elaborate courtesy which to Alec was as unmistakable a warning of peril as the skull and crossbones over a high voltage supply.

'Every woman in the country is going to make sure her man goes for testing. We could never have managed that. They've recruited half the population to check out the other half.'

'What a wonderful achievement,' someone muttered.

Surmising that the pathology laboratories had been able to test body fluid samples from all the killings, FIGHTBACK was currently demanding access to the results, to compare them with the data collected from—how many men was it so far? Nobody seemed quite to know. Alec wondered whether the vagueness of the generalizations about the success of the FIGHTBACK scheme masked a rather lower degree of compliance with it than the organizers were keen to acknowledge.

'We should give them what we have. Work with them. Not against them.'

'We have nothing.'

There was brief silence while they contemplated having to admit publicly that almost no physical traces had been left at any of the killings.

'Couldn't we,' someone volunteered tentatively, 'find a way of making *them* give us *their* data?'

Heads were shaken in gloomy doubt. Whether or not we catch the Carver, Alec told himself, the propaganda victory is already won. By FIGHTBACK.

Sandra Allen's body had been found almost fifty miles away, near Petworth. This was where attention now concentrated. This seemed wrong to Liz, even though she herself scarcely believed the Carver was still on the forest. 'What's wrong,' she complained to Alec, 'is that it's all negative. All the time we're working from the wrong end—trailing after him.'

Alec agreed. At present they were reacting to the Carver: going to where he had been two days ago. Moreover Oaks, having set so much store initially by the offender profile, seemed now to be making no use of it. He had become uncharacteristically mistrustful of the resources of technology and seemed content to plod in the Carver's wake and wait for information to come in from the public or— God help them all—another murder.

Liz proffered the clipboard on which she had assembled a CV for each of the murdered women, except Tina Lewis. 'I've been doing a bit of unofficial thinking, guv. And the thing I keep coming back to is that all the dead women were in the same generation—except Tina, and let's say she was killed for her mother. And that makes her mother the really important one. Because the other women we know to have been on the Carver's shopping list are dead, aren't they? If the Carver dated them all when they were kids, or something like that, and now he's taking some sort of revenge, Tina's mum is the only one who might be able to give us the key. I mean, if there's a pattern, why can't we use it to predict rather than plod after the Carver all the time? To identify other potential victims—and be there before him.'

'Every friend of the family has been checked. All negative.'

'Maybe someone was missed. Maybe someone turned up out of the blue claiming to be a friend of mum's.'

'She'd never have let him in.'

'Maybe,' Liz said stubbornly.

Alec said: 'It's worth having another chat with her. I'll

suggest it to Oaks, and see if he'd like me to ask Dyfed/Powys to go back to her.'

'You can do better than that, guv.'

'How?'

'Get them to send Pritch. Then I can go with him. Pritch and I want to see Tina's mum again. Really talk to her. No preconceptions. If there's anything, it's nothing obvious like all having gone to the same school, because we'd have spotted that. It has to be some little thing that nobody's going to notice. Then I want to put it on the computer—model it—and see what connections are thrown up.'

'You want to go with Pritchard?'

'It is his patch. And he's a bit sore about it. He's a romantic sort of a bloke.'

Alec looked doubtful. 'OK. If you two can manage not to fall out. But he's supposed to be here to do a job.'

'Sure, guv. If you find any wigwams on the forest I promise I'll have him back here before you can say "How!"'

'If the victim was supposed to be Tina's mother, and all the victims are linked, why hasn't she recognized the names of the other dead women?'

Liz said simply: 'Has anyone asked her, sir?'

14

'It's not that I grudge her the hospitality. And I mean she needs it. It's just . . .'

Liz sighed. It was a long drive to Trenant. They were in Pritch's car, and she was not quite sure how, when other topics of conversation had stumbled to a halt, she had come to be talking about herself and Rosie.

'It's just that it's my house and it's still new and I wouldn't mind a little space to enjoy it at my leisure. Tell me, Pritch, am I a selfish bitch? When I've got so much and she's got so little?'

'Honestly?'

'Honestly. Tell me. Don't be afraid, I shan't scream four letter words. At least . . .'

'Well, to be honest, it does sound as if it would be selfish to turn her out just now. But it isn't selfish to feel as you do. It's human. You can't stop the birds flying over your head, but you can stop them building nests in your hair. Which is as much as to say that we have all sorts of unpleasant impulses, but we don't have to let ourselves surrender to them. You're not doing that. You're fighting it and acting contrary to your inclinations. In fact, Liz, you're really being rather fine and noble.'

'I am?'

She eyed him cautiously. She was coming to know Geoffrey Pritchard, and one of the things she was beginning to appreciate was the extreme dryness of his wit.

'Does she really want to leave her husband?'

Liz shrugged her shoulders, suddenly weary of the whole business. 'God knows.'

'Want me to come and have a look at first hand?'

'There'll be kids' toys everywhere.'

'Fine.'

'And you'll have to watch Rosie feeding awful slush to Joy, which is not a pretty sight, to say nothing of baring her breast at the drop of a hat.'

'I expect I'll survive.'

'And the house'll smell of sick and nappies.'

'Liz, I'll cope. Don't worry.'

She cuffed him lightly on the shoulder. 'Pritch, you're a decent old bloke, did anyone ever tell you that?'

'I can't remember anyone putting it quite that way.'

Liz added after a while, 'For a Welshman.'

Bron Pritchard opened the door, releasing a baking smell Liz was used to only from the patisserie of the supermarket.

Liz said, when she had been introduced, 'This is a conspiracy, isn't it, to seduce me away from home. Lambs in the fields, sunshine, and now home cooking. I'm only a simple city girl. You'll have me babbling about my Welsh granny if you're not careful.'

'Have you got a Welsh granny?' Pritch asked, leading the way into the kitchen.

'I'm working on it,' Liz replied. 'She could fall off the twig and leave me her whitewashed cottage with honeysuckle round the door and I could come up here every weekend.'

'And we could burn it down for you,' Pritch observed comfortably.

'I suppose you've lived here since the year dot and Bron was the girl next door.'

'Something like that.'

They took coffee and Liz tried a Welsh cake, then another. Bron, approving a hearty appetite, pressed more on her.

'I've arranged we'll go round at half-twelve,' Pritch informed her as she picked crumbs from her lap with a licked finger. 'I've got to call in to the shop on the way.'

As they drove the mile from Pritch's house to the police station, Liz looked around at everything in the small town with curiosity. She felt Pritch's amused sideways glance. What she saw could not be more than the gloss—happy life in compact little towns set amid verdant country. The reality, no doubt, was as mundane and depressing as reality anywhere else.

The police station was set on a hill on the outskirts of the town: a modern, undistinguished block which had not yet spawned an accretion of temporary buildings or cheap extensions and so seemed spacious in its lawned site. Pritch showed her his room and left her alone while he attended to one or two matters. She stood at the window wondering what it must be like to work in a place with sheep in a field below and the hills rising wave upon wave to a horizon of hazy mountains.

'Looking at the view?'

'Lambs in the fields, Pritch. It's a bit much. And the hills.'

'The hills?'

'Don't tell me you've never noticed them.'

He grinned. 'The hills are always there. Ready?'

'As much as I'll ever be.'

'Let's go.'

Ruth had been so sure, as she drove over, that her journey would be in vain, that when she drew up in the lane and saw Anita's car on the muddy track that did duty as a driveway to Bracken Ghyll she was stricken with uncharacteristic hesitancy. What did she do now? She had been all ready to find the cottage empty and leave a note: guilt assuaged, duty done. Instead, here was evidence of Anita's presence—and evidence of what Ruth had feared, her deepening madness, for what but madness led to these crazy structures of wire and planks, these warnings written in the colour of blood, this self-incarceration?

She climbed out none the less, manipulated the wire barrier clumsily and pushed her way to the front door through the damp, bedraggled garden, the foliage spilling over the brick path clutching wetly at her skirt. There was no reply to her knock. Perhaps after all Anita was out. It was not a wonderful day, but quite good enough for an hour or two's riding on the forest. Diligently she made her way round to the back; not because she hoped to find Anita at home after all, but because the rituals had to be gone through before she could write her note and climb back into the car. The house was as she remembered it, though more shabby and dilapidated, and a branch blown by the autumn gales lay against the gable. The muddy track where Anita's car was parked led round behind some trees to the stable block, just visible from the back door. The doors were shut, but the wheelbarrow stood outside with the dung-fork propped in it, as if Anita had just that moment left it. The whole place depressed her, and there was a smell which was less than fresh. For a moment, Ruth felt an uncharacteristic anger towards her friend. Why must she let things go so? Why must everything she was associated with be rundown and messy and uncared-for?

The next moment her habitual charity reasserted itself. It was, after all, barely a couple of months since Anita's mother's death. What seemed to an outsider ample time for recovery from grief was nothing like it to the one bereft.

She pushed into the dingy back porch and knocked briskly on the peeling paint of the door. Rat tat tat.

And heard immediate movements inside. Though the door stayed firmly shut. Ruth made a face and waited. Inside the sounds of movement stopped. Out of the corner of an eye Ruth glimpsed movement at the window. With an inward sigh she turned her head and smiled at where Anita's face, framed in its ginger thatch, mooned through the smeared panes.

'Try again, Mrs Lewis,' Geoffrey Pritchard invited. He shuffled the photographs and handed them one by one to the woman to study. Liz watched her; watched the perplexity and the frown of anxiety and the remorseless lack of recognition. Yet there had to be a link.

146

'I'm sorry.' Gwen Lewis put the sheaf of photos down on the table beside her cup, looking small and bewildered. She sat with her husband at her side, coffee cups before them. A plate of biscuits had been handed round. Because that was how you had to behave when you had seen the body of your only daughter lying dead and savagely mutilated on a blood-soaked mattress. When they had arrived, Liz had offered the words of condolence she had prepared—she was a firm believer in offering, albeit briefly, that sympathy which so many people were too craven to voice—and, recognizing in Mrs Lewis's very posture that resolution she hoped she herself would present should she ever, God help her, be in so horrific a situation, had been unsurprised when the woman responded, 'Got to bear it, haven't you? What else is there to do?' What else indeed, except resign from the anguish of living.

She exchanged a glance with Pritch and took over, explaining the possibility that the killer had been known to Tina; explaining that it was possible too that he had been unknown to her but claimed to be known to her mother and so won the teenager's readily-given trust. The possibility that he had been known to his other victims also.

'I've been through all this.'

'I know. It's battering away at the problem. We're hunting for something, anything, that's a way in to the identity of the man who's doing these things.' Liz assumed a brisker air. 'We can go right back through your own history. Build up a CV. I'm doing this for each of the victims. Then we'll run all the data through a computer in a sort of—' she rejected the word game—'model. Try and identify patterns.'

'If there was any pattern of that sort,' Mr Lewis said, 'Gwen'd know the names of the other victims. And you don't, do you, Gwen?'

Mrs Lewis looked vaguely surprised, as if she was considering the possibility for the first time.

It was that moment—the cosy living-room, the bleak, ravaged features of the bereaved parents, the sullen rain running down the window panes, the light on against the dullness of the early afternoon—that moment when she saw a tiny furrow appear in Mrs Lewis's brow, that Liz felt the first tingle of excitement, the first trickle of adrenalin, like the first anticipatory intimation of passion, that whispered that the resolution of the case of the Carver, far distant though it might yet be, was no longer a matter of chance. She stamped it down quickly, but not quickly enough for some hint to appear in her face, for out of the corner of her eye she saw Pritch look up, curiously.

She ran through the names of the victims: Sonia Wright, Mandy Williams, Julie Warren, Sandra Allen; not worried when Gwen Lewis shook her head. It wasn't going to be so simple, but they were still going to get there.

They took the best part of the afternoon recording the details of Gwen Lewis's life. Liz had prepared a template designed to include everything that might conceivably be relevant; but the trouble with templates, as she knew, was that what lies outside them tends to get sidelined. And in this instance, if there was a connection between the Carver's victims and this woman, it would lie precisely in some area Liz hadn't thought of. So she asked Mrs Lewis to recount her history in her own words, and filled it in on the template as each item surfaced, recording the whole account on the portable tape recorder with the resolve that every word would receive full scrutiny. In her own mind, Liz was looking out for the occasions when women get together. She already knew that the victims had not all attended the same school or the same college or been neighbours or anything simple like that. But even if it wasn't obvious, she was convinced that at some time their paths had crossed. Privately, she still inclined to the hunch that they had all at one time been girlfriends of the Carver. She was certain his victims were not chosen at random. He was carrying out a programme of revenge or retribution of some bizarre and perverted kind.

As they came more up to date, Liz was aware of an atmosphere of constraint in the room. She felt it as a thickening of the air, and an electricity buzzing between Mrs Lewis and her husband, and wished she had contrived to remove him from the room before the reconstruction started. Undoubtedly, there was a guilty secret here somewhere.

'That's about it,' Gwen Lewis said. 'That's all.'

There was a silence. The electricity hummed.

Mr Lewis said: 'Hadn't you better tell them about Stephen Evans?' There was a faint tincture of acid in his voice.

'I . . .'

'I don't suppose it will embarrass them. If you are being totally honest . . .'

Gwen Lewis looked down at her hands, locked in her tartan-skirted lap. The fingers were interwoven protectively. In the end she said, 'There isn't much to tell. I didn't think you knew.' She looked up, guilt and unhappiness contending in her eyes. Liz was profoundly sorry for her. This was what murder did in families. This was the reality glossed over in television fiction; indignity, suspicion, denial of the decencies. Mr Lewis had been made to donate specimens of his body fluids in an attempt to confirm he had not killed his own daughter. The fingerprinting ink was scarcely dry on their hands. All the secret cupboards and lockers of their lives must be cracked open and the contents tossed out into the daylight for impersonal scrutiny.

More gently, Mr Lewis said, 'It doesn't matter now, Gwen. Tell them. I always knew.'

So Gwen Lewis added another name to the list of information: the name of Stephen Evans: the name of a lover. And, with a sideways, lidded glance of apology, a second. Her husband looked as if he had been hit. He didn't know about *that* one, Liz surmised. Another little bereavement, another negligible assault on the man whose daughter still lay, unburied, her body eviscerated by the pathologist's knife, in a cold store in a mortuary until such time as someone should have some idea who could plausibly be charged with the taking away of her life. Meanwhile, two beautiful leads to follow up.

*   *   *

There was one other tiny hint of light before they left: Liz, prompted by the space on her proforma marked maiden name, mentioned to Gwen Lewis the maiden names of all the other victims. It had almost certainly been done before. Or had it? For Gwen Lewis hesitated over one name, unwilling, or unable, quite to assert that she had never heard it before. Mandy Williams, the second victim, had been born Mandy Pascoe. No, they knew no one of that name. It was just a vague sentience that it held significance for her in some, unreachable, context.

Something?

They drove the few miles to the Pritchards' house for a snatched meal before the long haul back south.

Half an hour later they were on the road, Liz driving. Before they reached Shrewsbury, Pritch was asleep. Liz glanced at his recumbent form. He slept tidily, as he would do all things, breathing evenly and quietly through his nose. She settled herself more deeply into her own seat and turned her gaze back to the ribbon of concrete stretching ahead towards distant Sussex. Turning the radio on with the volume low, she drove on, relaxed, humming under her breath.

Anita locked the door behind her friend and waited until she heard the sound of the car recede down the lane. She had been interrupted unpacking the shopping and now she finished the task methodically, stowing cans and packets in the larder, frozen goods in the freezer, bleach and disinfectant and a big packet of loo rolls under the stairs.

She had left out some mince, and cooked herself a shepherd's pie on the stove, carefully rewrapping the unused half of the mince and placing the container in the fridge. She ate the meal at the kitchen table, a magazine—it was one of the new ones about true crimes which she found more interesting now than the liberated women's magazines— beside her. Afterwards she washed up, dried the few items of cutlery and sat in front of the television screen until the clock on the mantelpiece told her the day had drawn to a close, and it was time for bed. She never watched the news now. She didn't want to hear what others were doing about hunting the Carver; she didn't want to see the FIGHTBACK women and hear their educated voices. Resentment spread through her body like a bacillus, colonizing and multiplying. What had Ruth Samuels to do, snooping round like this? What had she wanted? What had she seen? Above all, what would she do now?

It had all been going so well . . .

15

That the Carver might kill again was both the fear and (though this thought was guiltily unvoiced) the hope. The date of his next killing, something known only to him (or did he indeed know nothing until the desire overwhelmed him?) was the invisible deadline lending urgency to their work. It seemed everything had been tried, and yielded nothing, and consequently there was an air of dejection in the building as if they were a team beaten before they'd ever encountered their opponents. And in time, as every opening was explored and proved barren, minds of senior officers turned towards those things their predecessors would have relied on: house to house enquiries and a yard-by-yard search of Ashdown Forest. 'If he's living rough,' Oaks pronounced, 'we'll find him.'

And the South Downs, Alec queried silently? The New Forest? Either was as near to the location of the last death as Ashdown. But recognizing another of the changes of policy that became more frequent as hope diminishes, he swallowed his objections and listened to Oaks outlining the form the search would take. Someone mentioned Crossland's name. Yes, confirmed Oaks, Crossland was not excluded from the picture. He was still unaccounted for, wasn't he? Alec groaned inwardly. They were back where they'd been six weeks ago.

Detective Chief Inspector Marjorie Weston and Detective Chief Inspector Alec Stainton were to set up the search, and officers would be drafted in from outlying divisions and neighbouring forces. Two coaches came down from the Met, carrying policemen who stood apart in prickly gangs jigging nervously like the hopped-up youths they resembled. Liz cut up more maps, with three constables to help her. The whole forest was to be searched over from the beginning, moving from east to west on the assumption that the Carver would be forced back towards the Petworth area; like beaters flushing game towards the guns, Oaks said. No credit was given for the work already done under Liz's direction; Oaks decreed that too much time had passed. Liz fumed. And amid media encouragement a famous survival expert was recruited, charged with examining any signs of the Carver's presence, picking up the trail, leading the hounds to the quarry.

'What's he supposed to do? Spot the bent branches and tell us Crossland peed against this bush last Thursday fortnight?'

Pritchard said: 'They found some stuff at his home. You saw the report. Outdoor stuff. A knife, a camping stove, a bivouac sheet. That sort of thing.'

'If they're at his house, then he's not using them out on the forest, is he?' Liz grumbled. 'And if we're going big on Crossland again, what about this woman he picked up in the Brambletye? Why aren't we concentrating on her? We've touted the photofit round the pubs and we've had it stuck up outside the local nick and that's it. But if she was tarting, she was probably an amateur, which probably means she wasn't on her home patch because of people recognizing her. She could be decomposing under a bramble patch on the forest by now.'

'If she is,' Pritch replied, 'the search squads will find her.'

'I wouldn't trust some of those woodentops to find their way to the canteen. There's something particularly painful about looking on while senior officers turn an important operation into a dog's breakfast. There's a man out there killing women. This whole thing's turning into a bad joke.'

'If you can't take a joke . . .'

'. . . You shouldn't have joined the police force. Thanks, Pritch. I knew you'd be a comfort.'

Alec looked down from the helicopter at the carpet of woodland and the barer uplands of heather and bracken and realized again the enormity of it. On the face of things, all they had to do was search a few square miles for a missing man. But on the forest you could pass within yards of a body and never see it. It had happened often enough. He remembered reading of a case on the North Yorks Moors where a corpse lay within feet of a wall on which families regularly sat to picnic, and yet it had decayed to a skeleton before it was stumbled over, and its identification was never known. A living man, committed to escape, could surely evade a ponderous police search without even breaking into a sweat. Even the dogs that were being brought in were little use. All they could do was track the path of human feet, registering the minute odours of crushed vegetation and human passage. But in an area like the forest, which was the exercise ground of probably half a million people, they would be hopelessly lost amid the conflicting scents. Six thousand acres.

Down below, the line of searchers came into view. They looked puny against the forest, and pitifully few. And he knew the ease with which a clue could be missed by a copper drafted in from the town to whom the whole exercise was a welcome change from routine and a nice day out in the country.

The survival expert arrived in a drab olive Land Rover. He was a civilian, who wore a subtly faded combat jacket and name-dropped wearisomely about Sass and the Falklands (the effect, which he could not have intended, was to draw attention to his tightly-strapped belly and his carefully arranged thinning hair). Taken to the place where Crossland's Audi had been discovered he looked around, asked if the cricket hut had been searched (it hadn't; unfortunately, since the survival man at once scored a gold), declared that there was no way of tracking Crossland until the following morning, and departed for his hotel.

He had set out his requirements for the searchers, laying great emphasis on looking for evidence of fire. If the Carver was on the forest, living rough, he must cook. Find the fire, and I will find you the man.

154

Alec looked on cynically. The man talked sense, but it was the obvious sort of sense that any senior boy scout could have recited as easily, and it only went so far. This was not Dartmoor or the Grampians. It was Ashdown Forest, ringed by villages and dotted with farms and houses with ranges of outbuildings. You could live for a long time on fish and chips bought in Forest Row; long enough to cross to Crowborough and stock up in the supermarket, long enough to pick a succession of night leaguers in tumbledown buildings. Only a fool or a fanatic would actually try and survive in the open with such riches all around him.

But Oaks could hear the press baying, and the blood they were baying for was his own. Therefore he needed to give them what they liked: camera shots of lines of bobbies crossing the forest, probing barns, quizzing householders on doorsteps. Visible evidence that Chief Superintendent Oaks was leaving no stone unturned in his tireless hunt for the Carver.

'A Mrs Lewis rang, skip. Mean anything? Said she'd ring back.'

'Why didn't you put her through to Sergeant Pritchard, you nerd?'

'One of them, is she?'

'One of what?'

'Well, if you want her put through to Pritchard . . .'

Liz stopped and looked at him. This was embarrassing, but it had to be done. 'Johnson, I'll say this once, so pin back your ears. DS Pritchard and I are working together now. Like—together. Get me? Everything you've heard me say about him in the past is superseded. The new issue gen is that he's OK. I'd be obliged if you'd revise your references to him accordingly.'

Johnson stared at her, then a huge grin of amazement creased his face and he rushed to the door. In the room opposite, DC Simms was stabbing one-fingered at a keyboard as if the keys were teeth he expected every moment to bite off his fingertip. 'Hey, Simmsy! Guess what! The skipper's fallen in love with Pritchard!'

'You what?' Simms was suddenly in the room with them.

'I have not fallen in love with anybody,' Liz protested. 'I have merely revised a first and erroneous impression.'

'Get that,' Johnson said in tones of awe. 'It's love.'

'Well, there's none lost on you two bright sparks, you can count on that,' Liz retorted tartly, and swept out. Only to return a moment later, rather destroying the impression of hauteur to ask: 'That call, Johnson. What'd she say she'd do?'

'She'll call back, skip.'

'Thank you.'

And Liz made a final exit, the giggles of the two DCs following her down the corridor. Babies at home, and a bloody kindergarten at work. She was beginning to feel as if she should take up childminding full time.

Mrs Lewis's call came through just after three. Liz took it with one of those distinct frissons of anticipation that illogically stabbed through routine work on occasions. She didn't know what Mrs Lewis was going to say, but she knew somehow it was going to be important.

So it was with a sensation of recognition akin to *déjà vu* that she heard Mrs Lewis, after apologies and excuses, say: 'I've remembered where I heard that name. Do you remember? Mandy Pascoe.'

Mandy Pascoe, latterly Mandy Williams, the Carver's second victim. 'Go on,' Liz invited.

'There was a girl of that name at ranger camp. We went to the Brecon Beacons. Mandy Pascoe was there. We became best friends for the fortnight.'

'Rangers?'

'Guides . . . you know.'

'When was this?'

'I've been trying to remember. It was just before my eighteenth birthday. That would make it 1977. I hadn't thought of it for ages, and then that name brought it all back.'

Statistically it was probable that Mrs Lewis should have at least one acquaintance with the name of one of the Carver

156

victims. Guide camp, nearly two decades ago . . . 'Let's try again with the names of the other women we're talking about,' Liz suggested without much hope. She read them out.

'I think there was a Sonia Vesey there,' Mrs Lewis said. 'It sort of rings a bell in my mind. The others . . . no. But it was seventeen years ago. Half a lifetime—I mean, my God!'

Liz thanked her and rang off. She sat briefly and pondered the conversation; then she took it—dismissively, with a wry laugh against herself—to Stainton.

'I wonder how we can follow it up without calling too much attention to ourselves?' Stainton asked, rubbing his jaw.

Liz leant against the filing cabinet, her habitual pose, less constrained than sitting opposite him, more on a level. 'It's nothing, guv. Almost twenty years ago. Guide camp, for heaven's sake. It's not much, is it?' Knowing all the time: this was all they had; this was important.

'It's not much, Liz. Agreed. It's probably a completely different Mandy Pascoe. That'll be Oaks's view. He won't be keen on the idea of us going up there when we should be working on the forest search. So we won't burden him with the knowledge. And you didn't hear me say that.'

'It's a long way to Trenant,' Liz reminded him. 'We won't be popular, muscling in on the local force a second time.'

'Can Pritchard fix that?'

'I dare say. But if I go . . .'

'Not you. Us. This time I'm coming with you.'

16

Afterwards, he had slept. Anita recalled it now, sitting silently in the sagging armchair in the dingy room in which the hum of the electric fire was the most distinct sound; the only company. She stared into the redness of the bars, recalling that momentous night with precise clarity, replaying events frame by frozen frame, as she had done so many times since that she scarcely knew now what was memory, what wish: savouring, exulting, wondering, regretting.

Afterwards, after they had made love, her Lover slept. (Love: strange word for a business which horses managed far more nobly.) He slept with abandoned limbs thrown out, one arm as if reaching for her embrace.

But she had lain more fully awake, more fully alive, than she had ever felt before. True, her body was sore, and to some extent she felt used. The skill he had employed in arousing her she knew for a practised trick, and her body's enthusiastic response equally a trick, a biological one, leaving her imperfectly fulfilled. The longed-for experience had not after all satisfied: the summit, finally achieved, revealed itself as a mere foothill with the real peaks as far out of reach as ever. In a few hours he would leave her, more impoverished than ever for the brief blinding flash of experience. Perhaps the first germ of the idea had sprouted even then.

He snored, his mouth open. His tongue fluttered on each out breath. His legs were pale and the hairs few and blond. On his chest grew a modest fuzz of hair which fascinated and repelled her. His shoulders were fleshy, like lumps of suet. And his belly. It bulged and sagged sideways with his posture, and rendered ridiculous the shrunken, sated appendage beneath its curve. She knew he was not much, this man. A stone or two of bone; a couple more of meat; a few handfuls of offal; a yard or two of skin to keep all decent. Yet naked, he both enthralled and repelled her. There was, in the intimacy of his flesh, something of the repugnance her mother had evoked. And yet . . .

And yet it was intolerable that he should snort himself into wakefulness, tug on those clothes, offer some crude, token sugaring of his departure and *go*. He wasn't much; but he was here, and her impotence to prevent his going infuriated her.

She looked at him lying there, proprietorially, on the new mattress. Now soiled. If he went, she would burn it. *If* he went?

In the past Anita had sometimes fantasized about capturing a companion—a little boy, it usually was, when she indulged the flight of fancy—and keeping him here, at Bracken Ghyll. Once she had gone as far as befriending a child on his way home from the primary school. She had walked with him until they came to where she had parked the car and he had easily been prevailed upon to accept a lift. But when he told her she had passed the end of his road she panicked and stopped the car and pushed him out in a gateway. Six or seven, she thought he had been: polite and innocent. He would have made a good companion, and she would have enjoyed looking after him. But this man was not a little boy; he would open his eyes and grunt and climb from the bed and leave. Unless . . .

That was the moment at which she had acted; and even now, when everything was falling apart, she hugged herself as she thought of her temerity, exulting all the more for the knowledge that she had so nearly let the moment pass.

For it was then that Anita swung her feet off the bed and reached for her clothes, covering herself swiftly. Crossland twitched and grunted and reached for the memory of her presence beside him but did not wake. She pulled on her skirt and thrust her shirt into it roughly and hurried on bare feet out of the room and along the passage to her own. They were in the drawer that contained her few bracelets and necklaces, her gold wristwatch and her good luck charms. She reached in and took them out and worked away at the shrink-wrapping plastic with her nails until she could free them.

Her mother's room smelled a bit; a curious feral smell: she was aware of it now, re-entering it. A rank, human smell that told of private pleasures. In her absence he had shifted on the bed, almost as if to make it easier. Delicately she picked her way round to the far side by the window, where his clothes lay neatly folded on the chair. She picked them up and threw them aside and shifted the chair out of the way.

The bed head was fumed oak, wood rendered hideous and twisted into contorted shapes and probably strong as steel. But Anita took no chances. The frame *was* steel. The mattress was a fraction narrow and the frame was exposed. She fastened one hasp of the handcuffs to the long steel angle which ran the length of the bed, and the other round the podgy, freckled wrist that hung so conveniently alongside. The metal engaged with a smart snap, and probably it was cold to his wrist, too. But she didn't look at him as she made her way round the bed towards the door, because she didn't want to be faced with questions to which she herself had not worked out the answers yet.

As she quitted the room she bent to turn down the wick on the paraffin heater. It expired with a weak pop.

No sense in wasting fuel.

Naturally there had been a good deal of shouting when he woke up. By then Anita was sitting in the armchair in the room below and she ignored the animal's caged roars because, though she was rather proud of her initiative so far, she had to work out what to do next.

There was his car, of course. If that stayed outside the house people would come looking for him. She would be arraigned, scorned, paraded, prosecuted perhaps. She must move the car. She thought of something else, as a result of which she went and hunted out a bucket. She hesitated before going back upstairs, but not for long. There wouldn't be much he could do so long as she kept out of his reach, but leaving the bucket where he could reach it, and yet without bringing herself within the orbit of his fat fingers might be tricky.

His fury when she opened the door and he saw her there, fully dressed, dominant, confronting his nakedness and impotence, was rather daunting; but Anita was not a timorous woman. Not now! Being back in his presence was a queer experience. There was the smell, and the fleshiness of his shoulders and waist and the narrowness of his hips and the pelt of hair on his chest and that fascinating few inches of flesh pendant beneath his stomach to which her eyes were drawn at once. So ridiculous—and yet . . .

She had scarcely got downstairs before she heard the smash of the glass and the clang of the bucket falling on the grass and the man's shouting.

She had smiled to herself, for there had been little chance of him being heard. It was then about midnight. If anybody did pass they would be cocooned in cars, with the radio playing and the heater fan on, eagerly intent on their homes a last few minutes' drive away. Besides, the road was on the other side of the house. The nearest neighbour was a quarter of a mile away. The man was shouting into the void where there were only squirrels and rabbits and badgers and foxes to hear; and they knew better than to have regard for anything a man needed. And smashing the glass would have let the winter chill in. He'd regret it.

She had better do something about the car straightaway. Then she would have to think what to do with the man. Tomorrow it would grow light again. He would hear hooves on the road as other horses were exercised by other women. He might hear the postman's van. If he shouted then, it was not impossible he could be heard, and that would be awkward. And the bucket, even if she replaced it, was no permanent solution to his requirements. It was all a question of working it out, and she would arrive at a perfectly satisfactory solution, of that she had no doubt. Her face clouded. If she moved him, how could she prevent him rushing her? He was far stronger than her, and even the DEF/AID knife would be useless if once he succeeded in grabbing her wrist.

After Anita had disposed of the car she walked back, enjoying the cloudy night (and it was true, you could barely hear the man's cries until you were close, because enough of a breeze had sprung up to whisk them away); then sat and worked everything out. She looked at her plan carefully from this side and that. It seemed, however, as good a solution as she could devise, and she had no doubt about her ability to carry it out. There would be a certain initial risk, but that could be minimized. The man was demoralized, which would make it easier.

She took her jacket and the big torch and went outside and looked around. It seemed feasible, and she set about her preparations with a curious sensation which she identified after a little thought as happiness.

Two hours later she entered the room and switched the light on.

He was lying on the bed, and turned towards her with a start. His skin was white, blotched with blue and red. The room struck her as cold, muffled as she was, and rain had blown in to soak the carpet. His foot was bleeding from a cut. No doubt he had intended to bluster. Perhaps to attempt to grab her. His mouth was open as if for words. But he closed it when he saw the shotgun, and his Adam's apple jerked as he swallowed. Anita felt the cosy surge of power she had always dreamed of. She had done it! And not a little boy, she exulted—a grown man! The ecstasy of power surpassed anything she had known before. All these years she had been chasing the wrong goal.

She raised the gun.

At last she had slept, but only after locking all the internal as well as external doors and setting a careful trap designed to cause a lot of noise if the man managed to gain entrance and stumbled up against it. And with the DEF/AID CS gas canister on the bedside table. And with the shotgun, loaded, by her side.

The shotgun was a comfort to her. It was old, and possibly that might affect its efficacy, though she didn't think so; and the cartridges were old too, which was more worrying. The shotgun had belonged to a neighbour who had expressed anxiety about two women living alone. Donating it to Anita's mother, he had told her with a wink that he held no certificate for it. Anita certainly held none. Bureaucracy, like rules, was for the control of the herd. Perhaps until tonight she had been one of the herd. But she was one no longer.

In the morning she found some pieces of plywood and laboriously painted warnings on them. NO HAWKERS; NO CIRCULARS; NO CALLERS EXCEPT BY APPOINTMENT; KEEP OUT—GUARD DOGS. She nailed them to posts and tied them to the front hedge. There was a plastic drum in the tack-room that had once held disinfectant. With a good deal of difficulty, Anita cut a slot in it, then slung it from the gatepost with baler twine. POST, she painted on it in irregular capitals of bright red. Not that there ever was much. Behind the stable was half a roll of sheep netting and a length of barbed wire, enough to make a crude barrier across the driveway. It would be awkward to dismantle every time she needed to take the car out, but she didn't think she would be doing that very often in the future. Already she had turned from contemplating the past to anticipating the future. He was out there now. Hers. As biddable, as susceptible to spur and rein, as JoJo had ever been. And what the future held . . .

In pleasurable languor Anita let her daydreams come. She had all the time in the world.

Now she had not. Now Ruth's visit had taken the future away. She began to wonder, sitting there, staring into the humming, hypnotizing electric element, what she must do.

After a while she roused herself. She crossed the hall and took her long riding mac from the hook. It was becoming more shabby, she noticed in the light from the overhead bulb; its brown waxed surface mottled with darker stains. She pulled it on, took her sou'wester from the pocket, slipped off her shoes and thrust her feet into the boots standing waiting.

Outside the weather was fierce and violent. Gusts of wind clapped round the house, battering her as she emerged from the shelter of the porch and flinging spiteful rain in her face. A dozen yards away the car rocked gently on its springs as the wind caught it, and moisture ran like tears down the glass. Anita bent her head into the storm and strode out for the stable. The double stable doors were firmly shut. That hardly seemed strange any more. The key awkward in her chilled fingers, Anita undid the padlock on the tack-room door and slid the bolt back. Within, after she had pulled the door to against the storm, all was very quiet. The familiar bridles hung on their wooden pegs, the saddles on their racks, the feed bins in the corner. A door led into the loose-box next door. Cautiously Anita slid the bolts and inched it open.

The straw on the floor. The smell. The stains. And in the corner, the mound which rustled rhythmically. The light shed through the door revealed pale gleams of dirty-streaked skin gleaming through the insulating heap of straw. As she opened the door wider the straw moved and, with a rattle of chain, Crossland sat up and stared back at her from the depths of bright, sunken eyes.

17

They had arranged to leave from Alec Stainton's: it was only a few miles from Liz's house and saved them the bother of driving south to the office before heading north again.

She arrived too early, but no one seemed to mind. Liz, who had scrambled to get herself out so early and was proud of having managed it, was disconcerted to find that in the Stainton household the day had evidently started some time ago. Frances was stacking the dishwasher; Alec excused himself to carry out a quick check on the car before the journey; and Liz was seconded to Lucy's company until he was ready to start.

Lucy swept Liz off to look at the rabbit—she was still young enough to want to show off a pet—and set about enlisting her support in the campaign for a pony.

'A pony needs an area of at least two acres,' Lucy explained authoritatively as they stood looking out across the two diminutive paddocks, 'and we've *got* that.'

Liz huddled in her sheepskin jacket. 'What about winter?' she asked.

'Oh, we'd need a stable, of course. You bring them in then, you see.'

'I see.' Liz swept the muddy grass with an eye rendered tearful by the wind. No stable was apparent. 'Do they just eat grass?' she asked.

'You have to give them pony nuts and things. I've looked it all up. And hay, but we could grow that.'

'If you're using the field for keeping your pony in, won't it eat all the hay?'

Lucy's face fell. 'I hadn't thought of that. That would mean we'd have to buy it in, and that would make it more expensive.'

Liz stamped her feet a couple of times. It was not an unpleasant day, the air sharp and vivid, stirred by a brisk wind out of the north-east. Lucy in sweatshirt and jeans and lacking Liz's body fat seemed impervious to the uncompromising weather. To Liz's relief she turned and they began to walk back towards the house.

'It's going to be hellish expensive, isn't it?' Lucy said sadly.

'It rather sounds like it.'

'They'll never let me have it.'

Liz, to whom at thirteen the idea of owning a pony had been a dream of the same order as the one in which she married a duke, felt illogical pity for the girl. So much anticipation, so much anxious study of ponies' needs and foods and care; all for nothing. Never mind that if she was given it Liz would regard her as a spoilt brat. Being denied it, she was a disappointed kid and Liz was sorry for her.

'Who's the problem?' she asked.

'They both are. I suppose Mum would at least see if it was possible.'

'Wouldn't Alec?'

'I don't know,' came the doleful response.

Liz glanced at her sharply. 'You aren't afraid of Alec?'

Lucy didn't at once reply, which rather suggested the answer to the question; but at last she said, 'Not *afraid*. I just don't find him very easy to get to know.'

Liz thought, and said: 'He's a good bloke, Lucy. One of the best.'

'Well . . .'

'I should know.'

Lucy looked more, not less, troubled. Something's eating her, Liz diagnosed; and she wants to share it. From here they looked back at the house, as at a photograph or a model; they were separate from it, standing in a little no man's land. Here it comes. Oh God, the agonies of being thirteen!

'You know DEF/AID?'

'Sure.'

'They're only selling things for women to defend them-selves with, aren't they? I mean, aren't they a good thing?'

'Well . . .'

'I mean, an offensive weapon isn't an offensive weapon unless you try and use it that way, is it?'

Liz gazed up at the bare trees. 'What have you bought?'

But Lucy took fright and quickened her stride. Liz caught her up and fell into step alongside her.

They were almost back at the house. Alec had backed the car out and was looking across as if ready to depart. 'Don't tell him,' Lucy pleaded at the last moment. 'You won't, will you? He wouldn't understand. He'd just be angry.'

Liz shook her head as if to discountenance both sugges-tions. Instead, she said: 'About the pony. Do you think you could talk your mum round?'

'I might. I think she'd quite like to have a pony. But I don't know how Alec . . .'

'How about leaving Alec to me?'

Lucy cast her a troubled glance, half hopeful, half dubious. What does she think I'm going to do to him, Liz wondered. Seduce him? Blackmail him? What am I doing? I don't even like this kid!

'Lucy!'

Alec, leaning on the car roof, had the door open.

'Coming!' She cast another glance at Liz. 'I don't know . . .'

'Leave him to me,' Liz said firmly. And received a raptur-ous smile in return. Oh no, she thought with a sinking heart; the kid's going to get a crush on me.

Lucy sped off indoors, presumably to get ready for school. Liz glanced at her watch and was amazed to find it was still not quite half-past seven. Alec treated Liz to a sharp look as she came up. 'You two villains hatching something up?'

Liz grinned with down-turned mouth and climbed in. 'Just a girls' heart to heart.'

He disappeared inside to say goodbye to Frances. Liz sat and wished people would resist the impulse to burden her with their confidences.

167

'I suppose,' he confessed, when he had emerged and was buckling himself into his seatbelt, 'that Lucy sometimes finds it hard being an only child. It's a pity she hasn't an elder sister, someone like you.'

'Oh, for Christ's sake!'

He turned to her in amazement. 'Why? What have I said?'

She sighed, her anger gone already. Men really could be the most imperceptive berks sometimes.

'Sorry,' he said.

'That's all right, governor. I'm sorry I snapped.'

They turned out on to the road and Alec accelerated away. 'She's a nice kid,' he said after a while. 'I like her a lot. Frances and I are very lucky.' She saw him smile reflectively. 'She's mad keen at the moment to have a pony.'

Liz said nothing.

A mile or two further on he said: 'I wouldn't be surprised if her wish comes true before too long.' And then: 'Sometimes, with all this Carver business, I wonder if there isn't some good come out of it after all. Everyone's been so scared of where he's going to strike next, feeling no woman is safe. If it's done nothing else, it makes men realize just how much they care for their wives and their daughters.' He cleared his throat briskly. 'Now: I'll tell you how I want to play this . . .'

'Susie!'

Her head turned automatically at the sound of her own name. Barker's Pool was unbelievably busy, and the tide of shoppers flowing into Coles's threatened to sweep her away. Susie peered through the thronging hordes and saw a car stopped across the road, and a figure standing in the half-open door, waving.

'Susie!'

She saw the big grin and a key clicked in her memory, and then she was pushing across the stream of pedestrians, and found she was grinning too.

'Debbie! My *God*! What on earth brings you here? I haven't seen you for—how long?'

'Ages. Too long. I'm literally just passing through. Amazing coincidence. I was sure it was you. You look great!'

She smiled up at the handsome face now, suddenly, so fondly remembered. How could they ever have lost touch? They had been so close. There had been a whole group of them . . . It seemed to have changed not a whit from that time—how long ago? Must be fifteen years, my God—when she had known it so well. 'How are you? What are you doing now?'

'What are *you* doing?' With a coy smile that suggested some acquaintance with Susie's life. The grapevine at work again! The car was double-parked where, she supposed, it had braked when she was spotted. The van trapped next to the kerb started hooting. Suddenly it seemed ridiculous that they should just disappear out of each other's lives again.

'Damn, this chap's getting impatient. Climb in.'

'I'm halfway through Christmas shopping,' Susie protested; but she was already slipping round to the passenger's side and reaching for the door handle.

'You live in Sheffield?' Debbie asked, buckling the seatbelt on.

'I've been here almost, oh, five years. Don't tell me you do too and I never knew!'

'I told you: I'm passing through. Business. When I spotted you I couldn't believe it.'

'Well, it beats shopping.' They were queuing at the roundabout by the post office, and they turned up West Street.

'Yes,' Susie admitted complacently, 'I'm married and Sam's at primary school and Amanda, would you believe it, is in her first year at the high school. I'm quite the establishment figure.'

'Just what I was going to say.'

So much had happened. Suddenly Susie herself could hardly credit that her life had contained so much, and felt a pang at the realization that the list of things which had happened was the typical list of a life half over. 'Where are we going?'

'Town's hopeless. We'll drive up on the moors and chat.

169

You can spare the time? You're not expected back at work?'

'I'm on a job share since the kids came along.'

'What a waste.'

'Far from it. It's magic.'

'I can't imagine it. I can't imagine you married. I remember you as a mousy little thing who scarcely dared say boo to a goose.'

That was a little uncharitable, Susie thought. She had never been like that, surely? A little edge of grudge, perhaps. 'You?'

'Never seemed to have the time. You know how it is.'

They climbed out of the city and out through Crookes.

'You seem to know where you're going.'

'I follow my nose,' said Debbie. 'If we keep going uphill we can't go far wrong.'

Houses started to fall away. The pavement narrowed, then vanished. The wind began to gust round the car and Susie felt it sway to the buffets. The hands on the wheel were capable. Yes, that was the characteristic one most remembered. Capability. Solid and reassuring. When the rest of us were children, you were even then grown up.

They came out on the moor. The car was warm; but even inside it was possible to be refreshed by the bright, clear air. They drove on, talking about her home, about how she filled her days.

'You sound so conventional.'

They slowed and turned into a track. It led them half out of sight behind a small copse.

'Is there anything wrong in that? I'm happy,' Susie replied. 'I don't know . . . I suppose it's being older. When we were young, it all seemed so serious. I can't believe we were so angry.'

'You don't look like a mother and—what were you saying?—a university lecturer?' They unbuckled their seatbelts and turned to each other.

'Oh, I bet I do.'

'You've had it easy, haven't you?'

'I wouldn't say that. I've worked damned hard.'

170

'Good job; happy children; devoted husband.'

'I'm lucky. I know that. But there's no need to sound so spiteful.'

'Everything a woman could want.'

'What about you? You don't seem to have done so badly for yourself.'

'The car? It's hired.'

'Well, all right, I have been fortunate and if you haven't had quite so much . . . luck, I'm sorry. But it's a bit unfair to blame me for it.'

'I'm sorry. That's how it is. You see, you've had it all so easy, you, who were such a little nothing. And I . . . I haven't. And that's why I am going to kill you.'

The competent hands moved as she spoke and before Susie could believe what was happening they clamped round her neck: those large, competent hands. The door came open and Susie fell back, her head over the edge of the seat, the other woman's heavy body on top of her pinning her to the cushion as if in a macabre parody of rape, and those competent hands with the strong fingers innocent of rings tightening round her neck.

She could only have had a matter of seconds in which to react. She never knew by what blessed instinct she did not even try to prise that inexorable grip from her neck. It would have been impossible, and she would have died. Instead, her hand dropped to the bag on the floor by her side. Her fingers scrabbled inside and came up with the canister of CS gas bought from DEF/AID in Fargate. Holding her breath was superfluous; but she forced her lids shut over her bulging eyes as she pushed the can in the face hanging over her and pressed the button.

She could have been unconscious only a matter of seconds, because when she came to, the other woman was pushing clumsily out of the door into the fresh air, screaming. The single glimpse she got sufficed to show the tears coursing down and the agonized scrunch of the features. Susie's own body seemed to be working to some miraculous scheme of

171

its own, as if it had been programmed long ago to save her life and Debbie's attack had been the finger on the keyboard pressing ENTER. She rolled out of the open door behind her, ripping her dishevelled clothing on the catch as she went. Tears streamed through her own tight-shut eyes, but as soon as she was out of the car her mouth opened to gulp in sweet clean air. Already she was scrambling to her feet. She opened her eyes to see through the blur Debbie stumbling in the heather fifteen yards away. She could hear the curses in between the sobs, and as clean moorland air whistled into Susie's lungs she saw Debbie turn and stagger towards her and she ran, but not away, and the CS canister was in her hand still.

The other woman groped for her as she came; but Susie evaded the grasp, reached out and emptied the canister full in her face. Then dropping it, she ran round the car and wrenched open the driver's door. The keys were in the ignition. Her fingers felt for them and turned them and the engine caught and roared. She slammed in the gear and the car leaped forwards towards the copse.

Her eyes and limbs were functioning now. At the end of the track was a circle of packed mud. Susie gave thanks for the week's hard frost as she hastily turned the car.

As she headed back along the track she saw Debbie lurch out into the centre to intercept her.

She pressed her foot to the floor and kept it there.

'I don't know,' yawned Detective-Superintendent Stan Jones, turning away. 'She's making it up.'

Detective-Inspector Gill Wightman fell into step beside him. The lift was five floors below and, as always, gave the impression of being broken altogether. They settled down to wait. Sheffield's Royal Hallamshire Hospital had been designed vertically, and the car park was too many floors below for the stairs to be a temptation. 'I don't know. If it wasn't for her neck . . . Strangling yourself, difficult . . .'

'One thing's for sure: one of them's lying. Know what I think?'

'Tell me, Stan.'

'That's a lonely spot, where they were, so what did they want to talk about that couldn't be said in a tea shop in town? East's got a husband. If we dig around, we'll find this Payne woman's been playing hanky-panky with him. Confrontation. It gets out of hand. They've both gone further than they meant. And East, respectable citizen that she is, is ashamed, so to cover herself she shouts rape. Or, in this case, attempted murder.'

Gillian Wightman shook her head. 'Typical man. All comes down to sex.'

'It usually does,' Stan Jones replied equably, 'in my experience.'

'So what do we do with her?'

'East? Slap her wrist and send her home,' he said. 'Have a word with her doctor. If she's going to go about telling people she's been the subject of an attempted murder she'll need quieting down. As for this one,' he nodded over his shoulder in the direction of the ward, 'she's not going anywhere for a while. By the time she's walking again it'll all be water under the bridge.'

'Do we charge either of them?'

The indicator started to blink as the lift ascended, and when it came they entered and stood amicably side by side. They would do nothing in the end. One unsubstantiated statement against another. Marks on a neck against a broken hip and two ribs. A tiff, lovers' or not; a jealous outburst; or summary vengeance by a slighted woman. One of those impenetrable vignettes that open to police view then close as suddenly.

'It'll all be the same in a hundred years,' said Stan Jones.

Seeing Stainton turn on the charm for Gwen Lewis reminded Liz that his attractiveness, to which long acquaintance and daily proximity had only partly inured her, was not in her eyes alone. Women do not always opt for beefcake. The lean, purposeful man who gives the impression of getting things done may set more hearts aflutter than he knows.

And Alec Stainton could be particularly winning when, as

now, a frightened woman was in the case, frightened and still traumatized by the death of a daughter and its brutal manner. As if he had all the time in the world, Alec set about securing Mrs Lewis's confidence. It was a hard job with her husband again present—protective, prickly as men are when raw emotion is in the case, ready at every word to leap in to his wife's defence as if it was her honour under siege rather than merely her memory. Slowly, like a well-trained sheepdog separating one timid ewe from the flock—now lying down, now taking a few quick steps, not scaring her, not making her panic and run, nudging her in the required direction—Alec guided Gwen Lewis into the sensible, dispassionate, meticulous conversation that was his goal. You had to admit it was consummately done, Liz thought ungrudgingly.

A photograph album lay on the coffee table. Liz had noticed it the moment she entered the room, and caught the flicker of Alec's eyes in the same direction, since when he had not so much as hinted that he was aware of it. Now, though, Mrs Lewis took it up and stared at the page before handing it to Alec.

'I got one of the leaders to take that. It amazes me that I never wrote everyone's names on the back,' she said. 'I suppose I imagined I could never forget them. I'm pretty sure that's Mandy Pascoe, though, on the left at the front.'

'Next to yourself,' Alec observed, making it sound like a compliment. Dammit, Liz thought, he'll have her rolling over with her paws in the air in a moment.

'The Mandy Pascoe we are concerned with,' he remarked, 'came from Rayleigh in Essex originally. You were brought up not far from here, I believe.'

She answered the implied question readily. 'We weren't all from the same brigades. We were seventeen and eighteen, you see. Rangers—that's what you go on to after ordinary guides. The camp was a sort of outward bound course. We were from all different parts of the country—we'd never met before we got there.'

'What about the other girls? Now you've got the photo to help you, perhaps you can recall some of the names.'

'You mean are they the same as any of the Carver's victims? Honestly,' she admitted, 'I've no real idea. The more I hear those names, the more familiar they seem. I never knew the surnames of most of these girls anyway. It's only because Mandy and I were so much in each other's pocket that I remember hers. I put it down in my address book, and we wrote for a while. There was an idea of going to stay with her, but it came to nothing.'

Laboriously they checked through each of the victims' names but Mrs Lewis could only repeat that Sonia Vesey's sounded familiar. They had photographs of the dead women and Alec compared them with the girls in the picture in the album. But the group shot was poorly focused and rather too far away for detail to be easily compared. Distinguishing features—ears, noses, hairlines—were difficult to make out.

Alec brought out one last photograph. 'We've asked every one of the forces involved for pictures of the victims when they were teenagers,' he explained to the Lewises. 'I've tried to put a measure of urgency behind it, but that's not easy to do. Obviously, I'd like to borrow this picture of yours, copy it, see if our people can find some clever way of enhancing the image. You haven't the negative, by any remote chance?'

'I might have.'

'It'll be in the chest in the spare room,' put in her husband with certainty. 'If it's anywhere.' Reassured by Alec's manner, and caught up in the spirit of the chase, he was letting his wife talk freely now and the closed suspicious expression had left his face. He leant forward eagerly.

'Well. If you'd have a good look for it I'd be grateful.' He passed Mrs Lewis the photograph he had taken from his document case. 'Meanwhile, have a look at that, if you'd be so good.'

Liz, watching him with the benefit of five years' experience of her boss, caught a glimpse of the excitement he was damping carefully down, and switched her glance to Mrs Lewis as she took the picture and began to study it. It was a studio portrait of Sandra Allen, taken many years ago for her eighteenth birthday, and when Liz collected it from the grieving parents there had been tears.

Mrs Lewis looked from the glossy portrait to her own snapshot and back again. When she looked up to reply it was with an almost timid air, as if she understood, and was afraid of, what she was about to trigger off.

'It looks like that girl at the back.'

'It does, doesn't it.'

Silently she passed the pictures back. Alec handed them to Liz. Now she looked curiously at the wavery snapshot of the ten, eleven, twelve ebullient teenage girls snapped against the outcrop of rock with the swelling mountains behind. Some of them were pulling poses, clowning around.

One of them, at the back on the right, standing on a boulder with her arms theatrically spread, was quite clearly Sandra Allen. Now dead. Strangled by an unknown man and her private parts branded with a spiteful, nullifying cross.

The room was very quiet. Strangely pregnant with unbearable grief. And, almost harder to bear, hope.

They stayed through the afternoon, leaving only when darkness had already closed over the streets splashed by pools of yellow light beneath the streetlamps. Methodically they quizzed Mrs Lewis about the other girls in the snapshot. She had thought she remembered Sonia Vesey, but now she couldn't be sure. What about the other girls? Had she written any names down—swapped addresses on the last night after the camp concert? No? Never mind. The names of the dead victims: did they ring any more bells now? No? Never mind. Could she remember anything at all about these cheerful clowning girls? One had parents who were schoolteachers: this girl, here. Yes. From some northern city: Halifax, Huddersfield maybe, and her name was, yes, Carol Swann, or Swanson, or Swainson. There you are, you see, it comes back to you. Now try this girl here, the handsome one. What about her? Oh, her! She was—of course, Debbie, how could I forget? Because she was—how can I put it?—look, you can see by the way she stands with her chin in the air. She was a Queen's guide and her father was in the diplomatic corps or something and she was going up to Oxford that autumn. Good Lord, I didn't know I knew all that! I tell you what else, she was the only one of us who had done it, you know, slept with a boy; doesn't it seem amazing now? I suppose we were terribly innocent. We used to get her to tell us what it was like over and over in the tent after lights out. Her surname? No; it's gone, I only remember she was the girl we all wanted to be. Debbie something.

OK, put it to the back of your mind, maybe it'll come to you later. This one? The one who looks homesick?

God, how wet she was; no, I can't remember her name. We called her, yes, we called her the Worm among ourselves. Who'd have believed we'd be so spiteful? (With an incredulous shake of the head for the malice of seventeen-year-old girls.)

'No other names? The name of your . . . guider? Leader? Is that what you called them?'

'Our guider didn't come; the course was centrally organized, I think. We applied to go on it from all over the country; there was a venture scout camp there too. Boys . . . When we arrived and saw there were boys there, God, what bliss . . .'

All the time Alec was making notes. When the scouts' camp was mentioned he wrote for a while, and a reminiscent silence fell over the room. Liz surveyed what they had, and found it tantalizingly scant, but by no means as scant as she had expected. She tried, as the one who would certainly have to trace these girls, to work out how she would do it. They had established the presence of three of the Carver's victims—or rather two victims and one supposed intended victim—at a guide camp in Wales almost twenty years ago. She would not now be surprised to learn that the others had been there too. It would be remarkable if they had not. But how to trace the unknown faces? Well, if Mrs Lewis had kept a photo, maybe others had; and if she had made a best friend and swapped addresses with her, chances were, others had too. They had Mandy Williams née Pascoe and Sandra Allen; and almost certainly Sonia Wright née Vesey; and a Debbie Somebody; and a girl cruelly dubbed the Worm; and a girl whose parents were teachers in Yorkshire called Swann, or something like it. Yes, they could probably find the remaining pieces of the jigsaw.

What fantastic pattern it would reveal was beyond her comprehension at the moment. The presence of a boys' camp was promising—obviously. So there'd be the boys to trace too. Impossible, after twenty years? No, she assured herself, just bloody difficult.

Alec stopped writing and asked Mrs Lewis, with an apologetic glance towards her husband, about the boys. A fortnight's proximity. Human nature said there would have been pairing off.

Gwen Lewis thought seriously, and shook her head with a half shrug. 'I suppose I might never have noticed . . .'

A dozen girls, Liz thought. Of whom, if we are right, four are dead and one grieving a dead daughter.

18

He believed he was more afraid now than he had been at the time of his initial imprisonment.

After his first days locked in the stable during which his personality disintegrated into painful shards, the woman had reappeared, after dark, with the shotgun, and thrown him the key of the handcuffs. At her bidding he had walked docilely from the stable to the house (the concrete gritty and chill, the grass thistled and sharp with frost, the cinder path like hot coals to his bare soft feet) and then up the stairs and into the bathroom.

She did not stay, but she made him leave the door open and her footsteps did not go downstairs, from which he deduced that she was keeping him under surveillance from nearby, the shotgun cocked against his appearance in the doorway.

Steam had filled the little room, wreathing round the ugly glass lightshade and thrusting probing fingers at the uncurtained moisture-running glass of the small window. She had left food—cheese sandwiches crudely cut—and milk in a plastic beaker, on the cabinet: his first nourishment since he ate in the comfort of the Brambletye Hotel, though there had been water in the stable. He almost could not eat: it was painful to do so.

The bath was old, cast iron, cold to the touch above the water level, even though the water itself was barely less than scalding. Crossland lay back and gingerly eased his shoulders against the cold enamel. Soap, a flannel, a pumice stone had been set in a group by the taps, but he made no move to reach for them. The thought of the pumice on his sores was agonizing, and meanwhile the hot water was softening the dirt and the skin beneath, so that patches of cherry red began to blossom in between the encrustations of filth and a blissful peppery heat spread through his limbs.

He lay back with his eyes closed, past trying to understand what change of heart or design had led the woman to order him indoors. Perhaps this bath was the precursor of his freedom; perhaps it was to be his last on this earth. Well, if it was to be the latter, it was a good one. He'd never enjoyed one more, because he'd never needed one as much. Funny how a bath could be the summit ambition, when you had had everything else taken from you. He raised one leg out, surveying it critically. Wavelets lapped at the overflow. A deep, hot bath.

A long time afterwards, when the water was no longer agreeable, the prospect of having to climb out brought back the contemplation of what was to come afterwards. He pulled out the plug reluctantly, watching the water beginning to swirl above the pipe, revealing a scum which remained as a tideline on the bath sides as the water ran away. He stood up, inspecting his limbs attentively. A film of dirt clung to them—a good shower would rinse that away, but of course in this antediluvian house showers were unheard of—otherwise he was not really in such bad shape. There was an angry red ring round his wrist where the handcuffs had rubbed, but in other respects he felt curiously healthy apart from the shakiness brought on by hunger and the stomachache from the sandwiches. There was a mirror on the wall, but it was too steamed up to show him his face. The worst problem was his hair, already tangled and feeling sticky. The woman had left shampoo, though, and he ran cold water into the basin and washed it as best he could, towelling it dry. There was no comb. For which he was glad, since to comb it would be agony; even though not to comb it would be to make worse trouble later.

She came in while he was trying to peer at his features in the mirror. He saw her reflection, standing in the open door.

180

Saw the shotgun. He swallowed. As he lay in the bath he had managed to believe that the next time he saw her they would deal as normal human beings. It was not to be. He turned, and waited.

She looked him over, her gaze resting finally on his penis hanging limp from the bath. Her mouth tightened a fraction. In laughter? In disapproval? 'I hope you can do better than that.'

She gestured with the gun and he preceded her along the passage to the door at the end. To the room where his ordeal had started. The room where, a million years ago, a man had idly copulated with a woman picked up in a country hotel. The broken window had been crudely patched with cardboard on which the word Kellogg's was garishly prominent. Under the unwinking eye of the shotgun he crossed to the far corner and turned. She threw him the handcuffs on their short length of chain and gestured at the bed. He knew what was required. He attempted no bluster, but meekly shackled himself to the bed's steel frame.

'Wait here,' she had ordered superfluously. 'If you try anything, you'll get more than you bargained for.' She left. He heard her footsteps recede. Not far. At first he made no attempt to move from where he was. Then he had put out a hand and felt the bed. So soft! He sat on it, fearful of creaking springs. Then abandoned caution and lay down.

'That's right.' She had reappeared. He saw with shock that she was dressed only in an orange satin nightgown even before he noticed that she was not carrying the gun. She seemed to have an uncanny ability to follow his thought processes, for she lifted her hand with a smug smile, and he saw that she held a knife in it. His stomach churned until he thought he was going to shit himself. Surely she wasn't going to . . . ?

'I'm not going to castrate you. Not unless you make me.' The smile was blithe, and thus terrifying. He was quite sure that if she used the knife on him, she would be persuaded in her own mind that it was of his doing.

She came round the bed so that she could lie on the

right-hand side of it beside him, with the hand holding the knife down by the side of the bed. She settled herself with little jerks of her body as if for a conjugal night's slumber. Then with her left hand she loosened the ties of the night-dress and spread it wide.

'Come on, then,' she invited.

That was how what he regarded as the second phase of his captivity had started. That was how what was unbelievable had come about. Once he got used to what was required of him, he had found the new regime curiously relaxing. He was kept in the stable, chained to the hasp in the floor, as before; but every day he was led at gunpoint into the house and up the stairs to the stark bedroom where he was required to perform. Afterwards they would lie side by side like any happy couple done with lovemaking; except that the woman lay on her back and he never, even when he woke after some hours and leant over her, found her eyes closed. And the hand with the knife was always ready. She never laid the knife down beside the bed, and she never put herself in a position where she could not use the weapon. It made her lovemaking very passive, but she seemed to like that: lying inactive and commanding his various performances. She came to orgasm very easily, but even in the extremity of her satisfaction she was in control; and the knife lay warm in her hand where she could at any moment bring her arm up and plunge it into his body. She never let herself be entangled in bedclothes, preferring to keep the room warm with a gas heater and have them lie uncovered on the bed. He could not escape, since throughout he remained fastened to the bed-rail. Nor was the chain long enough to enable him to wrap it round her neck, and the knife ensured he could not overcome her. He was required to be a bizarre captive lover. That apart, he had absolutely no responsibilities. After they had made love, and he had slept, she would go and get dressed then lead him at gunpoint downstairs, where there would be food—real food, if unadorned and unimagin-ative—on the kitchen table. Then he would walk before her back to the stable, loop the chain through the hasp and fasten with his own hands the shackle.

She rarely spoke. Once he asked her, 'Aren't you anxious that someone might call? How would you explain a man sitting at your table with no clothes on? The gun?'

She shook her head confidently. 'No one will call.'

Once, as they lay upstairs, they heard a car stop. The woman was crouched over him in an instant, the knife poised at his throat, her body twitching. A door slammed, the car drove away. The next day she didn't let him out of the stable.

He was obsessed with the fact that he knew nothing of her. 'What's your name?' he asked.

'You don't need to know my name. Names don't matter to someone like you.'

Once he tried telling her about himself. Trying to establish some communication. Her anger welled up, frightening him. 'Shut up!' she cried. 'Don't tell me anything. I don't want to know anything. OK?'

'OK,' he replied meekly.

How would it end? Was he doomed to live this bizarre life until his potency declined and the woman shot him as you wring the neck of a hen that doesn't lay, or send a barren cow to the knackers? Curiously, he did not find it repugnant to perform the services she required of him; and, life containing no other demands, no other matters he could influence (not even whether he lived or died), it was a ludicrously soothing existence. Perhaps one day he would find making love to the woman impossible, the intimacy of her flesh unendurable. Perhaps then he would forfeit his life. Or perhaps they would go on until her desire cooled, declining into undemanding old age together like any steady couple united by habit and a sort of love that has little to do with the heat of youth.

The thought was, disturbingly, guiltily attractive.

Anita could not have identified the moment when the idea finally took root in her mind, that the man she had eaten with in the Brambletye Hotel was the Carver. As it happened, the television, the radio and the newspapers entered only indirectly into the process of revelation. The name of Kenneth Crossland meant nothing to her. At the time when he was at his height as suspect, with his name and sometimes his face featuring on almost every news bulletin, Anita watched little television; and why should she buy newspapers? The need to find a job, a social life outside Bracken Ghyll, was behind her. But dimly she registered that another girl had died; and it began to be borne in on her that the photograph which appeared whenever the Carver was mentioned in the media was a photograph of—as she thought of him—her Lover.

She began again to watch the occasional half hour of television. On the screen Maria Tillotson talked heatedly about the brutal killer, describing once again his bestial cruelties. And this was what the man she loved was capable of! She saw his hands closing round fair necks, visualized sagging bodies, the hands relaxing, moving down to wrench at clothing, baring hirsute swollen flesh—followed the tip of the knife as it pierced the skin and watched the trail of scarlet open behind its passage. Rip, rip! Anita felt a ripple of apprehension shiver through her own pubic bone.

The seductive concatenation of images developed, as in a photographic dish manipulated by an amateur, into a wavery picture never quite fixed, always a little blurred. Sometimes Anita quite believed it. Occasionally a notion of its fancifulness brought a laugh to her lips. There was no conscious reasoning about it. But the knowledge that her Lover had been—was—might be—the Carver gave a hot spice of relish to her memory of that night.

As time passed, the media's focus on Crossland grew less intense. Other stories elbowed the Carver out of the news. But it is doubtful whether even photographs on a television screen could by then have affected Anita's inner certainty. It existed, as so much of her mental process now did, in a separate compartment of knowledge, a separate realm of existence which touched only at points with the existence of those living around her in her corner of comfortable, conventional Sussex.

The idea swirled round her mind like a seductive daydream. One evening, when it was at its most vivid, she wandered through into the kitchen and began rummaging through the drawer in the dresser.

Presently, from the back, she brought a carving knife, with a broad, unserrated blade. It was tarnished and when she felt the edge with her thumb it was disappointingly blunt. She pulled the drawer out to its limit and clattered through its junk.

Her hand closed on a carved wooden handle and she drew out the satisfying weight of the sharpening steel.

Perhaps, she thought, as the blade keened against the steel, the private video she played inside her head was erroneous? A man, surely, would prefer to enact his desires on a living, not a dead, victim? The knife first, then the squeezing hands? Yes. Perhaps she could ask him. She was doing them all a service, those cowering women, keeping him here as she was.

She tested the blade against her finger and then, tentatively, sat on the edge of the kitchen chair, pulled up her skirt, bared her own pubis and—no, she was not mad. But she teased out the wiry curls of gingery hair and watched the knife shear through until they came away in her hand. Her body shivered with pleasure. A coin-sized rough stubble remained; but she had a razor upstairs. A pity she could not let the man . . . But it would not do for him to be placed in the way of temptation; temptation to do to her what he had done to those others . . . As she laid the knife down, she saw on the table-top where it had been all along the DEF/AID knife, and stared at it for a moment, wondering what it was.

After she had sat down at the table and begun the letter to FIGHTBACK at their Wembley headquarters she realized that it was impossible. She couldn't find the tone she sought and knew they would think the letter came from a crank, and ignore it.

Next morning when she had done the chores Anita folded back the wire, coaxed the car into life and drove into Tunbridge Wells. She had little fear of the risk in leaving the house. The stable was padlocked. Post was deposited in the oil drum mailbox by the roadside. In all the time since that night no one had set foot within the gate.

Tunbridge Wells, always busy, was heavily congested with the press of shoppers. Queues for the car parks blocked junctions, adding to the chaos. Anita joined the drivers patrolling the common, where you could park free on the roadside if you could find a space. After three circuits she struck lucky and saw someone just climbing into the driving seat of a parked car. Another car had already stopped ready to back into the vacated space, but he had to wait for the leaving car to pass, and Anita was able to slip in quickly, ignoring the furious blast sounded on the horn by the thwarted driver. She thought for a moment he was going to climb out and come back and abuse her, and took the CS canister from her jacket ready; but with a rude gesture and mouthed obscenities he drove off.

Down in the town the pavements were narrow and crowded and it was difficult to keep any sort of steady progress. Anita fought her way through, pressing her shoulder bag to her chest and shielding it with an arm. It took her twenty minutes to reach the station.

She had the steps of her journey carefully noted down—and superfluously, for they were all impressed on her memory. From Tunbridge Wells to Charing Cross. From Charing Cross she would take the Northern Line to Euston, whence the trains left for Wembley Central. She pictured herself climbing the steps of the FIGHTBACK headquarters, being received into the presence of the leadership, telling her story to cries of amazement and congratulation.

At Charing Cross Anita made an error, and boarded a Bakerloo line train. She realized her mistake only after perplexed study of the route map opposite her seat, by which time the train was leaving Regent's Park. She hurried out at the next station, Baker Street, feeling raw and exposed to ridicule. The Circle line took her not to Euston but to Euston Square, so that by the time she stood in the concourse of the station she was thoroughly disorientated. People hurried by on every side, ignoring her, although she felt so conspicuous, the only person in the place who was muddled and ignorant.

The departures board showed that she had half an hour to wait for a Wembley Central train. A cup of coffee and a bun to soothe her frayed nerves felt very necessary. Her confidence was badly shaken; and the unceasing presence of so many people was in itself oppressive. She began to see people watching her; and the uninterest with which the multitude hurried by seemed artificial, a ploy.

She began to see that it would be like this too at FIGHTBACK headquarters. She began to see that they too would laugh at her, a woman who could not even take the right Underground line across London. She would never get as far as the presence of those competent, confident women who were the figureheads of FIGHTBACK; or if she did, they would be sitting in a circle from which she would be excluded, to stand and relate her unlikely tale as she had once, long ago, stood in the staff room accounting to an amused circle of mistresses for the fact that she alone, out of all the school, had arrived for school after Easter in her winter gymslip. The humiliation of that episode, never far below the surface of her memory, bobbed to the top causing her to flush and shift in her seat and glance around as if every eye must be upon her.

She finished her bun, meticulously picking up every crumb on a wetted fingertip. The indicator showed her which platform the Wembley train left from, and she went and stood indecisively at the top of the ramp, fingering her ticket. After some minutes the barrier was shut, and then with a warning beeping the train doors closed and it hissed into motion and drew away from her down the platform. It had been ridiculous to think of coming. And if she had been successful, and if she had been believed, what then? Then the world would have pressed in and left her bereft and solitary.

She turned away into the concourse, making for the big

Underground sign. This time she crossed London without error. She gained her seat on the Tunbridge Wells train with satisfaction, and as it rumbled over the Thames her spirits lifted.

Her car was where she had left it, and she drove happily through the stark winter landscape seeing only the encouragement of familiar scenery, and turned into the track which was her drive as pleased as if she had accomplished a successful expedition to a distant land. Climbing out, she rolled the wire across to close the entrance and pushed her way through the brown wilted foliage that hemmed in the path to the back door. Say what you wished, it was nice to be home.

19

When Liz mentioned that she'd invited a friend for a meal, Rosie made a histrionic performance of being required to absent herself, citing all sorts of things she and a baby of less than a year could do on a winter night, such as walking in the park, window shopping, and eating fish and chips on a bench in the High Street. This was Rosie at her most Rosieish, and Liz only regretted that Pritch wasn't there to appreciate just what she was up against.

Liz pondered phoning Pritch and suggesting they cancel the evening. But somehow she found she had begun to look forward to his coming and didn't want to give it up. With Rosie absent the *raison d'être* of the invitation might have gone but the evening in prospect looked a great deal more attractive. 'Surely I'm entitled to a simple bit of company,' she muttered to herself as she washed up the mess of dirty plates that seemed to cover every surface in the kitchen, while upstairs Joy squawked happily in her bath to the accompaniment of Rosie's encouragement. (And later there'd be the water to clear off the bathroom floor, and the towels left where they were dropped to hang up.)

Danger loomed. A meal *à deux* (even of her cooking), something classical on the stereo—she didn't want to project herself as a pinhead—Chopin, perhaps, or Schubert impromptus—and soft lighting; all would look as if contrived to give the sort of signal she did not want to give.

Liz found she was standing motionless at the sink, one of Joy's yukky dishes forgotten in her hand. Damn. It was all so complicated. They never had difficulties like this in Jane

Austen's day. In Jane Austen's day, on the other hand, I'd've been a fat peasant with a brood of snotty urchins and a sweaty husband stinking of pigs to give me another one every year, when he wasn't firing ricks or buggering sheep. Hey ho for the golden age.

She dunked the dish in the suds and watched nameless gunge float off to the surface. Let Pritch come. He was one of the few men she knew who might just take the evening at face value. If he didn't, well he and she need probably never meet again after this case. And she might yet prevail on Rosie to stay in.

Pritch came. Rosie left, throwing him a pretty, winsome smile. 'Joy's sleeping like an angel, Liz. I'll leave you two together.' Another coy look and she whirled out, all bouncing hair and flying fake fur.

Liz watched her go with a rueful turn of the mouth.

'A winning little minx,' Pritch observed, and she saw he was laughing at her, and felt instantly better.

They chatted easily through the meal. It was Pritchard who, as they waited for the kettle to boil for coffee, asked bluntly: 'Is it affecting your work?'

Liz glanced at him. 'I don't know,' she said glumly. 'If it hasn't, it soon will.'

'I suppose,' said Pritch after a long time, 'she *is* worse off than you, is she?'

'At least I have a house.'

'She has a house.'

'Occupied by a bloke who beats her.'

'What's she living on? You?'

'No. She seems to be able to buy nappies and things. To say nothing of clothes. Food and that we sort of share.'

'She pays her part of the housekeeping, then?'

'Yes. Well, sort of.'

Pritch looked sceptical.

'I don't think there are any miracles to be magicked,' Liz explained testily. 'I just felt I had to get it off my chest to someone.'

190

'And do you feel better for it?'

'Yep.'

'Good.'

'Right,' said Liz happily. 'That's that. Now how are we going to find these girl guides?'

Tracing the twelve girls who had camped together in the Brecon Beacons nearly twenty years ago was a matter of meticulous drudgery, the daily fare of CID. Stainton had taken what they knew not to Detective Chief Superintendent Oaks but to Detective-Superintendent Blackett, and as a result received an unofficial allocation of troops to assist Liz and Pritchard. Most of them, after all, she told herself, were standing around idle for want of direction from on high, so they might as well help her with her task.

Johnson drew West Yorkshire Education Authority as his area of search; Simms, protesting heatedly, got the Girl Guide Headquarters; Sally had the task of asking other forces to press distraught husbands and parents to hunt out their murdered wives' or daughters' snapshot albums and address books. Which had probably all been thrown out along with the clothes, Liz told Alec Stainton herself pessimistically, to exorcize the ghosts. But she hoped not.

She herself pursued the venture scouts. It gave her an eerie thrill to know that among this group of seventeen- and eighteen-year-old boys she was now, in all probability, trailing a serial killer. As to what might have occurred at that camp that led one of those boys to seek out the girls and kill them one by one so many years later, Liz confessed herself totally mystified. Some unendurable humiliation? Some violent initiation? Some precocious group sex session leaving a legacy of guilt or perversion?

'We don't have to understand, not at this stage. We just have to follow the leads.'

'You've said it, guv.'

'Sir.'

'Liz?'

'I've found what happened to Carol Swainson.'

'Yes?'

'She's dead, guv. She was found in an alley a hundred yards from her house, fourth March two years ago. Strangled.'

'Murdered? But that's impossible! Why . . . ?'

'Why has nobody made the link? I'll tell you. Because apart from the strangling, her body was unmarked.'

The knowledge that the killings had started at least a year earlier than anybody had previously thought threw several new factors into the enquiry. Crossland, this time, really was out, even though for the sake of appearances the forest was still being combed for signs of his presence. Two years ago he had attended a training fortnight in the United States during the first half of March. A verifiable and undoubted alibi.

For the Carol Swainson killing did seem, despite attempts to argue the contrary, clearly one of the Carver series: the first—or at least the first of which they were now aware. Everything tallied except the intactness of the body, discovered fully clothed and inviolate. After the inquest was opened (and adjourned) her body had been released for cremation; but the post-mortem records were comprehensive and revealed an exact correspondence in the method of killing with the later deaths. It would have been an outrageous coincidence if another of the guide camp girls had been murdered by a totally separate killer, but outrageous coincidences do occur. In this instance, it was a relief to be able to exclude them.

Given the absence of mutilation of that first body, attention focused afresh on the second killing, heretofore thought of as the first—the death of Mandy Williams, née Pascoe.

'It frequently happens,' Dr Carey told Alec, 'that a serial killer takes time to establish the so to speak characteristic signature of his crimes.'

'Something happened to provoke the mutilation of Mandy, and thereafter he included it in every killing?'

'Possibly. You note, of course, that the circumstances of Carol Swainson's death would have made mutilation of the body difficult at any rate. She died where she was found, and though it was not a very public place, there was a strong risk of detection if the murderer lingered on the scene. Plus, if it really was the first killing, there would be a certain amount of nervousness and perhaps panic.

'When we come to Mandy's death, we know she was not killed where she was found. We can speculate that there was opportunity for more elaborate ritual, and perhaps with growing confidence a curiosity to experiment.'

Alec nodded. All this dispassionate speculation left him with a sour taste. It was no doubt necessary to be so disengaged; but if you were not careful it was the path to callousness and moral indifference.

'I'd like to consider a little further before offering any opinion, even of the most tentative sort,' Carey warned, 'but it is not hard to deduce that some particular aversion motivated the mutilation. Perhaps the killer had experienced sexual rejection or humiliation. Have you read Lawrence?'

Alec nodded.

'You'll recall in *Lady Chatterley's Lover* there are references to women's sexual parts as predators; references that we would regard as almost vicious in their severity. In another context, they might be taken as evidence of mental imbalance. Perhaps the Carver had formed such a view. Perhaps, on the other hand, he was a sexual innocent able for the first time to explore the anatomy of a woman, and disgusted by what he found. Remember Ruskin, unable to consummate his marriage because, supposedly, his familiarity with the female form through the medium of art had not prepared him for the fact that his wife possessed pubic hair.'

'How long,' Alec asked cynically, 'before we get on to the Primal Scene?'

Carey's rather ponderous manner gave way to the grin that Alec found so irritating and he shook an admonitory finger. 'A little learning, Chief Inspector. Remember: a little learning! Dangerous! Anyway, leave it with me. I'll turn it all over in my mind. I'll try not to take too long about it.'

'I suppose,' Alec suggested, 'once the Carver had mutilated one victim it became something he had to do.'

'I think that is highly probable. It may well have given him sexual gratification. And of course, he will have realized, when the press went to town on it, that he had a ready-made trademark. Serial killers love attention; indeed, it can be hypothesized that even if some other occurrence starts them on their career, the urge to be noticed is sometimes the prime motive that keeps them on their course of murder. They don't want to be overlooked, or disparaged. As soon as the papers start to speak of him as the Carver, do you notice how there's almost an air of deference about their reporting? He's elevated to a monster, and a diabolically clever monster at that. It's the same pride that leads killers to address letters to the police. You haven't received any of those?'

'Not yet.'

'Pity.'

Slowly the picture came together. Literally. In the CID room Alec had a blow-up of Gwen Lewis's group snapshot pinned to the cork board on the wall and day by day, and then hour by hour, Liz wrote in the names above those clowning, carefree figures. The names of the dead, and the names of the living, and who would dare say at this stage that none of the living would become the dead before the Carver was captured?

When the women were identified they had to be located, contacted and warned that they were on the list of the Carver's intended victims. And as they warned them, so they ripped away security and certainty, replacing them with a lottery of violence waiting at the door. How was a woman supposed to react to being told that she had a very real prospect of ending up on a mortuary slab with a cross ripped through her genitals? The odds on being the next victim shortened with every death. They were down to one in seven now.

Counsellors were made available. Police watches were put

on houses, and special arrangements were made for the protection of Gwen Lewis, in case the Carver should attempt a second time to get at her, while plans to move the women to secret locations—thereby perhaps alerting the Carver, perhaps ensuring he was never caught—were heatedly debated.

Liz came in and wrote up another name. 'The one they called the Worm. Wendy Thomas. Durham have just rung. And there's a possible lead to that Debbie, Deborah Payne. Thomas saw her the other week, out of the blue. In Gateshead, at the Metrocentre. They went for a ride out in the country and had a good old chinwag. But she says she didn't get Payne's address.'

'Blast.'

'Ten accounted for,' Liz reminded him, gazing at the board, at the names and the ten ticks. 'Deborah Payne and Susie East still to locate.'

'Find them, Liz. Before we have another death. Find them.'

Alec set the telephone carefully down in its cradle as Liz came in.

'I've got on to Susie East, guv.'

He grunted absently, his mind still occupied with the telephone call. What on earth had he done that the chief wanted to see him? Then seemed to recall himself to the present and looked up attentively. 'Yes?'

'Sheffield. Trouble is . . .'

'Yes?'

'She's not answering the phone. I've put the word out to the local mob. They'll keep an eye on her place for us. I'll keep trying, and if there's still no reply I'll get South Yorks to make some enquiries.'

'Very good.'

She looked at him anxiously. 'Something wrong, sir?'

'Mm? No, no. At least . . .'

Liz read the signs quickly: he didn't want to talk about it, not to her, he wanted a clear room and time to think. 'I'll get on, then, sir. We've still this Payne woman to find, and I need a hand with the scouts, too. I'll be in my room if you want me.' The last piece of information superfluous, but the only means of indicating her concern she dared risk.

After she had left, Alec spared a smile for her tactful sympathy, decided the question of why the chief wanted to see him was not worth worrying over in advance, and turned his attention to the drafting of yet another interim report for the press office to turn into a news release.

'Thank you for looking in, Alec. Hope I'm not taking you away from anything too pressing.'

'Not at all, sir.'

'More's the pity, eh? That's good work Liz Pink has been doing. And I gather the Welshman has had a hand in it.'

'I think they've been working very much hand in glove, sir.'

'Bit of romantic attachment?' the chief constable grinned.

'I don't think so, sir. But they seem to make a good team.'

'I'll remember to mention it to his chief. Now: I expect you're wondering why I wanted to see you.'

Alec made no reply to this rhetorical observation except to indicate his attention. The chief constable passed him a letter. Alec, his senses preternaturally alert, took in the Home Office heading before the paper was yet in his hand.

'Take your time,' the chief invited.

Alec nodded, and set himself to peruse the letter thoroughly. A Home Office enquiry was being instigated, he read. Not an urgent analysis of an embarrassing blunder, but a study of effective methods of predicting criminal behaviour using computer modelling and Geographic Information Systems. He was being offered a six-month appointment; if the chief would release him. At the Metropolitan Police Forensic Science Laboratory. The post carried superintendent rank.

Alec read the letter a second time, more slowly, and looked up.

'Two questions,' the chief said with a twitch of a smile. 'Do you want it? Do you want time to consider it?'

Alec had arrived there before him. It was an exceptional

opportunity. He had been asked for by name. He was being offered the chance to place himself in that magic circle of officers from all forces 'known' by the Home Office and groomed for the top. He would have had to move on soon anyway—he had already arguably been too long with one force if he was to perform creditably in competition for more senior posts. South London was an easy commuters' journey. Regular hours . . . And after six months, who knew?

'Yes.' He smiled. 'And no.'

'Good.' The chief reached for the letter back. 'I'll get a reply dictated this afternoon. You'll hear about the personnel side in a week or two, I imagine. Keep it under your hat for the time being. And—well done.' His eyes twinkled.

'Thank you, sir.' And Alec left, giving the lift a miss and walking down the stairs to give himself time to adjust. Liz popped out of the CID room as he passed, her mouth opening with a query, but he waved her aside. 'Later, Liz.'

Just now he wanted a few minutes' solitude. To take in what had happened to his career since he walked out of his office twenty minutes earlier; and—Liz's appearance had prompted this turn of thought—to come to terms with what had so far not occurred to him: the fact that leaving was going to be curiously painful.

' 'Scuse me, ma'am.' The South Yorkshire sergeant had a worried look on his face as he hesitated on the threshold.

'What is it, Jimmy?'

'You know that East woman who was involved in that business out beyond Stannington?'

Gill Wightman nodded. East was already having sessions with the community psychiatric nurse. The Crown Prosecution Service office had declared in so many words that, with no better evidence than the unsupported word of one against the other, they wouldn't even look at a case against Debbie Payne. As it became clear that no charges were going to be pressed against her attacker, Susie East became a thorn in the flesh. Gill herself and Stan Jones were crossing their

197

fingers that the rumours of her MP getting involved would fade away.

' "A" Division have had this DS from Sussex on the blower, asking them to keep an eye on her house.'

'Do they say why?'

'Something to do with the Carver enquiry. They seem to think she could have had some contact with him, and he might come looking for her as his next victim.'

Gill Wightman's eyebrows rose expressively.

'That's what I thought, ma'am. Bit of a coincidence. Anyway, "A" Div've given me the number. A W/DS Pink. I just wondered . . .'

'I'll have a word. Good thinking, Batman.'

The two policewomen, the detective-inspector from South Yorkshire and the detective-sergeant from Sussex, spoke for some fifteen minutes on the telephone, during which Liz ran over the state of the Carver enquiry and the reasoning that had led up to the request that Susie East's house be kept under supervision. Gill Wightman listened and asked the occasional question but otherwise contributed little to the conversation.

Liz put the phone down with the vague feeling that the Yorkshire DI had been rather taciturn. Or maybe she was just slow on the uptake, Liz decided; and went off to seek out DC Johnson, whistling.

In her office in South Yorkshire Police Headquarters in Snig Hill, Gill Wightman cradled the receiver thoughtfully. Had Stan Jones been there to observe her, he would have noted the gleam in her eye that denoted the rapid whirring of a brain for which he had great respect.

After a while, she left her room and made her way to his.

'Stan.'

'Sweetheart.'

'You know that bust-up out on the moors, the woman who claimed she'd been strangled and drove the car at her attacker?'

He regarded her warily. Who, and where, was asking awkward questions?

'The one with the broken hip's out of hospital already, yeah?'

'Yep.'

'Do we have an address, do you know?'

'Gill, just tell me what's going through that beautiful head of yours without the Miss Marple act, huh? Yes, we do have an address. I forget where. Down south. Dorset, Somerset, would that be it?'

'What happened to the car? We didn't give it back, did we?'

'God knows. Now that's enough, Gill. Tell. That's an order.'

'Right you are, boss. It's like this.'

'Right.' There was a gleam in Stan Jones's eye now that matched that in his colleague's. 'Get a PW out to pick up Susie East pronto. Then check that address and speak to the local bill. Then get on the blower to Wetherby and tell them on no account to let that car go, but to put their best bloke on it PDQ. You didn't tell Sussex . . . ?'

'We'll have to tell them sooner or later.'

'I suppose . . .' He brooded, then winked. 'Good girl.'

'I'm right, aren't I? It seems mad, but . . .'

'I haven't been following this Carver stuff, since it's all down south; but I rather think you might be.'

'You'll have to see the big chief.'

He reached for the phone. 'He's going to like this, Gill. It's going to make his day.'

It was an estate on the outskirts of Frome. Not long ago it had been the council housing department's greatest headache. Even now, with many of the houses bought at discount by the tenants, its debris-strewn gardens and abandoned cars signalled the depressing conjunction of can't-afford with don't-care. PC Russell locked the police car with care, though it was the middle of the day and quiet enough.

'Hope she comes quiet.'

They pushed open the wire-mesh gate and walked stolidly up the concrete path. There was an alleyway through to the rear between the adjoining houses, but the front door looked more used than most. PC Russell banged firmly with his gloved hand.

She must have been looking through the window, for the door opened immediately. She was leaning on a stick, but appeared almost happy to see them.

'We've been asked,' Russell said, 'to call by South Yorkshire Police. We'd like you to come with us, please. We'll wait while you get your things.'

'What's it about?'

'It's some enquiries connected with the Carver hunt.'

Ten minutes later (could she have had her bag ready packed?) Deborah Payne locked the house and limped to the pavement. Russell held the back door open, surveying her overnight case in perplexity, and she climbed in, the WPC sliding dexterously in beside her. Russell closed the door with its child-proof lock. He wished he knew what the hell was going on.

The dispirited detectives were waiting for Oaks to open the discussion when the phone warbled. Alec took it, listened, and passed it to Oaks.

Oaks's face passed through an interesting spectrum of colour and range of expression. He slammed the instrument down. When he turned to them he was breathing heavily.

'That was the *Globe*,' he said. 'Wanting to know my reaction to the capture of the Carver.'

There was an instant's silence, followed by a buzz of curiosity which no one chose to articulate. The phone went again. Oaks looked at Alec, who nodded.

'Detective Chief Inspector Stainton . . . I'll see.' He raised an interrogative eyebrow at his superior, who shook his head and turned away. 'I'm sorry, Chief Superintendent Oaks is engaged . . . I see . . . I see . . . Congratulations. Yes, I'm sure. Yes, probably tomorrow. No, I can't say who it might be, but probably not Mr Oaks, who is rather tied up. Yes, thank you for letting us know, and congratulations again.'

He put the phone down. 'That was Detective-Superintendent Jones, South Yorks. They've got her.'

Oaks sounded weary and was still staring out of the window. 'Sure?'

Alec said: 'They're sure.' He paused, but Oaks didn't query it or ask how they were so certain. 'They want to know if someone is going up to interview her. Devon and Cornwall have somebody already up there. Norfolk are leaving it till tomorrow.'

Oaks turned round. He looked ten years older. 'Her.'

'I'm afraid so, sir. Nobody could have expected it. Nobody's to blame.'

But there would be plenty to blame. They all knew it. The atmosphere in the room was the more electric for the knowledge; the knowledge that Oaks would carry it. They watched him curiously, as bystanders watch a man condemned to die, for signs of his own awareness of his precarious mortality.

DCI Weston risked: 'I'm sorry, sir.'

'Keep your fucking sympathy for those who ask it!' The words seemed to be wrenched from Oaks, and as if overcome by shame as much as anger, he stormed from the room, slamming the door.

They watched him go, and the collective exhalation of breath was more expressive than words. Then the words began to flow. Alec, with no taste for it all, took his opportunity to slip out. Oaks was doomed. He himself, every bit as fortuitously, was on the up. He felt, illogically, ashamed.

Blackett and Alec drove up to Yorkshire. Alec admitted to himself that he was highly curious to see this monster who had killed five other women.

They found the South Yorkshire detectives quietly jubilant at having caused a sensation by capturing the Carver and revealing 'him' to be a woman. Blackett and Stan Jones understood each other well enough. Two of a kind, Alec observed. Gill Wightman he had met before: a clever woman, he had always thought, and seeing her on her own ground her competence was more in evidence.

Jones spoke deprecatingly of their 'luck' over the Carver. It was an accepted way of referring to callously stealing a march over another force. All fair in love and policing. Alec had left Liz Pink incandescent with anger against herself for divulging so much so readily over the phone to Gill Wightman. 'We slog away towards the capture of the Carver and all they do is stretch out a hand and grab her collar, and *they*'re the darlings of the press.' Just so.

'She did them,' Stan Jones assured them. 'Bang to rights, as they say. It was as much as we could do to stop her talking. Anyway, the lab at Wetherby've taken the car apart to the last nut and bolt and they've found a packet of Polos in the door pocket with Sandra Allen's prints on. I've told 'em you're here and you're welcome to go and have a chat after you've seen Payne.'

'We'll do that,' Blackett responded.

'You may not get anything much out of her. She sang like a bird at first; but now she's swung the other way and she's tight as ... hr'mm.' Alec, intercepting a look from Gill Wightman to her boss, was interested to note that it expressed not so much 'Mind your language in front of me' as 'Not in front of visitors'. He speculated about how they conversed when alone, recognizing the easy relationship senior and junior officers were sometimes fortunate enough to enjoy—he and Blackett, for instance; or Liz and himself.

Jones hesitated: an experienced policeman, at a loss to understand a crime committed on his patch. 'If it wasn't for the fact that she seems to swing from one mood to another so fast, I'd say she was as sane as you or I. So if you find out what made her kill five other women and do those things to them that she did, I wish you'd come and tell me. Because it's a mystery to me. I never thought I'd see the day I'd say this, but if I'd known when I joined the force that something like this would come my way, I swear I'd have gone down the pit instead.'

*　　　*　　　*

Anita found the news of the Carver's capture very puzzling. She was watching a lot of television now; watching it ten and twelve hours a day. It distracted her from the need to decide what to do. From the day of Ruth's visit she had stopped bringing the man into the house. Their relationship was over. He was a problem now. She fed him and mucked the stable out as a matter of routine, but that was only a temporary expedient while she waited for something else to happen. Often her mind assisted her in her wish that she could just forget about him. But after a day or two during which she didn't leave the house her remembrance that he was there would intrude again, summoned by some sense of responsibility too deep to erase: you didn't treat animals like that. If you kept them, you made sure you looked after their needs. Even when they were old and worn out and useless they were your responsibility—your responsibility to nurse and finally to help out of their pain and out of the world.

The police spokesman was trying to maintain a reasonable, matter-of-fact manner, but his satisfaction with the situation kept creeping in. Anita supposed that the police had been prepared for the tally of the Carver's victims to mount higher, and that to have caught her after only five deaths and one attempted murder was regarded as a triumph. Anita was troubled that there seemed to be no misgiving that the wrong person had been caught. She didn't understand all the references to scientific evidence, but surely it was only guesswork?

An interview with Maria Tillotson followed. There again, through all the clutter of accusation, claim, refutation and propaganda, Anita perceived that the accuracy of the arrest was not doubted. Everyone accepted that the Carver had been caught at last.

Anita sat on through the local news and the start of the children's programmes that followed, her sense of oppression rolling round and round her head. She had been betrayed by those confident, articulate women; by Maria Tillotson and Ruth Samuels. They spoke easy words, and she had obeyed them, and they gave no thought to the problem they were making for her. Out in her stable lay, in straw on cold concrete, the man they had told her was the Carver; and what was she to do about him?

20

If the capture of the Carver was the occasion for the party, the trigger was Liz, despatching Johnson for a takeaway, adding: 'And a couple of cans of Guinness. Why not?'

'A couple?' Johnson queried pointedly.

Liz looked round the crowded room. The buzz of voices hushed as everyone waited for her answer.

'What the hell,' she replied, quickly calculating the contents of her wallet. 'You'd better get a couple of boxes of wine while you're about it.'

Pritchard spoke up. 'Suppose I buy the food?'

'You could get some crisps and things while you're about it,' Sally said. 'I don't mind funding those.'

Soon everybody was chipping in suggestions for what was now, to Johnson's vocal consternation, a substantial shopping list. Eventually he departed. Someone raised the possibility of inviting colleagues. Everybody looked round the room. They were a team. Invitations to outsiders were vetoed.

'What about the governor?' Liz queried tentatively.

'Won't he want to get home?' Pritchard asked.

'He won't want to muck in,' Simms observed dismissively. Somebody made a remark about 'cold fish'. Liz bit her lip. Pritchard raised an interrogative eyebrow at Liz.

'Think he'd like to come?'

'I think he'd like to be asked,' Liz said, trying not to plead. 'No—he'd like to *come*.'

Pritchard looked round the assembled faces. 'How about it? Does he qualify?'

There was a moment's silent thought. Heads began to nod.

'If it wasn't for the governor . . .'

'He's done as much as anyone . . .'

'He's not such a bad sod for a governor . . .'

'He's deserved it after what Oaks . . .'

Pritchard nodded, and turned back to Liz. 'Better issue the invitation.'

Johnson returned to find desks pushed back, a corner reserved for the bar and a party in effect already in full swing. Sally swiftly commandeered the food and drink, releasing each item only as its sponsor paid up. 'Otherwise,' she reminded Johnson, 'you'll be paying credit card interest until Christmas.'

'Thanks, Fieldy,' he said humbly.

Liz proffered her wallet. 'How much, Fieldy?'

'Nothing, skipper. Everything's accounted for.'

'You mean the little so and so's forgotten the Guinness?'

Sally nodded in the direction of the bar, where Pritchard was holding up a can. A moment later he appeared by her side, proffering it.

'You fixed this!' she exclaimed.

'I don't know what you mean.' She almost thought she saw a wink pass between him and Sally Field.

'You're a pair of cheeky sods.'

'If you say so, skipper,' the girl replied. 'Next!'

'They're not a bad bunch,' Liz said, trying to sound judicious.

'And you love them, every one.'

She thought about refuting it, but it seemed pointless. 'Oh well,' she said.

Alec spent twenty minutes at the party. Liz could see from the expressions on the faces of one or two of the younger ones that they hadn't expected that a chief inspector, or rather *this* chief inspector, would permit himself to let his hair down quite so far. She was puzzled herself. It was as if he had some inner reason for wanting to show them all his benevolence. He's not really unguarded, Liz thought. I know

him better than that. And then she corrected herself: he *is*—
for some reason of his own. And he's enjoying the
experience.

After twenty minutes Alec Stainton looked at his watch
and excused himself. There was some daring barracking.

'If he's not careful,' Liz remarked to Sally in a voice which
was meant to be *sotto voce* but was almost a shout above the
prevailing noise level, 'he'll have them singing "For he's a
jolly good fellow".'

'Oh, I don't think anyone'll go that far,' said Sally drily.

'Why not?' responded Liz indignantly. At which Sally
turned upon her a speculative and impertinent gaze.

After Stainton had left the party moved up a notch. People
perched on edges of desks forking cold beanshoots out of foil
containers and arguing about football teams, cars and above
all people, as gossip flowed scandalously and happily. To Liz's
surprise, she found several of the constables forming a court
around her. She'd given these lads stick, and tomorrow or
next week she'd be giving them stick again. But gradually
Liz shed her followers and whether by design or accident the
drift of bodies brought her next to Pritchard.

'Well, Pritch?'

'Well, Sergeant?'

'You're a bloody fraud, Pritch, but I expect you know that.
Trying to get us believe you're just a boring Welshman. Sorry.
Racist remark.'

He looked meaningfully at the can in her hand, but it was
not alcohol that was keeping Liz high. She put her drink
down and began to fumble with an errant button. What was
it about this man that made her suddenly anxious not to
seem a tramp? Pritchard himself was holding a glass of white
wine, but his expression was relaxed, and she suspected it
was the same glass Sally had poured him when the bar
opened. Together they surveyed the scene.

'Time to leave them to it,' Liz opined.

'I think you're right. Are you fit to drive?'

'Is that an offer?'

'If needed. I can squeeze in a little one.'

'OK, *bach*. Isn't that how they talk in your part of the world?'

'*Duw*,' he replied. '*All hi siarad Cymraeg nawr?*'

'Right on, sweetheart. Let's go.'

'So: case complete.'

'No thanks to us.'

'You made the connection. Others followed it up.'

Alec smiled. 'Liz made it. In a way, it's been Liz's case all through, HOLMES or no. You should have seen Oaks this afternoon. Bears with sore heads isn't in it.'

Frances said: 'It'll do him no good, will it?'

'No, I'm afraid it won't. But these things die down. And policemen know they happen.'

'At least now he can't take you down with him. He's a vindictive man, I think.'

'Frances! Uncharitable?'

She smiled and came over to where he stood with his back against the worktop, so that he could hold her round the waist. In a relationship such as theirs, boundaries had little meaning and embraces were never solely comforting or solely consoling or solely erotic, but in each situation all the other possibilities were implicit. So now she felt the hardness of his arousal, thought how like a man it was to want a little sex in his moment of victory, understood and acquiesced, rubbing her hips against his.

'Did you know that the reason Deborah Payne became a killer is that men treated her badly?' she asked.

'That sounds like Maria Tillotson speaking.'

'You see, men are to blame after all.'

'I rather thought we might be.'

His face was suddenly bleak, so that Frances slipped her hands invitingly under his jacket, rubbing his chest and back. 'They had that other woman on, too. Wendy Thomas, the one who met the Carver and didn't get killed. The human touch. The Carver was sorry for her.'

'It's the only reason I can imagine why she wasn't killed like the rest of them. Because she had had worse luck than

the Carver herself, whereas all the others had been successful, in the conventional sorts of ways. Family, you know,
and jobs, and relationships . . .'

Frances involuntarily shivered as she was reminded of the
cruel signature the Carver had left on her victims. If all the
teams hunting for the Carver had been composed of women,
would they have guessed sooner that the Carver was actually
a woman? She could not comprehend the experiences that
motivated that terrible negation of the victims' sexuality.

'Alec, what . . .' It was a meaningless question, but she
had to ask it; 'What sort of a woman *is* she?'

Alec shook his head, recalling with exasperation the same
unanswerable question running round and round his head
as he sat opposite Deborah Payne in the interview room in
Yorkshire.

Blackett had left the questioning to him, but in the event
it had made no difference. 'You'll get nothing out of her,'
Stan Jones had predicted; and had been proved right.
Deborah Payne sat with a solicitor by her side with her handsome face closed, saying nothing while Alec ran through the
preliminary spiel.

'Where did you meet Sandra Allen?' Alec began.

Payne glanced at the lawyer. The lawyer moved his head
fractionally from left to right. Payne looked back at Alec. She
did not speak. She did not nod or shake her head. She just
waited for the next question.

'When you picked her up: what time was that?'

The same check glance at the solicitor. The same blankness.
At first Alec was determined not to be bested, but in the
end he acknowledged that he was beaten; not so much by
Deborah Payne's silence as by his own inability to understand. He could not have conceived that another human
being, man or woman, could be so inaccessible. He could
only speculate whether this impenetrability was proof of an
inner emptiness which had finally become intolerable, or
simply the psychopath's barrenness of emotion. She'd have
killed someone else, he thought, looking at her composed,
attractive features while on the desk between them the tape

machine faithfully recorded his failure. She'd have found some spurious justification, as she had with the women; and killed with as little compunction.

He continued framing the questions automatically for another twenty minutes; but he scarcely glanced up any more, and barely paused between the questions for the answers he knew she would not give, and left the room profoundly depressed.

He tried to explain some of this to Frances, and it seemed she understood, for she took him firmly in her arms and began to unbutton his shirt, smoothing her hands on the muscles beneath.

'I've never made love to a police superintendent before,' she murmured.

He made an effort to match her determined renunciation of the Carver, and said jocularly, 'I rather hope you'll resist the temptation a little while longer. I don't get promoted until my appointment begins.'

'Have you told Liz Pink?'

'Not yet.' He parted the buttons of her blouse and bent his head to her breast and she pressed it there.

'Don't leave it too long. She's going to take it hard.'

He nodded acquiescence without lifting his lips from her nipple, and she smiled to herself, knowing he didn't really believe her about Liz. For her part, she knew no jealousy, only smug pleasure that her husband was desired but she had him. Then she shivered with pleasure, other women forgotten, and played her fingers over his body. 'Talking of hard . . .'

But he was too occupied to reply, and they were soon too far down the road of pleasure for speech or thought.

The night was bitter as Liz climbed out of the car, but the rain, perhaps because it was too cold for it now, had stopped.

The grass was beginning to show white as the moisture froze. As the sound of the engine receded she wished she had asked Pritch in. He was a long, lonely way from Trenant. But she was not too drunk to realize that it was better this

210

way. 'Oh well,' she said aloud as she fumbled the key in the lock, 'he's probably a leg-man anyway.' And pushed in to the living-room.

Rosie lay on the sofa in a dressing-gown. It was, as it happened, Liz's dressing-gown. 'Hi. You're late.'

Liz drew in a deep breath with an effort. 'I don't suppose that's cocoa in that mug, is it?'

'Drinking chocolate, actually.' Rosie's expression remained petulant. 'Want some?'

'Lead me to it.'

Rosie shrugged, as much as to say: It's in the cupboard. Go and make it.

She had made no attempt to clear the clutter of toys away. The changing mat lay on the carpet, a disposable nappy, only too obviously used, pushed to one side.

Liz looked at Rosie without love. 'You lazy slut,' she said deliberately.

In the kitchen the worktops were hidden beneath plastic baby plates, cartons of food, and the sterilizer which had slopped its contents to drip steadily into the growing pool on the plastic tiled floor. Liz felt her limbs grow hot and her head throbbed. Slowly she counted . . . ten . . . twenty . . . thirty. Turned back into the living-room. Sat with great care on the edge of a chair.

'I think it's time you left.'

Rosie began to cry, sullenly, inelegantly, accusingly. 'She's only a baby! You hate her. Why don't you admit it? You hate her.'

Liz felt herself going hot over again. Hadn't she taken Rosie and Joy into her house in their moment of need? Hadn't she given up the precious privacy of her new little house before she had even had time to savour it? Hadn't she looked on as Rosie made herself at home, rearranged her kitchen, took over the washing-machine for Joy's endless clothes, the pedal bin for sacks of foul nappies, the bedroom, the bath-room, the living-room floor for toys and changing mats and paraphernalia—and never said a word?

I don't want thanks, she told herself, just . . . And then

she seemed to hear Pritch's dry, amused voice admonishing her: You do want thanks. What a selfless little angel you've been, Elizabeth, don't you think?

I never set up to make an angel. It's not Joy, of course, gurgling and wriggling and teasing with shows of affection. It's Rosie who's the problem, because she's grown up and imperfect and sometimes gets on my wick, which Joy does too but you can't blame a helpless little mite and you can a grown woman. It may be more blessed to give than to receive, but it's a damn sight harder, given the unlovely nature of the recipients.

'Right from the beginning,' Rosie snuffled, 'you've made it very plain we were unwelcome. We'll go. Right now.'

'For God's sake!' Liz sighed. At this time of night? 'You can stay,' she muttered.

'We aren't wanted.'

Liz swallowed. 'Stay. Please.'

From upstairs, a thin mewing was heard, swiftly swelling to a determined wail.

'Now we've woken Joy up,' said Rosie accusingly, rising from her chair.

Right on cue, you little blighter, Liz remarked silently. Right on cue.

The door swung wide open on to the night. The air was raw, and around the bulb in its wired shade hung a fog of moisture. Anita felt the dank chill which gathered and lingered beneath the trees probing icy fingers into her joints as she looked down at the man.

He was a funny colour, his skin mottled and his breathing shallow. The handcuff had worn an angry red wound on his wrist, crusty with yellow serum. Despite the pallor of the rest of his skin, his forehead was crimson and the hair matted on it damp. In his neck beneath the line of the rough beard, the pulse did not beat so much as tremble. As she watched, a shudder ran through his body from soles to scalp. She wondered whether he was going to die of fever or a heart attack.

She thought about it as she forked the straw out on to the concrete apron and shook a bale of fresh bedding on the floor of the loose-box. JoJo had died, and now the man was dying. Parking the fork on the wheelbarrow, she filled the water bucket then went into the tack-room and looked along the shelves. There was half a bottle of a drench the vet had given her for JoJo last year. What was that for? Some pills— but they were horse-size, huge. She might crush them, perhaps. A twisted paper of white powder. What was that, now? Anita put it into the pocket of her jacket and added, on second thoughts, the pills. She'd grind them up and mix it all into tomorrow morning's feed. If he was still alive. She looked down at him again, and he moaned and opened his eyes, but only the whites were visible and the lids fluttered shut again.

She felt the nagging of a headache forming between her eyes. They were forcing her. It was not her fault. Why must they force her? They could have been so happy together, she and the man. Angry tears streaked her cheek as she turned away and closed the door again on the stable where he lay.

As she crossed to the house, she considered where she might dig a grave without being visible from the road. The already-dug ground where JoJo rested was of course sacrosanct. The bonfire patch might be best: the vegetation was already flattened and partly burnt away. It was too dark to see it tonight, but she'd go and have a look in the morning. She fancied it would do.

Crossland believed himself to be near to madness, and clung to the belief, as the only proof that he was not.

It was beyond his capability to reckon how long what he thought of as the second phase of his captivity—that curiously domestic, curiously soothing period of undemanding subjection—had endured. He had fallen into the routine of being a kept stud as readily as ever he had pursued the routines of work and family life. He recognized, though it was a secret, guilty confession, that he had found the routine of servitude, with its bizarre admixture of sexual subservience, easier to come to terms with than he had in recent years found his life as an employee, a father, a husband.

Then a week ago was it, or more, it was difficult to keep track, abruptly and without explanation that phase came to an end and this last—no: mustn't say that: say latest—phase had begun: the more unbearable for following after that period of comparative laxity.

Now he was shut up in the stable all day and all night. Shackled permanently to the floor. His only food the foul mess of cat food scooped from the tin with his fingers. Hygiene was impossible and that, or the cat food, gave him perpetual diarrhoea which left him aching and shivering in the filthy straw. The nights were bitterly cold, the days little warmer, the lack of light demoralizing. He knew, with diamond clarity, that there was a very real risk that he would die.

Paradoxically, he no longer feared the woman so much: death was not in her gift alone. It would come from infection or hypothermia. But bitter, impotent tears crusted his cheeks. For a brief interlude he had been back in contact with something like normal human relations. (Normal to make love with a woman who holds a knife! Normal to eat bread and cheese naked at a table while she stands over you with a shotgun! Normal to fasten with your own hands the shackle of your daily reimprisonment!) Now again he was alone.

With what was left of his mind, he knew the woman was mad. He held on to that, as his only ground for believing that, with luck, given the irrational shifts of mood to which the mad are prone, he might not after all die by her hand. But the hope of survival flickered sadly and sometimes faded for days on end and he was bitterly afraid.

Sometimes he spent hours—he supposed they were hours—singing at the top of his voice. Initially he had shouted—until he was hoarse. Soon he learnt that he could make as much noise singing, and do it for longer. Singing was curiously comforting. Shouting simply emphasized his plight: he heard the stridency of desperation in his voice; but when he sang he produced, with whatever inadequacies, at

214

least the echo of something of beauty. He sang old hymns, long forgotten, resurrected from distant memory of Sunday School, with their naïve expressions of religious hope which he found unexpectedly strengthening; and songs from shows; and ribald rugby songs about extraordinary sexual encounters and women with bizarre physical characteristics, because they made him, almost, laugh. Singing everything he remembered, he ceased to do so in the empty hope that sometime, somehow, someone would hear, and began to sing for his own uplift. It was, after all, the expression of a mind still capable of activity. If you wanted to be blunt, you could say it was something animals couldn't do.

Yes, the woman was mad. His very presence there was proof enough. What sort of psychopath shackled another human being to a metal hasp in a stable and fed him cat food? And each time she appeared, with the bowl of food and cradling the shotgun, he wondered if she had tipped over the edge and he was looking at his own death.

He would see the light go on in the tack-room the other side of the wooden partition; and before she slipped the bolts on the stable door she put the light on in the stable too. But never outside, so that what was beyond the door remained impenetrable, for it was always night when she came.

The first time he had left the stinking mess of food untouched, nauseated by its very presence in the stable. And the second. And the third. The fourth night, hunger had brought him to regard it differently; but he gagged at the first mouthful, and at the second he was sick. Now, he ate it without a thought. Coming after several days' constipation, brought about because he could not bring himself to defecate in his prison, the cat food occasioned diarrhoea. After that, he accepted that the day's fresh straw was his bedding and his lavatory and his source of warmth all in one, and tailored his domestic arrangements accordingly. His movement was restricted by the handcuffs to the length of his own arm, so that though he did the best he could by way of isolating his living area from his lavatory, the best was not very satisfactory. The woman came every night and mucked out the filthy straw with a fork, and shook out a fresh bale; and he knew he had been reduced to the status of an animal.

And then she had become worryingly absent—literally, as well as mentally. For two days she did not appear even to change the straw in the stable or to leave a can of food; hunger gnawed at the lining of his stomach and he could no longer keep the cold at bay. Suppose she forgot him altogether, wrapped in her own, bizarre inner world? Suppose she simply left him there? How long could he survive without food? Without water?

He was amazed to find that the very fact of studying the woman so intently, gradually altered his reaction to her. At the same time, his survival became a matter not only of obvious personal interest but of abstract fascination. It was like playing a slow game of snooker against an infinitely devious, infinitely capricious opponent who might at any moment turn to smashing the table and throwing the balls against the wall. He spent at least as much of his time pondering the woman's psychology as he did trying to work the metal hasp free of the floor, and both tasks (the hasp had been designed to hold a horse, after all) seemed equally futile.

During the second phase of his captivity, with no demands except the most fundamental made of him, without a wife to snap at or children bickering and whining about Christmas presents, without the need to flatter company bosses or be matey with colleagues, with nobody to impress, none but the most basic of needs which the woman met in the most basic of ways, he had found himself surprisingly light of heart. He was puzzled, if relieved, to find that this outlook persisted now, when circumstances were so unpromising. It was something to do with having everything stripped away. If only he could be sure that life itself was guaranteed, he believed he could reconcile himself to living it on these brutally unadorned terms. But still, often, his imagination turned to picturing the woman flying into a frenzy and raising the shotgun. He saw the two implacable eyes of it staring and her finger whitening on the trigger. He saw the gun jerk and the woman stagger and the puff of the gases expanding from the barrel and the individual lead balls fanning out towards him and felt them press his skin inwards until it tore and press on through his flesh. Felt the air rush from his lungs; the acid explode from his stomach; his liver burst and his heart convulse and leap and seize. And his brain slowly starve and the message from his bulging eyes fade and the cloud descend. And he was afraid, and knew it, and knew that this was how he would die: in terror, in the mess of his own incontinence, in regret at the futility of his own life.

And resolved, in the end, that he did not want to die that way. There was a way, if he could find the courage to use it. He must begin to work on himself, seeking in the dusty corners and attics of himself, where he had rarely, or never, penetrated for the resolution and bravery it would take. He had, after all, plenty of time so far as hours in the day went. But his stock of days, he sensed, was running out.

On the third day the woman came and mucked out, wordless, unreachable as an automaton but the shotgun much in evidence. When she went, she left a tin of cat food with the lid turned back and a fresh bucket full of water. He sat down and pulled the blissful clean straw over him and set about calculating how long he could make the bucket of water last. He ate half the food. Then he twisted off the jagged lid of the tin.

He sat, holding it and afraid, a long way into the night.

21

Even as Deborah Payne was making her heavily-guarded way to Holloway Prison on remand, ranks from constable to superintendent were pushing aside Carver papers and reaching for towering in-trays.

The Crossland case too was to be 'disposed of'. Without the Carver element, what was there to the case anyway? A middle-aged man who fancies himself with the ladies leaves his wife without notice. He had briefly been important, when he was thought to be the Carver. Now he was not.

'He'll turn up,' Blackett predicted, 'when the woman he's with tires of him. Expecting his dinner to be on the table as if he'd never been away.'

Alec turned the pages of the file idly, momentarily self-indulgent, loosing the rein of his imagination. He lifted the phone. 'Spare me a minute, Liz.'

When Liz entered she took up automatically her customary position leaning against the filing cabinet. Alec scrutinized her carefully. Unless he was much mistaken she was tired. Or—which would be more unusual—dejected. The dark hair escaping from its clips did so less rebelliously than usual and was without lustre. Her shirt, though it was fresh and well laundered, hung slackly as if the body within were itself less lively, less charged with energy, than usual. She pushed herself off from the filing cabinet and stood rather more formally, her expression growing cautious, and he realized he had been frowning at her.

'Crossland,' he said. 'What do you think?'

Liz sagged back into informality. 'Where do I think he is?'

She ran her fingers through her hair, hitching a hip so that her body kinked at the waist. Some women seemed to have less in the way of a skeleton than others, like cats. With Liz, you were not aware much of bones; supremely aware of flesh, or rather, of contours, constantly fluid. What a gift she would have been to Degas or Sickert or those turn-of-the-century artists who painted fleshy tarts in Camden Town garrets. What an awful way to regard one's faithful and invaluable sergeant.

'Well,' she ventured, 'he's run away from his probably rather dull wife in Wilmslow. Which presumes that he's found someone rather less dull, in somewhere rather more exciting.' She chewed a lip. 'It's been a long time, though. His work hasn't seen him, and his bank account's intact. His wife was going to sling him out anyway.'

'But he didn't know that.'

'There's only one thing. Where has he been, not to see his name splashed all over the media in connection with the Carver case? And if he was lying low because he thought himself suspected, why hasn't he come out of hiding now?'

They were silent, contemplating the situation. The abandoned car, with no enquiries coming in for it. The good job, with its freedoms and its perks and its travel. The complaisant wife—for all Crossland knew when he last left home—who would iron his white shirts and brush his good suits and cook his large breakfasts before he set off on his travels. His lifestyle had reminded Liz of those sleek tomcats who, with a comfortable home, a regular supply of Whiskas and a cushion by the fireside, roam licentiously among the neighbourhood females each night—but always come home: because a secure and lavish home makes a promiscuous lifestyle enjoyable. Adultery flourishes more in affluent suburbs than in cardboard cities. It is the secure, she thought wisely, who can afford the indulgence of infidelity.

'He might have got wind of the fact that Sarah was about to throw him out. Though according to Greater Manchester's interview with her, she didn't go and see the lawyers until after he'd left that last week.'

219

'And we never found that woman.'

They both contemplated with the inward eye the expanses of Ashdown Forest: the dank rides, the frozen mud that the sun never thawed in winter; the undergrowth that never died back enough to yield the body that might have crawled in for a little shelter.

He showed her Blackett's memo. That, Liz told herself, put the lid on it. Two junior officers with a nagging feeling that a case should not be closed, and one senior one with an order to the contrary. An everyday story of police folk.

'I'd like you to put the file in order.'

'Right you are.' She gave him an oblique glance. 'I could take a day or two over it . . . ?'

He hesitated.

'No.'

Liz took her dismissal. Well, in the end, you couldn't spend resources looking for men who chose to leave their wives, and Crossland was no loss to his. She'd have liked to find the woman, for her own peace of mind, but she didn't intend to flog herself despite the governor's hint. She had something altogether more pleasant on her mind. She and Sally had a plan.

'Liz! Er . . .'

Liz turned, burdened as she was. Mike's big form was hurrying towards her and she shrank instinctively, before pulling herself together. Those hands . . . She had been trying to avoid this, but it had to come.

'Rosie's out,' she said firmly.

'I know. That's why. That's why now, I mean. I've been waiting for you, I mean until your car . . .' He hovered over her. The original man-mountain, she told herself. But, for a big man, exuding curious diffidence. Born of course of his guilt. She fumbled for her key.

'Let me help you. Let me carry something.'

'I can manage,' she said shortly. But somehow it was impossible to shut him out, once the door swung open. She had to push it wide to get herself in along with the carriers from the supermarket and her briefcase. Liz had never shut a door in someone's face in her life, and though she tried to do so now, habit occasioned a fatal hesitation. He may be big but he's like a kid, she thought; standing there with that supplicating, forlorn look. She sighed, gave in, and pushed the door wide once more, turning her back and leaving him to follow if he must.

The clutter of the living-room was so much a matter of routine now that Liz was startled when she emerged from the kitchen after dumping the bags to find Mike standing in the midst of the debris, turning one of Joy's teething rings over and over in those big hands. Those big hands that had left blue-black bruises on his wife's neck, she reminded herself. 'You'd better say what you want smartish,' she said gracelessly, 'because Rosie'll be back in half an hour and I don't want you here then.' But she relented to the extent of adding: 'I'm making a mug of tea. You can have one if you want.'

He followed her through, still turning the silly clown teether in his fingers as if it was a jewelled bracelet. Trying to efface himself while she crossed from worktop to tap to worktop to cupboard he contrived to form himself into an intransigent obstacle. She moved him out of her way three times while assembling the few necessities for tea, and each time he was more apologetic, more shamefaced. It'd be nice if he showed rather more brutality, Liz told herself. If he goes on this way I'm going to find it damn hard not to feel sorry for him.

'They're all right, are they?' he asked suddenly. 'Rosie and . . . and Joy.'

'Yes. Though I don't know what right you have to ask.' Telling herself directly: he's her husband, Liz. And Joy's father. Can a man have a better right, rotten though he is? Mike himself recoiled from her tartness like a cuffed puppy, taking refuge in silence.

The kettle boiled. Liz dunked teabags. Extracted them. Crossed to the pedal bin (moving Mike aside *en route*). Added milk. Proffered sugar. Found a packet of chocolate digestives

221

and broke two cutting it open. 'For God's sake,' she said at last, 'let's sit down and pretend we're civilized.'

In the living-room, the reminders of the absent woman, the absent child, all around, he asked: 'I suppose you don't know . . . she hasn't said anything about . . . coming back.'

Liz frowned. 'No.'

'It must be awkward for you. I know it must be awkward. She doesn't always think, Rosie.'

Liz felt grateful that he had at last begun to abuse his wife. It put them on predictable ground. 'You should have thought of that,' she observed, 'before you turned them out.'

He made her room look small. To sit on the sofa which was comfortable for Liz, he had to have his knees at an awkward acute angle. His jeans were the working sort, not for show: but clean and fairly new. Likewise the sweatshirt, plain but by no means scruffy, over a cotton check shirt such as a farmer might wear. His sleeves were pushed to the elbows, forearms richly haired. On his wrist a heavy gold (gold*ish*, Liz persuaded herself meanly) bracelet. Heavy, handsome head with abundance of dark curling hair. Regular cut of the jeans not wholly disguising a suggestion of generous endowment. Liz pulled a face. They're all the same, these builder types: part-time male models, or fancy themselves as strippers for the hen circuit. Full of themselves and dexterous with their hands. OK now, a nice fella, best behaviour, but he'll be down the pub tonight and think nothing of putting away seven or eight pints and having his hand up any skirt within reach before he staggers back to piss in his neighbours' back gardens and knock his wife about. And maybe his kid, his little, seven-month-old smiling gurgling kid that doesn't know when not to wail.

He said: 'You know why . . .'

'I know. I saw the bruises.'

'I'm scared it could happen again. I'm frightened for Joy.'

'Blokes who knock women and kids around,' Liz said, 'get put away when I have anything to do with it.'

'It's not right. Not for Joy. It doesn't matter what Rosie

does, I mean, she can make her choice, but Joy . . . I know she's only small. But it's not right.'

Liz felt as if she had missed a portion of the conversation somewhere. 'Not right?' Not right living here? Was that what he was suggesting, that she was somehow starving them, or making them sleep in the coal shed?

'I was wrong. At the time, it seemed like the right thing to do. I thought it'd bring her to her senses, you know, make her realize it wasn't worth it.'

'Sounds to me like a good way to make sure she never sees you again. You might call that coming to her senses, I suppose.'

He fetched a big sigh. What a thespian.

'I think,' he said, 'I could cope with it. I could let her go. If I was sure that he wouldn't knock her about again. If I could be sure he wouldn't ever lay a finger on Joy.'

Liz swallowed a mouthful of hot tea the wrong way. 'Hang on,' she demanded when she had done coughing. 'Hang on. Just say that again.'

'I just feel, maybe I'm being selfish. Maybe our marriage has just sort of run out. If she's really not happy, I wouldn't want to keep her against her will. But I'm afraid for Joy. You can't blame me for being afraid for Joy. Because if he doesn't want her, and let's face it, not everyone wants to take on some other bloke's kid . . .'

'Mike, shut it.'

'Wha . . . ?'

'Now listen. And answer in one word. The night Rosie left; the night she came here; the bruises on her neck . . .'

'I know, if it hadn't been for the bruises . . .'

'Mike, *will you shut it*! Right. The bruises. That was you, put them there. Wasn't it? Yes or no.'

The expression on his face, which had been wavering between hurt and incomprehension, froze into horror that would have been comical if she'd seen it in a cartoon. Now, it told her the answer to her question which he was too dumbstruck to articulate.

223

'Oh God,' Liz muttered. 'Mike, you didn't give her those bruises, did you?'

'Me?'

'OK, OK.'

'Is that what she said?'

'Yes.' She thought. 'No,' she admitted. 'I suppose I never asked, and maybe she just let me believe . . . Oh, I'm a first-rate downright prize-winning credulous cow. No wonder people take me for a soft touch.' She surveyed the baby-littered room. All this, all the upset, all the wailings and hardly being able to sit on the loo for the junk in the bathroom, and the sick and the messy gunge at mealtimes and Rosie's perpetual boobs—all her own fault. Because Rosie was engaged in a neat game of playing one fella off against another, and while she did it she needed a nice cosy base with a nice dumb host. The late nights . . . No wonder Rosie was reluctant to take Joy with her . . . No wonder she returned happy and shagged out. She was shagged out. Was probably getting shagged right this bloody minute with little Joy abandoned in her carrycot grizzling for a dry nappy forced to sit and endure the sounds (and, dear God, perhaps the sight) of her feckless mama having it off with a boyfriend who put marks on her neck.

'Let's get this straight, so's even I can understand it. That night, Rosie came home with bruises on her neck.'

'Yes.'

'Which she'd got somewhere else from some other bloke.'

'Yes. He . . .'

'So you threw her out?'

'Well, I . . . OK, I suppose it came to it, more or less. I said if she liked the way he treated her she'd better go to him. She said did that mean I was throwing her out, and I said yes. So she went.'

'As far as two doors away.'

'Yes, well I didn't know that at first. I thought she'd gone to him. Then when I learnt she was here, I thought you knew all about it. I thought you were on her side.'

'I'm not on anybody's side,' Liz said irritably. Least of all

Rosie's, she added silently. 'If this is true,' she said suspiciously, 'why'd you want to see me tonight?'

'To ask you to pass on a message. I thought maybe Rosie was finding Joy was cramping her style, sort of. And I've worked out a way I could have her. They've a place in the nursery in Lewes, and if I took her there before work . . .'

'She's not weaned,' Liz said sharply. But she thought: it must have taken a good deal for Mike to go in to the nursery and make enquiries.

A deep flush reddened his cheek, as if he was embarrassed by references to his wife's breasts even as oblique as this. Liz found herself liking him. If he wasn't such a poor sap, which he must be, letting all this happen and his woman go off with another bloke right under his nose, she'd have said Rosie didn't deserve him.

She stood up. 'OK. Push off.' She pulled a face. 'I'm sorry I've made things worse.'

'What are you going to do?'

'I don't know. Try not to be such a bloody fool in the future, I suppose.'

'But about Joy, I mean?'

'That's up to Rosie, isn't it?'

'She'll go to him,' he said miserably. 'He's a solicitor. She thinks he's class and I'm just a builder.'

'That's up to her,' Liz said, trying to shepherd him across the few feet of carpet to the front porch. 'She'll have to make her mind up.'

He stood on the outside step, uncertain. For the first time that evening their eyes were on a level. Liz said: 'Let her go. If she wants to, you've nothing to gain by trying to hold her back. She'll only hate you for it.' Thinking: but you've everything to gain. You love the bitch. 'But there's Joy.'

'But what can I do?'

'She won't be breastfeeding for ever. Go back to that nursery, check they can take her as soon as she's weaned. Get the whole thing arranged and make sure you've the money to pay for it. Then fight Rosie for custody. I'm not saying you'll win. But it's that or sit on your bum regretting it for the rest of your life.'

She watched him make his troubled way the few yards to his own door, then closed hers and went back in. They'll never have me doing marriage guidance, she told herself. Everyone takes me for a ride for the simple reason that I can't see beyond the end of my nose. They shouldn't allow me out in the wide world.

Then she checked her watch. Rosie was due back soon. And there was more than tea to sort out before she arrived.

She went through into the kitchen. In the warmth of the centrally heated room the frozen goods she had brought back from the supermarket were defrosting. Trickles of moisture wept across the worktop. Like me, she thought: soft and soggy when they should be firm. Ice, that's what's needed. Sort us both out.

22

Ruth found, to her annoyance, that far from quieting her conscience, her visit to Anita left her troubled. She might reasonably have expected, she told herself, to be able to forget about her for a bit now that she had reassured herself that nothing terrible had happened.

Yet it was not exactly conscience that nagged her; more some worrying incongruity about the visit. She did not think it was solely the increasing signs of Anita's mental instability. Over the years she had become accustomed to the fact that Anita had diverged from the path taken by the rest of their contemporaries. Not only in outward circumstances—her mother's valetudinarianism and later genuine illness could not, after all, be laid at Anita's door; and her muddy existence at Bracken Ghyll when most of their mutual acquaintances inhabited the comfortable world of town and suburbia followed from the tie to her mother—but in the way in which she approached life, Anita did not fit the template of normality. She had become, in short, more than a little odd. Neither Ruth nor Alan mentioned madness, but when Ruth saw her husband after visiting Anita, his question now was invariably, 'How was she today?'—which came to the same thing.

Ruth told herself that what had unsettled her was the fact that Anita had now blatantly crossed that narrow line that separates what is politely called eccentricity from downright mental imbalance. Far from freeing her to rediscover some sort of normality, her mother's death appeared to have removed the last curb on Anita's disturbed psyche. Though individually the things she said and the things she did were merely quirky, cumulatively they were quite unnerving for the onlooker, like a disorientating upset of perspective. It was like walking through a fairground hall of mirrors.

Ruth didn't try and explain all this to Alan. But one morning when she drove into Croydon to shop she found it all revolving in her mind, and set herself to try and decide whether there was anything more substantial behind her unease. Walking through the Whitgift Centre she asked herself what nagged. She went through the sequence of her actions on her visit and the words that had been exchanged. Was it the house: its all too apparent dilapidation, the lack of effort, the slatternly smeared windows, the piled crockery pungent with ancient meals? The garden, perhaps? How long before it ceased to be possible to call it by that name, the lawn full of self-seeded birch and sycamore, the borders a tangle of couch and flowers smothered in goosegrass? There was nothing else—only the stable. But the stable had revealed nothing more than a dung-fork in a wheelbarrow before the closed doors.

Ruth stopped abruptly. A man cannoned into her from behind.

'For Christ's sake!'

She looked round abstractedly. 'Sorry! Sorry.'

She began to walk again. The *closed* doors? And something else struck her hazy recollection as out of place. What was it? She thought herself back into that moment: walking to the car in the weak sunlight, that quick glance across at the stable with its closed doors, the wheelbarrow and dung-fork, the wisps of straw on the concrete apron.

Ruth found she was moving more and more slowly. Around her the other shoppers were parting like the tide round jetsam on the beach. Once more she pulled herself together. This was impossible. She was becoming as mad as Anita.

She found she was outside Alders and turned in through the glass doors and looked on the store directory for the cafeteria. It was busy; but by accepting a table which had not yet been cleared of dirty crockery she secured a place to sit down with her tray. A teenage girl came up and piled the used crockery efficiently on to a tray and wiped the table with a cloth. Ruth thanked her absently.

The wheelbarrow and dung-fork outside the stable. And those wisps of straw. Just as if Anita had been mucking out. And—yes, now she thought in those terms, she could see the other thing so familiar she had passed it by: a thin trickle of dark moisture staining the concrete from door to gutter. And smell the dung—a smell more acrid than it should be, strong and unwholesome, that had carried clearly over the intervening space. Maybe JoJo was unwell. Was that why the doors were closed where his head should have been craning inquisitively out?

It was none of her business, anyway. But next time—if after Anita's chilly reception she could nerve herself to a next time—she supposed she'd ask. To satisfy her curiosity.

If only she could be sure that Anita would do nothing cruel. She was so unpredictable. Just by neglect she might cause suffering. Ruth's tender heart was wrung. But it really isn't any of my business. Oh dear! Is it?

It had seemed all wrong that Pritch should be allowed to disappear off back to Wales without his leaving being, in some way, marked; so in the end, Liz and Sally had decided to give him a joint dinner party.

Liz thought they succeeded rather well. A small fortune spent at Sainsbury's and Marks and Spencer and Sally's natural flair and her own enthusiasm produced a meal that no mere Welshman could turn his nose up at, and afterwards they sat around in Sally's flat with the last of the wine laughing at *Who Framed Roger Rabbit* on video.

When the screen finally flickered white Liz looked across at the man she had labelled as an all-time prune and in her heart wished him very well. It would have been nice if he had been unattached, but you couldn't have everything, and it'd only have meant her and Fieldy squabbling over him. She glanced at Sally, briefly doubtful. They hadn't had they . . . ? But no. She wasn't sure she'd trust Sally wholly where a matter of the heart was concerned; there was a ruthless streak in her not too far beneath the surface; but Pritch was so wholesome you couldn't imagine him yielding even to the wiles of Sally Field.

'Pritch,' she decided, 'this wife of yours is a convenient ploy. If I hadn't seen her with my own eyes I don't believe I'd be sure she exists.'

'You're right,' he said. 'As a way of fending off importunate Englishwomen, she has her uses.'

Hell! He'd known all the time. Importunate, indeed. Liz said: 'Give her our love.'

Pritch said: 'Did I see a For Sale board on the house at the end yesterday?'

'You haven't been paying attention. We've had real drama. Mothers and babies thrown out on the street; weeping husbands accepting back their errant wives; Little Nell and Oliver Twist rolled into one. The upshot is, Mike's got a job in Scunthorpe on a road contract and Rosie and Joy have gone with him. It turned out her fancy man didn't want her all that much, and a bird in the hand, and all that.'

Sally said sternly, 'I hope it'll be a lesson to you.'

'I don't expect so,' Liz said. 'What else could I have done? In the circumstances?'

'Said no, and not been taken for a ride. You're lucky to have got out of it as lightly as you have.'

Pritch said: 'Being taken for a ride occasionally is one of the prices of taking risks. Maybe it's worth it. But I'm glad it's all worked out happily.'

Sally Field snorted, lying back in her chair, holding the last of her wine up to the light. Insubordinate minx, Liz thought affectionately. Pritch was right. You had to take a few risks occasionally. If you didn't, you ended up living in your own little armed camp, you against the rest of the world.

Maybe that was the way it was going. With FIGHTBACK to supply the weaponry. It's not for me, Liz thought. I'll be hurt; I'll be taken advantage of; but I'll have fun along the way and if I'm lucky, love too; real love that maybe Rosie wouldn't understand but Pritch would, Alec would, other people who take risks would. And when little Joy smiled at me . . .

Yes, I've made my choice. I'll bide by the consequences.

In the RSPCA office Morris Dempsey listened seriously to what Ruth Samuels told him, nodding sagely occasionally because he knew from experience that informants—they often were just such decent middle-class women with tender consciences and resolute wills as Mrs Samuels—needed reassurance that they were doing the right thing.

'Well, thank you for letting us know, anyway.'

'It's probably nothing at all. It was the door being closed, you see. And Anita being, well . . .'

'I do understand,' he said hastily. 'There probably is nothing in it, but we'll look into it. Leave it with us.'

'Will you need to say who told you?'

What they all wanted to know. 'No,' he reassured her. 'We're very discreet in that way. You've definitely done the right thing in confiding in us. Leave it with me now.'

'I'm sorry I've taken so long. I don't know why. I suppose I was afraid . . .'

'Of course.'

The man seemed stronger, so perhaps JoJo's fever drench had been efficacious after all. His brow was clearer, and though he said nothing the movement of his eyes showed he was in his senses. His skin was still a queer colour: cold, presumably, though she found it difficult to see why a man should feel hard done by where a horse had coped well enough. Another example of the vaunting of men not being matched by reality. Hypothermia, for that is what Anita supposed him to be suffering from, could take a long time to kill him. For all the empty tucks of skin, Crossland was well padded yet with muscle and fat.

Anita removed the empty cat food tin, pushing a new one within his reach. The straw was heavily soiled and the smell

231

of faeces ranker and somehow more strongly chemical, as if he had suffered another bout of diarrhoea. She saw that the backs of his thighs were crusted with dark matter. There was an alert glint in his eye she did not like, and Anita decided to postpone mucking out until the evening.

Back indoors Anita began to hunt through the shelves. She was beginning to regret destroying all her mother's medicines so comprehensively; there would certainly have been something among all her painkillers and hypochondriac's stores which would have served. How long did she have? Ruth was a weak creature; it would take her weeks to work up resolution to do anything; still, Anita was vaguely puzzled that nobody had come already. But they would, sooner or later. So she had to do it. It was all over now.

There was nothing on the shelves that looked particularly lethal. Anita got out the car and drove in to Forest Row. In the chemists there she looked on the shelves for something to help you sleep, but there was nothing. She vaguely remembered that these days you had to ask. Maybe they wouldn't give her anything without a doctor's prescription anyway. She bought a bottle of Paracetamol; and one of Aspirin; and then in the little supermarket a bottle of gin, and three six-packs of cat food.

Back home, the little bottle of Aspirin looked unimpressive. Then she remembered she had heard somewhere that Aspirin had been used in some way to ward off heart attacks. That was not what she wanted at all.

That left the Paracetamol. It was a bottle of fifty, and she hunted along the mantelshelf to find the packet she kept for colds and period pains—that was almost full too— and tipped them both into the blender attachment of the mixer and switched it on. It stuttered for a few moments against the load and then, as the tablets began to shatter, picked up speed. A white cloud of powder began to fill the bowl.

The noise of the blender was powerful, so that only when she switched it off did Anita hear, outside, the sound of an engine running. Somebody was parked outside the house.

The engine was switched off. Abruptly, jerkily, Anita began to move.

As soon as he drew the RSPCA van to a halt in front of Bracken Ghyll, Dempsey realized that this had all the signs of being no empty tip-off. A little eccentric, was that the phrase that Mrs Samuels had used? Well, eccentric was one word for barricading yourself in your house with barbed wire and posting notices round the perimeter as if it was Fort Knox. What people did on their own property was a matter of supreme indifference to Dempsey provided no animals were involved; but mad people were not always very nice to animals, and the roof of the stables Mrs Samuels had spoken of was visible behind the house. Dempsey pulled on the handbrake but left the engine running to keep the heater going while he wrote the preliminary details on the report sheet and attached it to his clipboard. Then he switched off, checked his identification was to hand, and climbed out.

Unfolding the wire far enough to squeeze through took some minutes' concentrated attention and strong fingers. He managed it eventually and straightened up. Used to isolated cottages, he headed for the back.

Round the corner of the building appeared a woman with flaring ginger hair outlining a white face, in a muddy skirt and torn body-warmer.

She held a shotgun.

She lifted it; as Dempsey froze.

He stood very still. Then, gently, he began to ease himself backwards, keeping his eyes towards this lunatic. He made his feet move slowly, smoothly, until he judged he was near enough to the road to feel for the wire behind him. He pushed backwards through it, trying not to panic as the barbs caught at his jacket threatening to trap him; the woman standing all the time motionless, not a word passing between them. She did not come after him, but he could see her index finger plainly, and it twitched as it lay against the trigger.

When he gained the van he started to shudder and his stomach fluttered and sent a sour fizz of fear up his throat.

233

He dropped the keys the first time, reaching for the ignition, and scrabbled blindly for them on the floor.

Anita turned away behind the house as the van roared away.
There was not much time now.

'All the time she just bloody *stood* there,' Dempsey explained to the sergeant at the police station. An inspector came, and he told him the same: 'She just *stood* there. Oh, God, where's the loo?'

'She made no attempt to stop you leaving?'

'I wasn't hanging around. Christ! The place was done up like a concentration camp. 'Scuse me.'

When he returned he was shunted aside. Phones began to ring. The inspector had disappeared, presumably to consult higher authority.

Twenty minutes: roadblocks are set up across the lane three hundred yards either side of Bracken Ghyll. Thirty minutes: officers begin knocking on front doors, evacuating house-holders. Forty-five minutes: the helicopter is in the air and making the brief flight for a first pass over the site. An hour and ten minutes: the incident control vehicle is set up at the crossroads and the radio links netted. An hour and twelve: the first pressman arrives. An hour and fifteen: Alec Stainton completes his cross-country dash and finds Liz Pink has beaten him to it. An hour and a half: the tactical fire-arms team arrives, bereted and body-armoured and begins briskly checking over automatic shotguns, Heckler and Koch machine pistols. Two hours, midday, good visibility, the world still turning, aeroplanes going over, and in this little niche of Sussex countryside time slows down as the directing chief superintendent decides he is ready. No rush. Speed kills. Time to begin.

They stood in silence at the stable door. Liz gagged and swallowed hard against the foetid air. Twenty, twenty-one, twenty-two open tins of cat food, she counted, piled neatly as if in Tesco's, plus two empty ones, and a bucket full of water with a plastic mug and two wisps of straw floating in it.

Suddenly she said: 'There's something on the floor, sir!' Starting forward. Something mottled black and pale, shapeless, yet . . .

Liz turned for the door but the surge of her stomach was too quick for her and the unstoppable tide of her vomit exploded from her mouth to shoot over her skirt and the floor, and she thought, Oh God, what are Scene of Crime going to say . . . as the tears of nausea came to her eyes.

Alec turned away. 'I want the place searched. Not inside: every inch of the grounds.'

Liz pulled herself upright. (*And for the rest of my career I'll be known as the girl who threw up over a severed hand.*) 'I'll organize some spades and stuff. There's a couple in that little room next door to start with.'

'Better treat those as evidence. Bag them up.'

'And . . . that?' She gestured at the severed hand lying beside the encrusted tin lids and the empty handcuffs.

'Leave it. Scene of Crime will see to it. Or the pathologist.'

'What're we looking for, sir?' someone asked, thicker than the rest. Liz looked at him pityingly. 'A grave, son. A grave.'

She turned away and began ineffectually rubbing the mess off her skirt with a paper tissue. Someone shouted, from the far side of the fence, in the small paddock. They looked at each other, and Liz ran, her heavy skirt banging against her knees, grateful for the excuse to gulp mouthfuls of clean raw air down into her lungs. There was a triangle of freshly dug soil in the corner of the paddock. A handful of bare saplings, more dead than alive.

'Bit big?' she queried as Stainton came up. As a grave, it was extravagant. A week's work for a woman on her own to dig. Presumably a futile effort to camouflage the location of the body.

'Have it up,' the governor said.

Alec went through the gate into the road and along to the

incident control vehicle where already the tactical firearms unit was packing up, breaking open weapons, signing rounds of ammunition back to a team leader who was ticking off each batch against his issuing inventory.

'Crossland's been there all right,' he said, arranged for the notification of the pathologist, and agreed to be available for an *ad hoc* news briefing.

'Won't be long,' he confirmed to the pressmen gaggled beyond the tape. A video crew was taking stock shots of the lane, the incident vehicle, the policemen dismantling their weapons. He wondered whether the severed hand would be shown on prime-time news.

They hadn't had many days as splendid as this during the winter. Crisp, bright, invigorating. Bizarre thoughts in this country lane littered with vehicles, prominent among them the ambulance, backing up to the cottage, blue lights idling.

The doctor was still bent over Anita, feeling the pulse in her neck, examining the crust at her lips, his nose wrinkled at the smell of her.

'There's those,' Alec said, indicating the Paracetamol bottles in their evidence bag. 'In the wastebin.' The gin bottle still stood on the table beside the single glass, but both were bagged.

The doctor's mouth set grimly. 'Get me two men and a bucket and a lot of water. I'll wash her out straightaway, and then they can get her to the Queen Vic. Give her a few hours and you'll be able to talk to her.'

'Great.'

Liz put her head round the door. 'We've found some clothing in the garden. Partly burnt. A man's jacket and shoes.'

'I'm on my way.' He gave her instructions to detach two constables from the digging party to help the doctor, and she nodded and vanished.

Alec turned back to the doctor. 'I was afraid you wouldn't be able to save her.'

'I can't.'

'You said . . .'

'She'll be fine in a while. Like any other drunk with a

236

hangover. Sitting up and talking. Until her liver packs up. I give her three days.'

'You mean you can't stop it?' Alec protested.

'If she's swallowed all those,' the doctor replied smugly, 'the president of the Royal College of Physicians couldn't save her. But we may as well go through the motions.'

Anita had been removed to hospital. Already the short winter day was fading. The pathologist had been, cast an eye over the hand, said the obvious, and gone. The team of diggers continued to dig. They had made slow progress, mainly because it had become plain that the hole was a deep one. Alec ordered them to stop at three feet, fearful of cave-ins. Tomorrow he'd bring in a mechanical digger. Arc lights were set up. Blackett arrived, and then Oaks; to watch the line of constables turn over spadeful after spadeful of wet Sussex clay on to the untidy heap raised beside the excavation. The saplings lay where they had been tossed aside in a forlorn heap.

They were about six feet in towards the field corner when one of the constables straightened. 'Something here, sir!' Alec hurried over.

'Felt the spade hit something, sir. Sort of solid, but soft, if you know what I mean.' He lifted his spade to examine the edge of the blade then swallowed. A dark greasy stain glinted in the artificial daylight.

Alec knelt down. 'Keep digging. Trowels. Liz! Get two more here to help Chapman. The others can stand easy for a minute.'

Slowly the mud was removed. A surface was revealed. Mud made it impossible to discern its outline or even its colour. It was extensive.

'It's too big, governor,' Liz said dubiously.

'Bring more light.'

They were using their hands now.

'Well,' Alec announced, 'we've found a body, but it's not Crossland.'

Oaks surveyed him frostily. There was not much room for humour in Detective Chief Superintendent Oaks's world— his rather precarious world—just now.

Blackett said interestedly, 'She made a habit of keeping men, then?'

Alec said: 'This one's not a man.'

Blackett whistled, but not very loudly. Nothing much perturbed him, in his forty-second year as a policeman.

Alec grinned. 'It's not a woman either.'

Oaks's face was contorted. 'Cut out the fucking backchat, Stainton. Is it a body or is it not a fucking body?'

'It's a horse, sir. I'm afraid it's too early, sir, to say whether foul play is involved.'

Oaks turned on his heel and marched out of the control vehicle without a word. A car door banged. They heard the engine start and fade away.

Blackett said: 'You may regret that, son.'

Alec, who didn't really know what impulse had made him behave so childishly, silently agreed. 'Come and see where she kept him.'

They walked across the trampled mud. The spade party were still, though with less enthusiasm, digging: Alec had instructed that the horse must be fully disinterred, just in case there was another body underneath. Though how devious would a woman have to be, to bury a man and kill a horse to conceal his grave? But in his heart he did not believe Crossland was dead. And the evidence of the stable seemed to reinforce that belief. It was only too plain that a man or woman had been kept in that stable a very few hours before. He showed Blackett the bucket, the handcuffs ('Wonder where she got those,' was Blackett's comment, in a tone of voice that suggested he was only too sure of the answer) and the twenty-two full and two empty cat food tins.

'Two or three dozen more empty tins in a binliner next door,' Alec said. 'Nutritious, but not exactly a balanced diet.'

The hand had gone. 'Pathologist offer any comment?' asked Blackett.

'Only,' replied Alec drily, 'that it was cut off while its owner was still alive.'

Crossland was lost and cold and though the crusted mess at the end of his arm had ceased to drip he knew he had lost a lot of blood. He had no energy any more to keep the arm raised, and it hung lower and lower, and he felt the circulation returning, trying to force his chill blood out of the leaking vessels. If he had known the way, he would have gone back, risked the woman's irrational fury. His feet, for all their hardening in the stable, were torn and bloody, and winter scrub had snatched weals and tears in his skin. His legs were watery and he staggered. Where were the lights, the lights he had glimpsed a moment, or was it an hour, ago? He shook his head to try and clear the dark fog. Was there not at least a bloody road across this wilderness?

He was on the track before he recognized it for what it was, and turned along it doggedly. After an aching bone-juddering age it petered out at a gateway. Crossland crouched down miserably, hugging his body, just able to recognize that the cold was steadily sapping his will, his ability, to act, to live. Then forced himself upright and began to retrace his steps. Foot before foot. On and on. Now grass beneath his bare feet, now harsh stones and broken brick. Finally, tarmac, and other tracks joining, and looking up he saw the light before his eyes, not twenty yards away beyond the wrought-iron entrance gates.

Anne Baker tutted peevishly as she put down her book and swung her elegant legs from the sofa. Bill home early, and too lazy to hunt for his key.

As she passed through the hall she pressed the switches to turn on the outside lights. She opened the door into the porch. It had to be Bill, because everybody else rang the bell a second time, underestimating the time it took to reach the door in this lavish house.

'You're early,' she began, 'and where's your . . . Good God!'

She thought at first the porch was empty. But no: at her feet squatted, huddled, a form. Slowly, teeth chattering, it uncoiled itself, a shivering form at first barely recognizable, so smeared, matted and discoloured, but then in its naked-ness only too plainly a man. It opened its mouth like a cavern in mute entreaty and slowly lifted a misshapen arm.

Anne slammed the door at once; then uttered, as if convention demanded it, a brief sharp scream. And then, recollection of what she had seen thrusting itself on her with horrific clarity, a genuine cry of repulsion. Outside there was a thump as the man either fell against the door or threw himself against it.

'I will not have hysterics,' she adjured herself, heading for the phone. 'I never have, and I won't now. Hello? Is that the police station? I want someone to come out *at once.*'

23

'Ken Crossland, the released Sussex captive, has today been celebrating his release with his family. Mr Crossland, who was kept in an outside stable for several weeks while temperatures sank below zero, was reunited with his wife Sarah and daughters Beth and Amy after being driven from a police station in Sussex where he has been giving detectives a detailed account of his ordeal. Doctors who have examined Mr Crossland say he has emerged from his captivity remarkably fit and well. Surgeons say his hand, amputated in his horrific escape bid, cannot be sewn back on, but doctors have praised Mr Crossland's remarkable stamina which enabled him to survive his drastic plan. One of them today described the conditions in which Mr Crossland had been kept as "unsuitable even for a dog". Mr Crossland and his wife Sarah have now left for a brief holiday together at a secret location.'

Frances Stainton yawned, stretching. 'The media. What would we do without them?'

'What do you mean?'

'Well, why do they persist in peddling this myth of the happy couple? Why always this "reunited with his family" bit—as if family life is necessarily happy? Whereas they must know very often that the truth is a rather hopeless, rather gruesome daub which the people most concerned were in process of consigning to the dustbin.'

'You notice there's nothing about the woman.'

'What is there to be said?'

'After all, she did keep another human being captive for three weeks. If she had been a man it would be an outrage.

But she isn't. It seems we haven't yet achieved equality of the sexes.'

'Alec, darling, you're talking rubbish. And don't become too cynical too quickly, will you?'

He glanced across and smiled. She was right. The trouble with being a policeman was that you started to believe that so much that was the norm in the world in which you worked, was the norm for the wider world too. You dealt with fraudsters and began to look on everyone you dealt with as out to trick you. You dealt with vicious teenagers and saw all teenagers as vicious. You dealt with murder, rape, arson, violence of every sort and became cynical about the very possibility of human goodness. You dealt with Anita Simpson who locked a man in a stable and Deborah Payne who killed women and even people like Liz's neighbour Rosie (that story had come to his ears too) and despaired of human beings ever living in any sane relationship.

'Men and women have an equal capacity for evil,' he said after a little thought. 'That's all it is. But we are not allowed to admit as much.'

The phone went. Frances said parenthetically: 'I'll go.' She swung her legs off the sofa. 'I suppose you're right. But I've never had any problem accepting the human disposition to wickedness. It's where you begin from if you believe in redemption.'

'I'm glad it's not my job to diagnose it, that's all.'

'Hello, Frances. It's me. Er, Liz Pink.'

Liz trotted out what she had prepared to say. She had had a story ready if Alec answered the phone. 'So I wondered if you would like . . . if there was some way . . . I did hear that Lucy had got her pony.'

'I think,' Frances said, 'you'd better come over on Sunday afternoon.'

Liz hesitated. 'Er . . . Won't . . .'

Frances's dry smile almost seemed to travel down the phone wires. 'Alec has to go and see his sister. I, on the other hand, get on with my sister-in-law—who is a delightful person—like vinegar and sugar, and Lucy will definitely be glued to her pony. There's nothing better she'd like than to have someone to show it off to.'

'That,' Liz agreed happily, 'will do fine.'

While she was out of the room, he thought: Frances is the reason I shall not become one of those embittered policemen with the black dogs on my back. Every policeman should have a Frances at home: someone good, without being unworldly. Someone who believes in evil, but is not content that the story should stop there.

When she reappeared he asked: 'Who was it?'

'Just a girlfriend ringing about something.' She settled back into her place on the sofa, swinging her legs up. 'You were saying . . . ?'

'Oh, I was just thinking that I'm glad that I'm not the one who has to distinguish between evil and madness.'

'Meaning Anita? Or the Carver?'

Against the doctor's prediction, Anita had lived. Some people, it seemed, had an inexplicable tolerance to doses of Paracetamol that in anyone else would be lethal many times over. Which meant that Anita was still a problem unsolved. A person—not a problem, he corrected himself. Could only someone who was mad confine a fellow human being naked in a stable in mid-winter and feed him cat food? Could only a mad woman persuade herself that what FIGHTBACK preached sanctioned such behaviour? Could Anita Simpson have been saved by love—her father's, a lover's, friends'? Could she have been saved if her mother had died years ago, suddenly, instead of lingering as a demanding, tyrannical invalid? Did circumstances make tragedies? Did circumstances make Deborah Payne a strangler of her fellow-women, or Anita a torturer of men?

If so, then circumstances had made him. Well, he could believe that, to a degree. He could recognize some of the circumstances that had contributed to his character, just as he could recognize some of the traits he had inherited from his family.

But I can't, he thought, let myself off the hook like that, can I?

Frances had settled back to her book, relaxed on the sofa, legs up, head bent. OK, he thought, I love her for her body—look at the way her neck curves; look at the way her skirt falls back to show that her thighs are strong, woman's powerful muscles leading into the grace of her calves, the fineness of her ankles. But don't I love her primarily for who she is? All the sum of the impenetrable characteristics that *are* Frances? Her sense of humour; her ability to undermine pomposity (in me, too, let it be said—thank God!); her capacity to love; her forthright beliefs, whether in original sin and the possibility of redemption, or in Lucy, or in our marriage, or in radical politics. When she and I make love, all those things make love to me, and I make love to all of them.

Which doesn't, he thought ruefully, make the answers to any of the big questions any easier, but is some sort of consolation; and perhaps is in some way the answer.

Alec, returning from his sister's on Sunday evening, found the number of women at home swollen to three, and a general air of complacent self-satisfaction.

'Lucy will have bored you to death with that wretched pony,' he said to Liz. 'I don't know why we ever bought the thing. It does nothing but eat its head off and the vet's been out twice as a result of pure ignorance on our part, at fifty pounds a time. I used to wonder how they could ride around in such expensive cars.'

Lucy pouted.

'It's going to get worse. I've been told a long list of things a well-kept pony just *must* have,' Liz teased.

They chatted amiably over tea and toast, then Frances began making stern noises about bed and school tomorrow and Liz looked at her watch and found it was after nine and she had been there ten hours.

'Don't go yet,' Frances told her.

Lucy trailed from the room. At the door she turned, and said to Alec timidly: 'Come up and say good night, Dad?'

When Alec had disappeared upstairs, Frances said, 'She's never called him that before. I always hoped one day she would.' And Liz saw she was biting her lip, even as she smiled.

When Alec came down he held something on the palm of his hand: it was the DEF/AID self-defence knife in its waist sheath. Liz tried to look moderately surprised. He said to Frances: 'Did you know she had this?'

'She told me this afternoon.'

Alec turned to Liz. 'I suppose you've had a hand in this too, have you?' he enquired sternly.

She looked him straight in the face, working out what she should reply. Frances said: 'She gave it to you?'

'Straight out. Said she'd something to show me and she knew it was wrong and she wanted me to take it. She's got a dye-spray and an alarm. She asked if it was all right to keep those. Honestly, I understand it a good deal less than I can understand her getting them in the first place.'

Liz ventured an oblique remark. 'I don't envy the kid, guv, being a copper's daughter.'

She saw his mouth open, feared it was to remind her that Lucy was not his daughter at all but Frances's; saw, thankfully, it close as he gave a perplexed shake of his head and a half smile. She's his daughter now, Liz thought. And he's her dad. God, this halo's heavy. Involuntarily, she grinned in his face.

No doubt it was meant as a sort of expression of gratitude, a repayment of intimacy with intimacy, that he told her, there, in his own house, when Frances was out of the room, of his impending move. But driving home, the congratulations she had lavished ringing insincerely in her own ears, Liz's spirits were as deep in the abyss as they had earlier soared in the heights. I'm tired, she thought; and stale. All that's happened in the last couple of months has used me up. The Carver enquiry, the urgency and the fear of a killer on the loose; the Crossland case; my new house; God, it seems I've lived there for ever and it's barely seven months;

and Rosie, and little Joy; and Pritch, thank God for Pritch to keep me sane; and mates like Fieldy and Frances and Alec.

And now Alec's leaving. As he was bound to, because he's going a lot higher than DCI; but that makes it no easier to face. I'll have to work for someone else, Marjorie Weston maybe, starting from scratch again to build that relationship of trust and mutuality that makes a good team.

And then she thought: but I'm taking my exams for inspector. And if I pass, and there's a vacancy—who knows? Suddenly she felt itchy to be away: if Alec was to go, then smash it all—let them all disperse to the four winds.

But he'll still be living there in that house I've just left, he and Frances and Lucy, and if he's no longer my governor we can be free to be friends properly without the superior/subordinate thing getting in the way . . .

Anyway, she told herself, locking the car and letting herself in to the blessedly silent house, that's all in the future.

'I remember Deborah Payne now.'

Gwen Lewis was more poised, less withdrawn, as if the identification of her daughter's murderer, even before any trial or punishment, had satisfied some deep need and allowed her to enter the process of acceptance and healing. Why is it, Liz pondered, recalling photographs of rows of relatives trudging along lines of war-dead searching for the features of loved ones, that we have this compulsion to know? Why is ignorance so much harder to bear than certainty that a terrible thing has happened?

'In many ways,' Mrs Lewis was saying, 'she was the one we all wanted to emulate. She was tall, and very attractive, and somehow so confident in herself that there seemed nothing she had not done or could not do. The rest of us were emerging from adolescence; she was positively glamorous, we thought.

'Strange. It must have been just her manner, somehow,' she remarked. 'For we all thought her by far the most attractive girl there. And as far as boys went, streets ahead of us. And then, she was going to Oxford, and she had this glamorous background, you know, her father was in the diplomatic service, they were always moving to some exotic posting . . .'

Pritchard took the photograph back. Her eyes lingered on it. He thought: she remembers someone who never existed.

He said: 'She had no father. She was illegitimate, and her mother brought her up alone. She never went abroad. She never went to Oxford.'

Mrs Lewis looked doubtful. 'No?'

'No.'

'I'm sure she said . . .'

'I'm sure she did. The truth was, she was sponsored on that camp by her local social services.'

'Oh.'

'I'm not surprised she seemed sophisticated. She'd packed a good deal into her life. She'd had an abortion the year before. She was on suspension from school that very Easter while she was at camp. When she went back she was expelled.'

'Surely she was due to take her A-levels. Or was that all fabrication too?'

'No, that was true. She was a bright girl, very bright. She'd done all she could to escape her background, though in fact it was nothing to be ashamed of, her mother put all her life into bringing her up. Eleven-plus; scholarship to the grammar school; did well at O-levels.'

'So why did they throw her out?'

'For having an affair with a member of staff. It was a bit messy. He was married. The education authority had to suspend him. There was a deal of publicity, and he put his head on the railway line. I've got an idea that Debbie wouldn't have let that upset her A-levels, in fact; but there was no question of her staying on at school to sit them.'

'If she had, would she have gone to Oxford?'

'No. She'd been for interview and failed to get a place.'

'Because she was illegitimate, because of her background?'

It was uncanny, how Mrs Lewis had become partisan for her daughter's killer, now she was emerging as an underdog apparently rejected by society.

247

Pritchard shook his head. 'Because she told the dean who was interviewing her that the college and governing body system was corrupt and doomed. In the nineteen-seventies those were not uncommon sentiments, but they weren't very endearing expressed by a cocky teenage vamp who hadn't even gone up yet.' He paused. 'I suppose your camp was the last time she felt in command of things. Since she left school she's had a succession of very ordinary jobs, most of which she was too bright for and fell out with. We haven't been able to find any particular event that would account for her setting out to kill. I suppose she just reached a point where she seemed to have had such a rough deal, and you were the ones she had once lorded it over and who had done so well. You weren't hard to track down, for someone who was persistent enough.'

Two days after Liz heard the result of her examination, the flap of the letterbox clattered as she was spreading Marmite on her breakfast toast and she wandered through, knife in hand, to see what the postman had brought; anticipating (as always) disappointment; hoping (as always) for the exciting or unusual.

There were two circulars, a red council tax reminder (I've paid it, the berks, she expostulated; weeks ago).

And a letter in a hand familiar from a very different context, on a businesslike buff envelope. In the corner, the stamp bore a small heraldic dragon. Briefly, Liz saw broad hills rising in ranks of every hue of green towards a purple horizon, before the walls closed in once more and she found herself standing in her tiny lobby reaching for the envelope with fingers sticky with Marmite.

She bore it back to the kitchen. Toast would have to wait. The drawer seemed to be empty of knives, so she used a buttery one to slit the envelope. Within there was no fat, gossipy letter. Only a clip from a gazette and, pinned to it, a sheet of notepaper blank but for a single brief sentence.

She read the clip first. An advertisement cut from the *Police Review*, inviting applications for the vacancy for an inspector

248

in the Dyfed/Powys Constabulary. Liz glanced at the pile of magazines and junk mail waiting on the sideboard. Her own copy of the *Review* was no doubt buried somewhere in it. The words on the notepaper were enough, but she seemed to hear Pritch's voice, soft but insistent, shot through with gentle mockery, as she read them.

The lambs have gone, she read, *but the hills are still there.*

Liz looked from the note to the advertisement, and out of the window across her tiny back yard, beyond the rows of houses, to the broad sky and the waving tips of the leafless trees on the edge of the park. It was fanciful to think she could see the tiny buds already unfurling with the first warmth of spring.

She could never leave here, of course. Never leave her coveted CID posting and the happiness of good mates and the busy life of home counties England. Not for some godforsaken one-horse town in the middle of nowhere. Welsh nowhere at that. To go back into uniform, too.

Pity. Spring in Trenant, the lambs and the hills . . . And if Pritch came from there, perhaps there were others like him: solid, comfortable men at ease with the natural rhythm of life. It couldn't be done, of course. Could it?

She took another slice of bread from the packet and pressed the handle of the toaster down.

24

So, Sarah Crossland told herself as she looked at her husband in weary resignation, he has finally beaten me.

The last of the policemen had left; and the last of the journalists. There had been literary agents and book packagers eager to secure signatures on contracts. Crossland had refused to speak to them. Sarah supposed he felt shame. She had heard men speak as if being held captive by a woman was a titillating, exciting prospect. What had Anita Simpson done? How often, and in what devious ways, had she forced him to have sex with her? It was a dream to delight the masochist in every man; and how many women had fantasized about keeping a captive, since Crossland had been released? But there could be little room for pride in the man who had been kept as a slave for six weeks.

It made it no easier that Sarah sensed the depth of his self-repugnance. Ken Crossland, that confident, cocksure man, had been reduced to the status of an animal in a cage. By a woman. Made grateful for cat food spooned from the tin. Made to defecate like a beast and bed in his own soiled straw. Confined in darkness at the whim of a woman, denuded alike of clothing and modesty, subject to the throwing back of the door at any time of the day or night to reveal his nakedness to the derisory gaze of anyone she might choose to share her cruelty. His ironed shirts, his gold wristwatch, his expensive suit, his opulent car, his polished leather shoes, his mobile phone, his occupation: taken from him to show him for what he was without them, a pitiful, ugly animal.

Now she hated him not for what he had been: the philandering boor, the selfish taskmaster, the sexual tyrant. Not even for what he was now, the subdued, thoughtful, emaciated victim with the cocoon of white bandages where his hand had been. She hated him for coming back.

They had the hotel to themselves. A newspaper was paying: a small investment for a large return, when Ken, as they were confident he would, succumbed to the lure of telling his own story to a million readers. The weather was indifferent. You could call it good, for the time of year. For want of anything more purposeful to do, they walked most days. Sarah wondered when they had last been on holiday together, alone. For so long the children had been the reason for the things they did, and the factor determining how they spent their time, and a distraction gratefully seized on from the possibility of being alone together.

After a few days they fell into a routine. After breakfast in the near-deserted dining-room—just a few commercial travellers, and an elderly couple taking an out-of-season break—they walked out of the hotel and down the drive and over the coast road. The dunes formed a barrier between the sea and the land. Crossing them to the deserted level sands of the tideline was somehow like crossing into limbo, a place detached from here and now, the speeding cars, the school bus, the petrol signs on the garage, to a place where anything might be said, anything posed, a place of pax.

As they walked they could look ahead to where the estuary narrowed like a bay into the rounded hills; the town and the harbour, their goal, spilling like a child's bright discarded bricks from the foothills. A bridge crossed the water and sometimes a blue and white train snailed across it, precariously balanced above the water on iron stilts. When they reached the town they would have coffee—a particular café, soon found, thereafter always made for. The comfort of rituals.

Sarah was grateful for them none the less. Grateful for the time bought: the time before they must confront, resolve,

251

unite or part, before they must construct the story they wished to tell when they went back. It was not, Sarah found, straightforward after all.

For one thing, Ken was changed physically, quite apart from the fact that he was now a man with but one hand. It was almost like a trick unfairly pulled to disorient her: he was sunk in on himself, thinner in the shoulder, thinner in the face, with a hint of grey in his hair (and surely that was not as abundant as it had been).

The hotel room had twin beds. They had not slept together; had maintained a delicate modesty by mutual unspoken consent, neither approaching the other. Yet still, Sarah was aware that the confident full belly was wasted. This was not the man she had been married to, the man she was so certain about, the man she meant to dismiss, but a person strangely free of physicality. And always the white mound of bandage in which his arm ended.

And her, what did he see when he looked at her? A woman harder, colder, older, unwilling to venture charity.

Sarah felt time passing and began to panic. What would happen when they finally had to leave this limbo? Would Ken forever refrain from pressing her; would they forever shrink from confronting the future, and the past?

They walked out on Monday, the second week, across the dunes, along the dry sand above the margin of seaweed. Talking of the girls mainly: nothing dangerous, like what should happen to them in the future, but safe reminiscences of things past (but what was safe? Sarah felt the treachery of being drawn into recalling good times shared). On Tuesday they talked of her family, mainly; and of her teaching. On Wednesday she began to tell him what had been arranged. The separation. The divorce. The hectoring, admonitory solicitor in Cross Street. And Ken listened judiciously as if considering a plan she had for the garden, new shrubs, perhaps, that she had always been promising herself for the bare patch behind the garage. Even now he would not help her by reacting with the anger, the derision or the spurious sym-

252

pathy that formerly she could have counted on, that would have helped her keep her resolve.

The storm that night woke her and she lay listening to its moans and whistles and the pattering of rain dripping off the balcony for a long time. Ken slept on with an even, untroubled rhythm she envied, and in the morning woke with every symptom of that bewildering inner peace he had been exhibiting since his return: as if he waited on events, and knew they could not overwhelm him. She, by contrast, was short and tired and snappy and picked at her breakfast.

She walked out resentfully into the chilly, rain-washed day. There was no sun, but between clouds a fitful gleam suggested it might be there still, to return one day, and from time to time a stray gleam of watery yellow escaped and spotlit a tree, a patch of snowdrops, a roof.

They crossed the road, and Sarah noticed how the children stood waiting for the bus like travellers waiting to embark on an ocean voyage, and wondered how it is that reality comes to be seen as a drab and depressing thing.

At the seaward margin of the dunes she paused, and he waited. The water of the estuary shone with a metallic sheen and the gulls rose and fell as if on wires, shrieking shrilly. It was now or never.

'Let's go the other way,' she said.

'All right.'

So they turned tight, away from the town. Away from the encroaching hills and the necklace of the railway bridge. Towards where the estuary merged into the sea, a flat vista with no perceptible horizon, washed of colour. On this wide, featureless page, Sarah thought, there are no lines ruled and no margin drawn. Anything might be written.

The sands ran on for five miles before the next town. She need not make a hasty decision. She could still postpone the moment of speech. She—they—would get there at last.

Perhaps even today.